Mao scra...
the seat, ...
spattered with blood

She bent to the driver's legs as Bolan fought the wheel, the hillside and the running people a blur out the window.

"I can't get him to budge!" she called. "He's wedged tight."

Bolan checked the rearview mirror. The other Mercedes was following them down the hill a hundred feet distant and trying to close. Red tie gunners were leaning out the windows.

"You drive," he told her, releasing the wheel and drawing the Beretta from its webbing, trying to get a clear target.

A red tie with an AK-74 cut loose from the front passenger side, the Executioner ducking as a short burst took out the back window. "Your father was waiting to have a meeting with me when he died."

"That's why he was at the hotel," she said. "I warned him to stay out of public places. But then *you* had to come along—what kind of meeting?"

"I don't know. He was going to tell me."

"Wrong answer, American," she stated, and suddenly a MAC-10 was in her hand, pointing over the seat at Bolan.

The woman pulled the trigger.

Other titles available in this series:

Stony Man Doctrine
Terminal Velocity
Resurrection Day
Dirty War
Flight 741
Dead Easy
Sudden Death
Rogue Force
Tropic Heat
Fire in the Sky
Anvil of Hell
Flash Point
Flesh and Blood
Moving Target
Tightrope
Blowout
Blood Fever
Knockdown
Assault
Backlash
Siege
Blockade
Evil Kingdom
Counterblow
Hardline
Firepower
Storm Burst
Intercept
Lethal Impact
Deadfall
Onslaught
Battle Force
Rampage
Takedown

Death's Head
Hellground
Inferno
Ambush
Blood Strike
Killpoint
Vendetta
Stalk Line
Omega Game
Shock Tactic
Showdown
Precision Kill
Jungle Law
Dead Center

DON PENDLETON's
MACK BOLAN.
TOOTH AND CLAW

A GOLD EAGLE BOOK FROM
WORLDWIDE.

TORONTO • NEW YORK • LONDON
AMSTERDAM • PARIS • SYDNEY • HAMBURG
STOCKHOLM • ATHENS • TOKYO • MILAN
MADRID • WARSAW • BUDAPEST • AUCKLAND

First edition August 1996

ISBN 0-373-61449-7

Special thanks and acknowledgment to
Mike McQuay for his contribution to this work.

TOOTH AND CLAW

Printed in U.S.A.

Who but shall learn that freedom is the prize
Man still is bound to rescue or maintain;
That nature's God commands the slave to rise,
And on the oppressor's head to break the chain.
—John Quincy Adams
1767-1848

The quest for freedom drives ordinary men and women
to do extraordinary things, to continue the fight against
oppression regardless of the consequences. These
people are truly heroes.
—Mack Bolan

PROLOGUE

Potala Palace, Lhasa, Tibet
December 12, 1993, 7:16 p.m.

Colonel Li Soo watched two of his men fight bare-handed, to the death, in the center of the Great Hall. Sweat ran down their naked chests as they pummeled and wrestled before the huge fireplace that heated Potala's rooms.

Both men had committed regimental offenses. One had initiated sex with a local; the other had stolen supplies and sold them to a local lamasery. Whoever survived would keep his place in the regiment. It was customary.

Li, in full dress uniform, sat at the dignitary table with Dr. Oskar Werner and the two men from Beijing he hoped were here to take him from the hell of Tibet and give him his life back. One, lean and wearing a silk suit, never talked. He just watched from behind a haze of cigarette smoke. The other was Pei Chai, one of Jiang's puppets from Party headquarters. He had a great deal to say, none of it good.

A loud cheer went up from the regiment as one of the combatants' arms snapped at the elbow, the man swallowing the pain without a whimper, answering instead with a roundhouse kick to the other man's ribs that sent him sprawling on the cold stone floor.

"How can you eat this slop?" Pei asked, staring at the untouched plate of barley cakes with yak butter sitting before him.

"Sir," Li said respectfully, "we live in a land twelve thousand feet above sea level that gets no rain. We must eat what the earth provides. One learns to...accommodate."

"*Accommodation,*" Pei replied, "is a word your brother used a lot also."

"I am not my brother. I am loyal to the People's Revolution."

"You have not publicly condemned your brother."

"We are of one flesh, sir. He has been my responsibility since childhood. I will not condemn my responsibility."

"The kind of thinking that got you sent here, General."

"You know I am no longer a general," Li replied, working now at holding his anger in check. "Tiananmen Square happened years ago. When will I stop being punished for my brother's indiscretions?"

"Perhaps soon," Pei said with a smile, sitting back and turning to stare at the action.

"Have you something to tell me?"

Pei turned to Dr. Werner. "What's remarkable," he said, pointing to the combatants, "is that they're able to take such an extraordinary amount of pain and still fight."

Werner smiled, raising a finger to stroke his precision-clipped mustache. "The administration and reception of pain are merely opposite sides of the same coin. If you convince someone to love pain, they will love it in all its forms."

"Extraordinary," Pei replied.

Blood and sweat had made the floor slick. Both men were slipping and falling as they continued to fight, the man with the broken ribs bent over trying to protect himself from the kicks of the man with the bad arm.

Finally the kicker slipped. The man with the broken ribs grabbed his leg and flipped him hard to the floor, then jumped on him. He slammed his opponent's head to the stone floor several times before the man was able to flip him off and crawl away, coughing blood.

"They're all this tough?" Pei asked Werner.

"Tougher," the man replied. "These are the weak ones, ones who broke the code."

"They're animals, all of them," Li stated. "You sent me animals to train to be vicious animals."

"And you've done your job splendidly," Pei told him. "Can you control them?"

"I am their commanding officer. They treat me as such."

"Excellent."

Spitting teeth, the crawling man got dizzily to his feet as the other man charged him, head down, with an animal roar. He caught the man chest high, propelling him backward, both men crashing heavily onto Li's table.

The colonel grabbed his barley beer and slid his chair back as yak butter splattered a terror-stricken Pei, and the cheering in the room rose to a thunderous crescendo. The man on top yelled and shook his head, sweat and blood falling like rain, then jammed his thumbs into his opponent's eyesockets and applied pressure.

He came away with his prizes, holding up the eyes for his comrades to see and cheer, the still-living victim sliding soundlessly to the floor. One of the watchers hurried over to end his pain with a bullet in the head.

"Is it possible for me to leave here tonight?" Pei asked as he brushed at his suit with a napkin. His companion, Wang Wushen, simply smiled.

"The morning," Li said. "Nothing flies here at night."

Pei frowned, then with the shrug of the petty bureaucrat, said, "Perhaps we should take care of our business now. Is there a place...?"

"It's a palace, sir," Li reminded him, arching a brow. "There are many places, but perhaps my office might be best."

"Indeed. Lead on. Dr. Werner, I'd like for you to join us, too."

The four men, plus two of Pei's uniformed bodyguards, moved through the excitement and up the long stone stairs.

Li's heart had fallen when they'd asked Werner to come to the meeting. He'd been hoping for reassignment. Ever since his younger brother, Li Yun, had been arrested as a ringleader of the failed democracy movement at Tiananmen Square, he'd been punished by assignment to Tibet and loss of rank in the Red Army. His brother had it worse, however. He was still in jail. But this had passed. He'd hoped that Jiang had forgotten and forgiven.

They walked up endless stairs, Li smiling as he heard Pei wheezing behind him. This had once been the Dalai Lama's palace. Now it was the seat of the power bosses who had crushed the once-independent state. The electric lights were weak and dim, the stone walls cold and still ornamented with statues of Buddha right beside the red star of China.

Pei was gasping for breath by the time they reached Li's office on the top floor. The colonel opened the door, and a Lhaso apso jumped down from a chair and barked loudly, nipping at their feet.

"Silence," Li said sternly.

The dog quieted immediately, its tightly curled tail wagging as it moved to a warm corner and lay down. The room was austere and serviceable, lighting provided by oil lamps that had made it stuffy. The electricity didn't go to Li's office; he needed no typewriters or computers or paperwork for the job he was doing in Lhasa. Horror needed no paper trail.

One of Pei's bodyguards carried an aluminum suitcase. He placed it on the wooden desk as Li moved to the windows and flung them open to air out the room.

"Will your men work as a unit, General?" Pei asked. Li turned back to the room to see the suitcase open, revealing a small television and VCR.

Li ignored the reference to rank this time. "They are the most disciplined, prepared regiment in the army, sir."

"Good," Pei said, taking Li's seat behind the desk and putting his feet up. Wang slithered into a chair away from the window. "Who's your best man—smartest, toughest, meanest?"

Li and Werner shared a look. "That would be Corporal Chao," Li said, Werner nodding. "As close as I can tell, he lives to cause pain, thrives upon it like his mother's own milk."

"Get him," Pei said to Werner. "He'll be your second-in-command."

"My second-in-command . . . *where?*" Li replied.

"In the field."

When Werner hurried out, Li turned to Pei, incredulous. "You sent me here to train these beasts, not command them."

"But they already respond to you so well."

"I'll resign my commission before I lead this regiment."

Pei smiled. "That's what colonels do, *Colonel*. Lead regiments."

He pointed to the bodyguard by the suitcase, and the man turned on the battery-operated machines. Li moved closer and stared in horror. It was a video of his brother in prison. Gaunt and dirty. Tortured. The tape was meant for him. It was a plea.

"Please, brother," Li Yun begged, his voice raspy, breaking as he spoke. "I don't want to be a coward, but they are going to kill me if you don't help them." The man began to cry. "Help me. Do whatever they—"

"Turn it off!" Li said, moving to the machine and punching the keys. "Turn it off now!"

He grabbed Pei's lapels, dragging him out of his chair, shaking him. "How could you show this to me? What kind of a man are you?"

"A man who does what he's told," Wang Wushen said, speaking for the first time. "Are you going to do what you're told?"

Li turned to the man and knew true authority when it stared him cold in the eyes. He also knew the man had to have the power of life or death over his brother. "What do you want?"

Wang reached into his pocket and withdrew an envelope, handing it to Li. "I have some good news for you. You'll be leaving Lhasa, bound for Hong Kong."

Li had already opened the envelope to stare at a long list. "It's names," he said. "Just names."

"Enemies. Names that should be expunged from the list of humanity," Wang said casually around the stem of his cigarette holder. "I also have some... special needs that must be addressed."

"Who do I report to in Hong Kong?"

"Me, Colonel. You'll report to me. I look forward to a fruitful association."

Dr. Werner had returned with the man they only knew as Chao. He was a large man but moved well, tightly coiled for trouble, some terrible fire raging in his brain.

Pei regained his composure and stood. "Corporal," he said, "you're about to get a field promotion."

The man just stared at him.

"Is he loyal?" Wang asked.

The colonel removed his side arm and primed it, handing it to Chao. "Kill that man," he said easily.

Chao, expression never wavering, moved up to a startled Wang and stuck the gun in his face, pulling the trigger. Nothing happened. He pulled it again to no effect. Li watched Wang slump back in his chair, composure ruffled for just a second.

"I don't keep it loaded," Li stated.

"Well," Wang said, reaching into his suit coat and removing a small .22 automatic, "I *do* keep mine loaded."

He handed it to Li. "And what about your loyalty, Colonel?" Wang asked quietly. He looked around the room, then pointed to the bodyguard near the window. "Kill that man."

Li's breath was coming fast as he dropped the gun to the floor and sprang at the bodyguard, who was fumbling with his own weapon.

He hit the man hard, razor-sharp nails slamming into soft belly under the rib cage until the flesh gave way. His momentum carried the man to the window-sill. Li jerked his own hand back and shoved the man out, watching as he plummeted down the sloping side of the palace, then down the mountain.

He walked back to Wang and opened his hand, dropping the bodyguard's heart onto the man's lap. "I'll do your killing for you," he said. "You have my word."

CHAPTER ONE

The Present

Mack Bolan didn't like the word *easy*. He'd never found one easy thing that didn't have a high price tag connected to it. Hatred was easy. Killing was easy. So was dying.

So he watched the manic bustle of downtown Victoria, Hong Kong, slide past his taxi window and worried about the "easy job" he'd been given. He had to attend a meeting with a man who didn't trust information not given firsthand, then he was free to, as Hal Brognola had put it, "take a few days to wind down."

He'd flown commercial under the Mike Belasko passport, his weapons and a hundred thousand Hong Kong dollars arriving at the U.S. Consulate by way of diplomatic pouch. He'd picked them up on the way to the meet.

"You all alone, mister?" the driver asked over his shoulder. "Don't need to be alone in Hong Kong. Maybe you want a nice girl to keep you company, heh?"

"No, thanks. Just get me to the Hilton in one piece."

The driver, laughing, swerved across two lanes of traffic to the bleating of horns as he cut a swath through the heart of the shopping-and-financial district of Connaught Road. Victoria Harbour, one of the world's best deep-water harbors, sat to the left, massive buildings to the right, the tree-shrouded island itself rising in majestic emerald splendor beyond.

He'd been here on R and R during the war, and was unsettled by the changes he saw on his return. On the surface, things seemed just the same—a mixture of the commercial west and the mysterious East. Eight-sided mirrors called *pat kwa* hung from modern office-tower windows to deflect evil; the waterfront buildings, including the famous Harbour View Hotel, were still heavily glassed in to allow the free passage of the neighborhood dragon down from the mountains on his way to bathe in the harbor. But inside, everything was different.

The change was frightening. Everywhere Communist Chinese influence was being felt as they took control of more and more of the 410-square-mile area of 235 islands, plus Kowloon and the New Territories. He saw a desperation in the faces of the citizens, most of whom had come to Hong Kong to escape communism. Uniformed Chinese regular-army soldiers walked the streets as if they already owned them. And soon they would. Everyone wanted out. Heung Gong—the Fragrant Harbor—was dying inside, and Bolan knew there was nothing easy about that.

"Maybe you'd like some jade, huh?" the driver asked as he hit the horn and took the corner of Connaught and Murray on two wheels, scattering a crowd of pedestrians in all directions. "I get you a good price...best in Hong Kong."

"Maybe you can get me some aspirin. You're giving me a headache."

The man threw his head back and laughed. "That's good. Very funny." He turned back and looked at Bolan. "You want aspirin...really?"

"I want you to watch where you're driving. That's what I want."

The driver nodded knowingly and turned back to the front just in time to slam on his brakes at a red light. He pointed through the windshield to their right. "There's Hilton," he said. "See, I didn't kill you."

Bolan reached into his pocket to retrieve his billfold. "Not for lack of trying," he said, then nodded toward a building across the street that dwarfed the hotel. "What's that?"

The driver's smile faded. "Bank of China," he said, face set in a hard sneer. "Seventy-four stories tall."

The light changed and he hit the gas, screeching them across the street only to hit the brakes again on the hotel's circular driveway. The taxi had two speeds: fast and off.

They jerked to a stop, and Bolan gave the man a handful of Hong Kong dollars before getting out. The Executioner slung his heavy tote over his shoulder and stepped out from under the hotel's awning to get a better look at the Bank of China.

It was all glass and shiny ostentation, dwarfing to insignificance all the other buildings on the harbor. It tapered to a peak, like a giant fist thrusting defiantly into the sky. It was China, thumbing its nose at the world.

He turned to walk to his meeting in one of the top-floor suites, but stopped on pure instinct. He heard a whoosh, followed less than a second later by the man hitting the ground directly in front of him. He landed with a loud thud, on his back, and Bolan knew everything inside of him had disintegrated into pulp.

As people yelled from the hotel entrance, Bolan knelt beside the man. He wore a gray suit, and all of the pockets had been turned inside out.

Bolan looked up and saw curtains fluttering from the top floor of the twenty-story tower. He looked at the man again, recognized him. Mao Hsing, his contact.

Amazingly his eyes fluttered open, staring at nothing, vibrating.

"Easy," Bolan said because there was nothing else to say.

The man opened his mouth to a rush of blood that slicked his neck and joined the rapidly growing pool beneath his head. His lips quivered, sounds bubbling red from deep in his throat. He was trying to talk.

Bolan leaned close to his head.

"U-under...Man," Mao said, the words frothing out, then choking him. His brows relaxed, his eyes stationary in death.

The soldier looked up again at the windows, then got to his feet, charging full speed toward the hotel, pushing his way through the considerable crowd that was gathering.

He jostled through a group of men dressed alike in blue suits and white shirts—hotel security. They called to him to stop running, but he ignored them. Passing the mammoth marble ball held aloft by jets of water, he zeroed in on the bank of elevators on the far wall.

The lobby was wide open for three stories straight up, double mezzanines giving a spectacular view of Victoria Harbour. He raced across it and grabbed an elevator just as the doors were closing.

American and Japanese tourists filled the car. He pressed the button marked Suites and dropped his tote to the floor with a loud clang.

"First time we stop, get off," he told the tourists, grabbing his Beretta 93-R from the bag and jamming a clip into the butt. "Understand?"

There was wide-eyed, nodded agreement as Bolan snapped a shell into the chamber, then picked up the tote to sling over his shoulder.

The elevator stopped on three, and everyone crowded to get out. Within ten seconds Bolan was alone on his ride to the top. He had no game plan except forward momentum. Whoever had killed Mao had turned his pockets inside out looking for something. He intended to help them find whatever it was.

The elevator stopped on ten, and the doors opened. An overweight American in a bright yellow shirt stared at the gun, eyes wide. "I think we'll...wait for the next car," he said.

"Good call," Bolan agreed, focusing into the warrior mode. He was in a building full of civilians; the situation called for the utmost diligence and care. Before his job was done, he was going to have to deal with the security people, too. So much for the "easy" assignment.

The elevator jerked to a stop on twenty, Bolan flattening himself against the inside wall as the doors slid open. Then he dived out in a shoulder roll, coming up on his feet, the Beretta at the ready, to empty teakwood halls.

He moved quickly down the corridor, dimly lit by brass fixtures, the safety off the Beretta, its barrel pointed toward the floor.

He reached the Albert Suite, its door ajar. Without hesitation, he put his shoulder to it and dived in, rolling behind a couch.

Someone opened up with a submachine gun, filling the room with a chain-saw rattle, answering his question. A wet bar on the wall behind him promised solid protection.

He crawled through the confusion and made the bar, coming up immediately into the firing position. His quick glance took in two Chinese dressed in identical black suits, with thin red ties and sunglasses, ransacking the suite, searching. One of the men had used his entire clip and was trying to reload as the other brought a sawed-off Ruger Red Label over-and-under shotgun to bear on the Executioner. Bolan fired twice, taking out the man with the shotgun chest high, his charge exploding into the ceiling as he fell, plaster raining to the floor.

Bolan swung to the loader and tried for his arm. He wanted one alive. His first shot shattered the MAC-10 at the breech, splintering metal shrapnel into the gunner's arm, knocking him back against the wall.

Bolan was out from behind the bar immediately as the man staggered toward the dead man's shotgun. It was strange that neither man had made a sound when he'd taken them out. Though the man still on his feet was bleeding from his right side, his suit cut to ribbons, he seemed unimpaired as he reached for the shotgun.

"Stop!" Bolan yelled. *"Zantingqianjin!"*

The man never hesitated. He grabbed the shotgun with his good hand, pumping it against his side. Bolan fired again, hitting his shoulder, spinning him into the beige walls.

Falling, the gunner fired wide, taking out a chandelier in a cascade of sparks and broken glass. Bolan fired again, shattering the man's elbow, the shotgun flying out of reach.

Arms dangling uselessly at his sides, the man moved for the door. He still hadn't uttered a sound.

"Come on, pal. Give it up," Bolan said, blocking the man's escape. "We're going to have a nice little talk."

The man's eyes were like dead things as he stared at the Executioner, all animal cunning without a trace of humanity. Then, without a hint of conscious thought, he turned and ran toward the balcony.

It took a second for Bolan to realize what he was going to do, and it was already too late to stop him.

"No!"

Soundlessly the Chinese ran through the open balcony doors and dived headfirst over the rail. He was gone. Just like that.

"Drop the gun!" a voice said from the doorway.

Bolan swung around to see the hotel's security people pouring through the door, armed with 9 mm automatics.

"Hey, take it easy," Bolan said, setting the Beretta gently on the floor. He couldn't shoot it out with these people. "I'm on your side."

"Hands behind your head," an older man said in a clipped British accent.

"These boys pushed one of your guests out of the window," the Executioner said casually, slowly locking his fingers behind his head. "I was just trying to help."

There was a commotion at the door, and a Briton in a suit walked into the room with several uniformed policemen.

"Thank you, gentlemen," the Englishman said. "You've done your usual good job. Now please clear the crime scene."

"This man is heavily armed," the security supervisor said, nodding toward Bolan's tote on the floor. "Maybe he's a terrorist."

"Thank you, Mr. Noda," the Briton said. "I'll get back to you if we need anything else."

The security men just stood there.

"Out," the Briton said, shooing them from the room, then looking down the hallway to make sure they were truly gone.

The Englishman slowly walked around the room, holding up a hand for silence when Bolan began to speak. "Quite a mess," the man said, bending to inspect the body on the floor. Then he walked through the fluttering balcony curtains to look over the rail. He made a clucking sound in the back of his throat.

After shaking his head at the room, he walked up to Bolan. "My name is Chief Inspector Ian Crosswaithe," he said, fixing the Executioner with hard eyes. "Royal Hong Kong Police Force. For the moment this is my town. Who the hell are you?"

"May I put my hands down?" Bolan asked.

"You're not going to do anything crazy now, are you?"

"I just want to get my passport."

"Whatever," Crosswaithe said with a gesture of dismissal. As Bolan retrieved the passport from his jacket pocket, the inspector walked to his tote, groaning with its weight as he picked it up and dropped it to clank on one of the sofas.

"Those are my personal belongings," Bolan said, moving to place himself between Crosswaithe and the tote and handing the man his papers.

The inspector took a cursory glance at the passport, but Bolan couldn't help but notice that the man didn't really seem to care. He looked at the date-and-time stamp on the entry visa.

"Well, Mr.... Belasko, is it?"

"Yeah. Mike Belasko."

"Got into Hong Kong an hour ago and already you've put your foot in it. What is it with people like yourself?"

Two men in white wheeled a gurney into the room, Crosswaithe pointing toward the dead man at their feet. "Load it up. Another John Doe." He winked at Bolan. "Isn't that how you Yanks say it?"

"That man killed Mao Hsing, the man staying in this room," Bolan said, pointing. "Aren't you going to—?"

"No, I'm not," Crosswaithe replied, then sighed loudly. "God, I get so tired all the time. Is it old age or uselessness?"

"I wouldn't know," Bolan said. "Look, Mr. Mao's death needs to be investigated. Your government—"

"Please," Crosswaithe interrupted. "I really don't want to hear about it. I've already investigated. Two men out the window, one dead up here. Two murders and a suicide. There, happy?"

"What kind of cop are you?"

"The kind who's sick to death of being here!" Crosswaithe said loudly, then sat on the sofa and watched the body of the dead Chinese being loaded onto the stretcher. "Look, in a few months it's gone, all of it. We're out, the Reds are in. Do you think they give a bloody hell about our investigations, our trials, our jails?"

He pointed to the man being wheeled away, a trickle of blood running down his left arm and dropping from his index finger. "I've been seeing people dressed like him all over the island. They've been seen on the other islands, too, and in the New Territories. They're killing people, lots of people."

Bolan sat next to the man. "Hit squads?"

"Chinese hit squads. They want to take out all the dissidents who escaped them over the years by settling here. I'll venture that your friend was a Chinese expatriate."

Bolan remained silent.

"That's what I thought," Crosswaithe said. "Mr. Belasko, your friend Mao is the ninety-seventh dead man to turn up in the last three months, all linked to these red-tie killers...that's what people around here call them. It's like a lottery. Everyone waits for their number to come up. They're professional, highly trained, absolutely vicious and—"

"Silent," Bolan said. "Very strange."

"You should be proud of yourself. The two you...sidetracked are the only two ever taken out of the action. Whomever they want, they get."

"And you won't do anything about it."

"Can't," the man replied. "Can't do anything about it. We have a large pool of illegals from the mainland who sneak into work and commit crimes here. The red ties come in with the illegals, then go and live with people sympathetic to their cause. It's almost impossible to ferret them out. And if we do, we have to take them. If we take them, the Chinese let them out as soon as they gain complete control over the territories in '97. It's all a monstrous exercise in futility. And it makes me very tired."

"What about me?" Bolan said.

"Double murder, suicide," Crosswaithe said. "I don't see you fitting into the equation at all. So, Mr. Belasko, or whatever your name is, I want you to pack up your guns and go back to the United States, where people enjoy killing and being killed. I don't want to see you again. I don't want to hear about you. Your joss, your fortune, has been good today."

"Do you mind if I look around here for a few minutes?" Bolan asked. "I just want to see if I can turn up anything useful."

Crosswaithe stood, stretching. He was a curious man with thick red hair and a bushy red mustache. "You and I have never met," he said, motioning for the rest of his squad to follow the gurney out of the room. "But I would urge you to close the door behind you when you leave. There's no telling what sort of people could be lurking in the halls."

Bolan got the message. The red ties took care of their own. "Thanks," he said.

Crosswaithe moved to the door, then turned back to the room to stare at nothing. "Did I hear someone?" he asked, then shook his head. "No. Must be the wind talking to the dragons in the hills. Dangerous, those dragons."

With that he left Bolan alone, closing the door behind him.

The Executioner moved to the balcony and stared down at the two bodies being loaded into separate ambulances. He knew that Crosswaithe was right, that he should call the whole thing a wash and take the next jet back to the States. But that was the easy way out, and Bolan didn't believe in things being easy.

CHAPTER TWO

Wang Wushen sat in absolute serenity, fixing an American cigarette into his long holder as the *hong* representatives glibly tossed around words as if they were hand grenades.

They sat in the clouds, on the seventy-fourth floor of the Bank of China, surrounded by glass that looked out over the People's Republic's new, sprawling empire.

The wheel of life had turned China's way. At midnight on June 30, 1997, everything changed. The trouble was, nobody realized it yet. It was Wang's responsibility to teach them.

The conference room was spacious, luxuriant in the capitalist way, to calm the money grubbers. The room's woodwork was teak, its long table walnut, the plush easy chairs surrounding the table Algerian leather.

"The business of Hong Kong is business, Mr. Wang," said Londy Than, new head of the Hutchinson Whampoa syndicate, the largest trading house on the island. "We all have a great deal of respect for the People's Republic of China, but the form of subjugation you propose is tantamount to slavery in a free-market economy."

"'Slavery' is a very pejorative term, Mr. Than," Wang said softly, lighting the cigarette. "We would like to think of this as a simple cooperative effort."

"There is nothing simple or cooperative about the plan you have proposed," Than said.

"You're very blunt."

"It's the Western way, the way of commerce. You'll need to learn it."

Wang stood, walking slowly, gracefully, around the table, carefully watching the eyes of the other six men seated there. The *hong* were the big trading houses on Hong Kong Island. Though the island boasted 165 licensed banks, these seven men controlled nearly ninety percent of the money going in and out of the country.

"Gentlemen, don't we all wish for Hong Kong to remain a viable financial entity?"

"Of course we do," said Kwong Ying-wai of the Inchcape Conglomerate.

"But all the money is leaving the country, isn't it?" Wang replied, continuing his slow march, his voice gently singsongy in Cantonese. "My proposal is a way of keeping it here where it belongs."

Than stood to face the man as he passed. "Quite frankly no one trusts your government to continue free-enterprise policies when you take over. If China honestly intends to continue free-market operations in our city, then the money will return after you've been here for a while."

"Why should it?" Wang asked, staring at the man who had anglicized his name, dishonoring his ancestors by putting his family name last like the British. "Once you've moved all your capital, there's no reason to move it back."

There was some murmuring around the table. Wang rolled with it. "Our...community is an organic entity," he said. "It grows from its internal pressures and needs and is at the mercy of the world of trade and the shifting winds of history. We seek a perpetual state of dynamic balance in a nastily fluctuating world. Flexibility, gentlemen. I'm offering you the opportunity to invest in your own future. Has not the People's Republic already become a trading partner with Hong Kong?"

"China," Than said, "has already promised to squash our democratic reforms and refuses to honor government investments past June 30, 1997. That frightens our investors and it frightens me."

"We can handle this right now, today," Wang said, moving past the man and staring out the window. "All you must do is assign all your investment capital through the Bank of China in a brokerage capacity. We won't even take a percentage."

"Why should you?" Than laughed. "Once we sign things over to you, you'll control all our assets anyway. I'm sorry. Everyone in this room has clawed his way to the top of the financial heap. I doubt if there's a person here who's going to be willing to trust you enough to consign his capital to you."

Wang turned to face the nodding heads. "That is most unfortunate, then. You are all making a terrible mistake. I'm trying to work with you. All of you know that we can take this island whenever we choose with a phone call to the British. No one can stop us."

"Where's your spirit of cooperation now, Mr. Wang?" Than asked, his face set in a sneer.

"You have an amount to learn about human interaction, sir," Wang said. "I'm afraid you've been around the Westerners too long."

"Why not?" Than asked. "Look what it's done for me. I live my life a free man." He looked around the table. "Except for a sixteen percent income tax, anyway." Everyone laughed.

"You must learn your place," Wang said, jaw tightening.

"From you, sir? I think not." Than moved to the door.

"I did not dismiss you!" Wang said loudly.

"Bloody hell," Than replied, and walked out the door, the others following close behind.

Wang took several long drags from the cigarette to calm himself. He'd tried to befriend them, to show them the error of their ways, but they just wouldn't listen. Well, now they'd have to cash that check.

He turned and walked through the door leading from the conference room to his office. Colonel Li Soo, in a business suit, sat at his desk, playing with a large abacus. Major Chao and his two lieutenants were perched on the sofa. They'd been watching the meeting in the conference room over closed-circuit television. They were dressed in black suits, sunglasses and red ties.

"Well, you certainly took control of that," Li said, his eyes fixed on the abacus.

"Your pathetic humor does not amuse," Wang growled, going to his bookshelf and taking down the songbird cage as the yellow bird chirped loudly. "Persuasion now falls to your department."

"My men are already busy," Li told him.

Warbling to his bird, Wang moved to a filing cabinet and removed a stack of file folders, the bird cooing in response. He walked back to the desk and dropped the folders atop the abacus. "Perhaps we could convince your... brother to help change your mind."

Li's eyes just flicked to Wang, then fell to the file folders. "This is no occupation for a soldier," he said. "Isn't there some other way?"

"I'm going to call those men back here tomorrow," Wang said, Chao standing from the sofa to join them at the desk. "When they come in, I want it to be on their knees, begging me to sign over anything they have to the Bank of China." He pointed to the folders. "Here are all their vital statistics. You *will* take care of this."

Li handed the folders to Chao. "We'll do it tonight," he said. "Take one member from each family. We'll return them after the powers of attorney have been signed."

Wang moved up close to Chao. "Put fear into their hearts," he told the man. "Especially Londy Than. Start now."

"Not now," Li said. "They have a funeral to attend first."

"Yes," Wang replied as he admired the bird, whistling softly to it. "Yesterday's 'incident.' Do you have the facts on it?"

Li frowned. "Our Hilton contact reports that our men were killed by an American. He came in on a tourist visa. The name on his passport is Mike Belasko. He was there to meet with Mao Hsing, but no one knows why."

"Is this trouble?"

Li stood, stretching. "Anything we don't control is trouble. The American was carrying a bag full of weapons."

"But he's just one man."

"Indeed. One man we can't find. He's not registered in any of the hotels."

"An American," Wang said, shaking his head. As he put his lips to the cage and kissed the air, the bird moved on his perch to peck gently at Wang's lips. "Why are they mixing in here?"

"Happenstance?"

"No. Mao Hsing was a well-known dissident with a large network of supporters. The fact that the American was here to meet with him is important. Find the man. Kill him."

"That's why we're going to the funeral," Li replied.

MACK BOLAN SAT cross-legged amid the headstones of the old cemetery on Mount Nicholson, eating his steamed dumplings and roast pork with chop sticks and watching the picnickers dig up the graves of their ancestors.

It was the beginning of spring, the 106th day after the winter solstice, annually celebrated as the Ching Ming Festival. Traditionally Chinese families received blessings from their ancestors at the onset of a new undertaking. The bones were dug up and cleaned, then a picnic was held at the gravesite.

Children laughed and played as their fathers washed the skulls and bones. It was a good holiday, a time for happy communion with one's forefathers.

People were everywhere, taking bones from the ground, offering food. Even the harbor vendors had made it up here; Bolan had purchased his food from a man with a cart.

It was a warm, sunny day, and Hong Kong's islands and the New Territories stretched out resplendently amid the glittering diamond brightness of the South China Sea—a nice day for a funeral.

He saw it then, a hundred feet distant, a hearse climbing slowly up the ever-rising peak peppered with graves, a taxi following behind.

Bolan stood, walking slowly in that direction. The previous day he had followed the ambulance containing Mao Hsing to the Hollywood Street morgue, waiting outside until a young woman showed up to claim the body. Later a hearse from a local mortuary arrived to take it away. He called the funeral home and asked about the Mao Hsing interment and was told that the man would be buried the following day at Mount Nicholson. He'd taken the Peak tram up the island, then a taxi to the cemetery, camping there. He didn't trust the hotels.

As he slowly closed the distance to the funeral, he saw the young woman, dressed in a traditional white *nufu,* climb out of the hearse along with several older men. Two Buddhist monks in full ceremonial robes climbed out of the taxi to lead a procession to the gravesite, a statue of the goddess Quan Yuen carried on a pillow before them.

The soldier didn't want to have to pump his dead contact's daughter for information, but he'd promised Hal Brognola he'd find out what was going on if he could.

He drew within thirty feet, the pallbearers lowering the coffin into the ground as the young woman burned stacks of fake money for her father to take into the next world. He'd seen the custom in Vietnam. Then the cars came into view, three black Mercedes sedans. The tension snapped like a rubber band, and the Executioner automatically scanned his surroundings for good killing ground. There wasn't any. Everything was in the open, and full of civilians.

He broke into a trot.

The young woman saw both him and the cars at the same time, her head jerking toward what she thought was a two-pronged attack. Spouting Cantonese to the men with her, she spurred them to action, the pallbearers pulling guns from inside their jackets as the cars screeched to a stop, red ties pouring out of them.

Bolan reached into his own jacket, coming out with the Beretta and his equalizer, the Desert Eagle .44 Magnum. Both were already primed.

A hail of automatic gunfire from the red ties chewed the old men to pieces as the monks scattered along with the hundreds of people on the hillside. Two of the red ties sprinted forward to grab the woman. Bolan, jostled by fleeing people, was unable to make headway.

The woman fought back, jumping high to kick one of her assailants in the head, the other taking her down while her legs were still in the air. She wriggled away and tried to run, but by now other red ties had come to aid their partners. She was surrounded, then carried, kicking and screaming, to one of the sedans.

The Executioner broke from the crowd and headed toward the gravesite. "Hey!" he called. "Forget somebody?"

They turned, MAC-10s and AK-74s in their fists. There were twelve of them, and all he could hope for was one at a time. He raised both pistols to head level and fired them alternately, stiff armed, each shot taking out a red tie at chest level.

Bolan dropped into the grave with the coffin as the chain-saw babble of ten weapons split the air and the dirt around the grave spurted into the air. He waited it out, then jumped up during a lull and rolled out of the grave, coming up on one knee to fire twice more. Four red ties were dead or dying on the ground as the others jumped back in their cars to drive off.

The Executioner charged.

The lead car left the road and veered toward Bolan, who jumped out of the way, then fired both guns to take out the back window. Two more shots made sure he had the driver, and the car jerked hard to the left, then flipped to roll down the long hillside.

The car bearing the woman was in the process of driving away. Bolan ran hard, charging beside it, then past, since its speed was restricted on the small cemetery road.

He grabbed a small headstone from an open grave and faced the vehicle as it barreled straight at him. Unable to use his guns with the woman so close to the action, he charged the car, the passenger in front firing at him from out the window, gravel exploding all around him.

Bracing hard, he threw himself at the car, headfirst, over the hood, the headstone leading the way. He banged with a grunt on the hood, then slid into and through, the windshield. The gravestone took out the driver at head level, snapping his neck as Bolan slid sideways over the front seat.

It happened in flashes. He'd come down hard in the back seat atop two red ties, the woman between them. As he wrestled one man for his gun, he wrapped his legs around the other's neck, while the woman grabbed that man's gun hand. She jammed his finger on the trigger to take out the front passenger in a long, bloody burst.

Twisting wildly, Bolan jerked his knees, breaking the spine of the man caught between his legs. He managed to pull down the other man's hands, and the woman bit him until he dropped the gun in her lap.

"Cover him!" the Executioner yelled, hoping she understood English.

"No problem," she said, and put the gun to the man's ear, pulling the trigger immediately.

His head popped, and everything in the back seat was drenched in blood and brain matter.

"Great," Bolan said, opening the door to toss the headless corpse out. They were moving fast, picking up speed. "I wanted that one alive."

"And who the hell are you, Charlie?"

Bolan was trying to get over the seat. The dead driver lay almost flat, the headstone resting on his lower legs, his foot jammed hard on the gas pedal.

"Name's Belasko," he said while trying to steer the car from over the body. Through the front window he could see them descending at a forty-five-degree angle, bouncing crazily over headstones and coffins. He couldn't reach the key to turn off the engine.

"Angela Mao," she answered, opening the back door to kick out the other red tie. "I thought you were with them."

"Can you get up front?"

"I'll try."

He watched her scramble over the seat, her white silk dress and her face splattered with gore, to kick the passenger out of the car. She bent to the driver's legs as Bolan fought the wheel, the hillside and running people a blur out the windows.

"I can't get him to budge!" she called. "He's wedged tight, thanks to your big entrance."

"It's all I could come up with at the time," he said. "Turn off the key and pull the emergency brake."

"I don't think so," she said, pointing past him out the back.

He checked the rearview. The other Mercedes was following them down the hillside a hundred feet distant and trying to close. Red ties with guns were leaning out the windows.

"Any bright ideas, Charlie?"

"Yeah . . . you drive." Bolan released the wheel and pulled the Beretta out of its webbing. "And my name's not Charlie."

"All Americans are Charlie to me," she said, grabbing the wheel from beside the corpse and steering from the center. "What are you doing in the middle of all this?"

"There's a question," Bolan replied, trying to get a clear target in the out-of-control bouncing. A red tie with an AK-74 cut loose from the front passenger side, and Bolan ducked as a short burst took out the back window. "Your father was waiting to have a meeting with me when he died."

"That's why he was in the hotel," she said. "I warned him to stay out of public places. But then *you* had to come along and—what kind of meeting?"

"I don't know," Bolan answered, turning slightly to her. "He was going to tell me."

"Wrong answer, Charlie," she said, and suddenly a MAC-10 was in her hand, pointing over the seat at Bolan.

She pulled the trigger.

CHAPTER THREE

The hammer dropped on an empty chamber. Bolan stared hard at Angela Mao, her face dripping blood, her eyes deep and unreadable. "Here," he said, handing her the Beretta. "Do it right. This one's loaded. But I didn't kill your father." He pointed at the other Mercedes. "They did."

She nodded once, her face strained hard with anger and tension. "I'll trust you for now," she said, holding on to the gun.

"Okay, then. Look out!"

They topped a small rise at full speed, going airborne. They seemed to poise in midair for a second, then came down hard on the roadway, both of them bouncing up, hitting their heads on the roof.

The Executioner shook it off and drew a quick bead on the shooter with the Kalashnikov. He breathed out, firing one shot as the trailing car flew over the same rise. The man's left eye spurted blood as he fell limply, flopping, in the window space, the automatic dropping from his grasp.

The trailing car fishtailed on contact with the ground as a rear tire blew loudly. "They've dropped back," Bolan said.

"Good news," Mao called from the front. "The driver's dislodged." She tossed the headstone out the window and jerked the man across the seat, climbing over to take his place.

The Executioner scanned the surrounding hills and saw other black Mercedes sedans bearing down on their position. "Where does this road go?" he asked.

"Down. I don't know...Repulse Bay on the left, Aberdeen on the right. It's a small island."

"Aberdeen."

"I don't want to go to Aberdeen."

"Look." He pointed. Five other cars were closing in on them.

She nodded. "Aberdeen," she said. "Can you keep them off us?"

"No easy job. Might have to do something radical."

"Do whatever it takes! And, tell me, how did you know my father?"

"I didn't. Did you know anything about his involvement with the U.S. government?" They were two hundred feet from an intersection with a dirt road. A Mercedes was speeding to intercept them, a long plume of dust trailing after it. He levered his arm on the windowsill, trying to work with the bouncing car. He still had five shots in the Desert Eagle before reload. He'd have to use them right here.

"My father was an important man," she said, hunching over the wheel as Bolan settled himself to absolute calm, his eye tracking down the barrel of the

Desert Eagle. "He worked with many people. My mother was an American. She was killed."

"Rough," Bolan said, then watched guns poking through windows. He concentrated on the driver, then fired five times just as their guns fired at him.

The Mercedes left the road and flipped into a roadside rice-cake stand, scattering customers. Seconds later the gas tank exploded, the plywood kiosk rising fifty feet into the air, then crashing onto the asphalt just behind them.

"Your left!" he shouted as he dropped the .44's clip. Mao fired the Beretta at a car coming up to the other side of the intersection, taking out the front passenger and shattering the windshield. The vehicle fishtailed to a stop.

"Nice gun," she commented as Bolan slammed another clip home. The harbor was coming into view several hundred feet below them. Aberdeen was the home of the boat people, and thousands of junks filled the small harbor.

The trailing cars were dropping back. Bolan's attention was drawn to a Mercedes parked several hundred yards farther up the hillside. The trunk was open, and the red ties were removing an ordnance box from it. They bent and took out several weapons the size of sawed-off shotguns with huge, rotating cylinders.

"Hang on," Bolan said quietly. "They've got grenade launchers."

"What?"

The roadway in front of them exploded, Mao jerking the wheel as they drove into thick smoke. She left the road to avoid the crater, and another explosion slammed into the ground right beside them, rocking the car as fire climbed the windows.

Bolan scrambled over the seat. "I'm driving!" he yelled, shoving her aside as a grenade erupted behind them.

He slipped behind the wheel and goosed it.

"What's the matter with *my* driving, Charlie?" she said venomously. "I got us this far."

The road sloped steeply into Aberdeen, Hong Kong's oldest settlement. The Executioner gunned the engine and roared into the city, explosions following in his wake.

He started to turn down Main Street but was cut off by two carloads of red ties coming the other way. He jammed on the brakes, skidding the car sideways, then turned and took Wu Pak near the Lin Hau Temple.

He turned again, looking for water. The red ties were everywhere, their cars blocking most escape routes as he kept steering for the harbor.

"You keep going this way, you're going to run out of road," Mao warned, her head turning to look from window to window. There had to be ten cars after them now.

"That's the idea," he said. "We've got to stop this now, before anyone else gets hurt. There."

Bolan turned down a weed-choked dirt alley, at the end of which was a clear view of the harbor beyond.

He gunned the engine just as another Mercedes entered the lane from the other end, coming right at them.

"They're crazy," Mao cried. "They won't stop."

"I know," he said as they picked up speed, two cars in a narrow alley with nowhere else to go. "Crack your door. When I say, jump, get the hell out of here."

She looked at him, incredulous. "You're crazy, too."

"Ready?"

The two cars sped toward each other, men leaning out the windows, firing wildly. The speedometer hit ninety kilometers per hour, and when Bolan could see the determination on the other driver's face, he yelled, "Now!"

He dived out the door, crashing immediately into a hurricane fence that broke his fall and threw him into a dirt yard. The cars collided with a monstrous rending of metal on metal, car and body parts flying in all directions. A red tie shot headfirst into the yard with him, his trajectory taking him into a large chicken coop. He was followed by one of the engines, which came down hard on the ground, raising a dust cloud, as hundreds of chickens flocked madly into the yard.

Bolan climbed to his feet with some back pain. But everything still worked, and he consigned the pain to the part of his brain he didn't visit very often. Mao ran into the yard, her arms and face scratched from her fall into a briar patch, her once-lovely white dress shredded and filthy.

"Let's go!" Bolan said, waving his arms to drive off an onslaught of chickens.

They hurried out of the chicken yard to squeeze past the wreck. Dead red ties, thrown through the windshield, littered the alley.

They headed for the harbor.

"Do you know why your father wanted to talk to us?" Bolan asked as they ran.

"No," she replied, keeping up with him. "And I wouldn't tell you if I did!"

"Why?"

"Your government has turned its back on us."

"No way."

"You're just a stooge, Charlie! Face it."

They broke from the alley, crossing into the harbor area as several Mercedes squealed to a stop near them, closing the noose. Whoever ran these boys knew what he was doing.

"The pier!" Bolan yelled. Mao followed him onto a long wooden pier jammed with boats and people.

Gunfire rang out behind them, the decks clearing quickly as the end of the pier drew close. Bolan chanced a look over his shoulder and saw the men with the grenade launchers running onto the pier with them.

"Can you swim?" he asked.

"Like a fish," she answered.

"Good. Don't lose my gun."

The pier exploded with a *whump* just behind them, the concussion throwing them fifteen feet in the air and out into the harbor.

Bolan hit the water on his back, closing his eyes and holding his nose against the water's toxicity. He swam blind until running into a boat of some kind. Breaking water, he grabbed a breath, got behind the junk he had bumped into and looked for Mao.

"Over here!" she called from behind a sampan twenty yards from him. He immediately went under again, swimming to her side.

The blasts on the pier had sent boat people scurrying, their junks filling the harbor with confusion. Good.

They could see the remnants of the pier, red ties scanning the harbor for them, but the miasma was too all encompassing.

"They won't quit this easily," Mao commented, black hair plastered all over her face. "They never quit."

"We need to keep moving," Bolan said.

"Hey, cowboy...you need a ride?"

He turned to see a woman in a coolie hat standing in a small, self-propelled junk the size of a rowboat. Water taxi.

"You sure you want us?" he asked, angling his head toward the pier as he tread water.

"Red ties," she said with a sneer, then spit. She picked up a small tarp. "Quickly...under here."

Bolan hoisted himself into the small junk, then helped Mao up, the two of them rolling together under the tarp. The woman got under way immediately, using a long pole to push them farther into the confusion.

They lay together under the hot tarp, their breathing ragged, their faces nearly touching. "You still got the gun?" he asked.

"Yeah."

"We'll need more ammo."

"No sweat, GI."

"Stop it," he said. "I'm not Charlie, I'm not a stooge and I haven't been a GI for a long time."

"Then tell me what you are...really."

The tarp came off, the nearly toothless middle-aged woman smiling down at them. "You come out now," she said. "It's safe."

They sat up, checking for damages. Bolan was battered and sore but didn't think he'd done any permanent damage. If Angela Mao was in pain, she didn't tell him about it. They'd need new clothes, though, and they smelled like petroleum, dead fish and decay from their swim in the harbor.

From his position Bolan could see nothing but boats. Their pilot was taking them through small channels between several yachts and larger junks. Thousands of masts jutted into the late-afternoon sky, atavistic appendages for craft largely run by motor now. It was a whole society on water. Dogs and cats sat on the junks as old women hung laundry to dry, and small boats full of steaming kettles delivered hot food. In Hong Kong everyone was an entrepreneur.

"You okay?" the woman asked. "Need doctor?"

"Don't think so," Bolan replied. "Thanks for your help. You risked your life for us."

The woman grunted. "We have no love for Red China here," she said. "We're all IIs or boat people."

"IIs?" Bolan repeated.

"Illegal immigrants," Mao said. "Tanka and Hoklo, egg people, who bartered their taxes. The Chinese never wanted them, not even before the revolution. They've lived on these boats for two hundred years. When the Reds take over, they will be killed."

"Just like that," Bolan said.

"Yeah. Don't be so surprised. Hong Kong will be a wasteland before they're finished killing the people who don't agree with them. You never answered my question—who are you?"

Bolan looked at the feisty young woman sitting beside him and decided to give her an abridged version of what he did. "My name is Mike Belasko. I'm a consultant for the American government, helping it to resolve certain situations. Your father contacted us with information, but refused to pass it along any way but in person. A friend of mine in the government asked me to come here as a favor and take the message. I arrived at the hotel just as he... You sure you want me to go on?"

"Yes, please."

"He came out of the window and fell twenty floors right at my feet. None of us knew what he wanted to tell us. All the U.S. government knows is that Hong Kong is going through a trying period right now, and any information that will shed some light on China's role in all this is extremely important."

"That's it? That's all you know?"

Bolan shrugged. "You've got everything I've got."

"And what are your orders now?"

"Find out what your father knew."

"Pump me for information."

"Something like that."

"You realize your meeting is what got him killed?"

"I don't understand."

"He's on the list. We were in hiding. He came out to meet with you. He's dead."

"I'm sorry. What list?"

"You'll see. You were with him when he died, then. I don't guess he said...I don't suppose there was any..." She shook her head. "I'm being silly. Of course not."

"Yes," Bolan answered. "He had last words."

Her face lit up expectantly, the Executioner shrugging. "'Under man,'" he said. "That's it...'under man.' Mean anything to you?"

He watched her face run through a gamut of emotions in several seconds. First she looked puzzled, then her eyes lit up with a kind of understanding that turned quickly to a downcast sadness that metamorphosed into a wry grin and a shaken head.

"What?" he asked.

"I probably should be hurt," she said. "Papa's last words were a message to you, not to me. But hey, that was just part of my papa's vision. He was an irreplaceable human being, a great writer, a great man."

"You know what the phrase means—'under man'?"

She smiled coyly, brushing hair out of her face. "I think so."

"What?"

"Why should I tell you? What have you done for me besides get my father killed?"

"Your father and I are fighting the same war against oppression," Bolan answered without hesitation. "His message came from the battlefield, and he was killed in battle. We were both fighting for freedom, for democracy."

"We've already got democracy here," she replied, looking him straight in the eyes, without rancor. "Democracies are easily taken away."

"Help me with this information. Your father wanted to. His legacy has fallen to you."

"Go to hell, Charlie," she said, "and take your speeches with you. You don't know anything about my father *or* me. You don't know what it's like to live under a death sentence, to be a name on a list."

"You've mentioned this list twice . . . what is it?"

"Hey!" asked the taxi driver. "Where you want to go?"

"Can you get us to Repulse Bay?" Mao asked.

"Can do."

She looked at Bolan. "I've got contacts in Repulse Bay. I hope you can pay for this."

"Wet money dries and spends just the same," he returned.

"You really don't know about the list?"

The Executioner shook his head. "I've told you everything I know."

"Messenger boy," she said. "Errand boy. America doesn't care what happens to you, either."

"*That* I'm used to. What's the list?"

"It's a list of names the Chinese have sent out to every country in the world, asking they deny asylum to anyone on it. A 'criminals list' they call it, all dissidents, expatriates who escaped the horror of the Cultural Revolution. My father was a leader in the dissident movement, writing and speaking out about human-rights violations in the People's Republic. The red ties have the list, too. They are eliminating everyone on it while the world sits by and watches. My father has been trying for three years to go to America. Your people have said no. They don't want to ruin their relationship with the Communists."

"I don't believe it."

"You better believe it. You think we want to stay around here and be shot down one at a time?"

"Maybe the right people need to know. If we can get this information out—"

"Nobody cares, GI. Nobody."

"I care. America cares."

"Prove it," she said. "Hong Kong is a city for business, for trading. Here's what we'll do. You get asylum for my people, and I'll tell you where to find your information. Fair enough?"

"Sure. As soon as we can get to a telephone, I'll call my contact and find out what's what."

"Good."

Bolan smiled, but it was hollow. He worried that the United States might be more interested in expediency than decency.

CHAPTER FOUR

Colonel Li Soo, in full dress parade uniform, reconnoitered from the high ground of the Stanley Peninsula. The night was silky, lush, a warm trade wind playing with his hair, the kind of wind he'd dreamed about in Lhasa. Through the infrared lenses he could see the ostentatious house of Londy Than nestled within the green, gently rolling hillsides that made up the peninsula. While the poor huddled together in urban squalor on the north shore, people like Than spent millions leasing overpriced land on Hong Kong's southern side, where they could be away from the rabble, from the company of their brothers.

Li shook his head and put down the glasses. It wasn't working. No matter how hard he tried to hate the man he was sent to violate, he just couldn't separate it from Wang and his agenda. This wasn't why he'd been sent here, and he didn't want to do it. He didn't like Wang and he didn't trust him. The man seemed to have his own scenario that no one else was aware of, and aiding that scenario made Li Soo feel on the razor's edge.

But what was he to do? As long as Yun was jailed, Li Soo's soul was no longer his. He worked for the butchers now, sharpening their cleavers, and at this point it was kill or die. He knew there were worse things than death, but he couldn't accomplish them without the sacrifice of his brother. So be it. Fate wasn't an eagle. It crept like a rat.

He put the glasses to his face again and saw the flashing light from the home's south side, six hundred yards distant. "Major Chao," he said, "the rest of the squad is in position. Give the order."

"Yes, sir," Chao replied, then went down the line of men, moving them forward as Li gave the responsive flash to begin the assault.

They converged on the house swiftly but silently, their forward man having already killed the gate guards and gained them entry. He watched Chao move ahead, scurrying like a spider up and down the hillside.

He assumed Chao was to be his executioner if he ever got the urge to step off the treadmill of horror he'd climbed upon after Tinananmen Square. His punishment had been assignment to the atrocities of disturbed men, men who trafficked in depravity out of the pure enjoyment of it. It was without honor and made his entire life seem like a lie. He had been a good soldier, a good Party member. Now he was living death. They all were.

He kept moving.

They reached the perimeter gates, which were gaping open, the dead guards pulled behind shrubbery. The gates were heavy iron, attached to walls of brick and mortar. The house that sat fifty yards within the gates was redwood, imported from the United States, and wide open in the Chinese way. Lanterns danced happily on the wind from the gables. It would soon be a house of sorrow.

And then there was the American.

Li motioned his squad to divide into teams and surround the house. They closed in silently, Li and Chao walking directly across the concrete driveway.

Than was the first to taste Wang's wrath. All seven of the men attending the *hong* meeting were due to experience it this night also, in order of importance.

Li moved up to the front door, a sculpted jade *pat kwa* built into the wood to ward off evil. He turned the handle, and the door swung open silently.

As he, Chao and several other red ties entered a darkened entry hall, the sound of a television drew their attention to a room farther back in the mansion. Li put a finger to his lips, and they crept through the mostly darkened house filled with elegant, overstuffed furniture and French Impressionist paintings.

The colonel was unable to get the American off his mind. One man had managed to destroy four cars and kill eleven of his men in a fifteen-minute period. Who was he? Why was he here? He would have to be stopped, certainly, but so far that hadn't been easily accomplished. Every moment the American roamed freely through Hong Kong Island, Li was losing face and precious manpower. The man would have to be a priority.

Li moved confidently through the darkened house to the lit back room. Every possible exit was covered, all contingencies accounted for. He reached the den and strode in without hesitation, startling Than, his wife and their ten-year-old son, Ying-wai, all dressed for bed.

"Mr. Than," Li said, his men, guns at the ready, following him in. "It is time to pay the debts you owe to your country."

At that moment windows started breaking all around the house as his outside team closed the net completely.

The woman began to scream. Than grabbed his son to his chest and stood. "What do you want?"

"You already know that," Li replied as Chao and two other men grabbed the wife and pried son away from father. The woman screamed loudly now. Li had to raise his voice to be heard. "Mr. Wang laid it all out quite succinctly at today's meeting."

His men were in the house now, ransacking it, the sounds of wood and glass breaking filling the air.

"L-look," Than said, his eyes wide with terror as they dragged the screaming wife and struggling child out of the room. "We can negotiate this. Tell Mr. Wang we'll work something out to his satisfaction, I'll work very hard. I'll—"

"Mr. Wang appreciates and expects your cooperation," Li said, moving to block the man as he tried to pass. The wife was shrieking in the next room. "But the time for idle promises is finished. We've been sent to *insure* cooperation.''

The sound of a single gunshot quieted the entire house, Li's stomach jerking. The woman was no longer shrieking. There were several seconds of silence, then the boy screamed, ''Mama! Mama!''

''No!'' Than roared, running for the doorway. Li grabbed him and tossed him back into the room.

''The world is full of women, sir,'' Li said, ''several billion. But a man has only one firstborn son. If you wish to keep him alive, you'll do as you're told.''

Than staggered back to fall heavily to a leather couch. ''Please don't hurt him,'' he said, his hands shaking uncontrollably, his face drained of color, his eyes overflowing tears. ''I'll do...whatever you say.''

''Of course you will. Mr. Wang wants to take a meeting with you tomorrow at 10:00 a.m. Please be prompt. I promise you that your son will be released as soon as everything is taken care of to Mr. Wang's satisfaction. Of course, any mention of this to the authorities will have disastrous results.''

''I'm to take your word?'' Than asked. ''The word of a thug?''

The rebuke stung Li like a punch. ''I am a man of honor,'' he said. ''My word is golden.''

The man just stared at him, and Li could only imagine the words he was choking back.

There was nothing more to say. He turned and walked from the room as his men tore a series of Degas paintings from the wall and set them afire. He barely looked at the body of the woman on the dining-room floor before moving quickly to the living area, where the insides were now ripped out of the overstuffed furniture.

Chao held the boy at the door, a large hand wrapped completely around his neck like a choke collar.

"Let's go!" Li called. His men immediately stopped their rampage and moved quickly through doors and windows to the outside.

They became one with the night, retracing their steps at a brisk jog, Chao throwing the boy over his shoulder as they ran. "I didn't tell you to kill the woman," Li said to Chao. "You overstepped your bounds."

"As squad leader I took it upon myself," Chao replied. "She wouldn't have remained silent. She went out of her head."

"Kill no one else unless under direct orders."

"As squad leader I will exercise my best judgment in the field, sir. With or without your permission. Perhaps you should spend your energies in catching the American."

"You're being insubordinate," Li said harshly.

Chao turned and looked at him, his eyes smoldering with madness in the dark. "Yes," he said simply, then jogged ahead, leaving Li alone in the darkness.

BOLAN SAT CROSS-LEGGED on the floor of the beachfront luxury apartment, the Beretta in pieces before him as he cleaned it after its run-in with the pollution of Aberdeen harbor. Repulse Bay was another story— clean, sandy beaches, the haunts of the very rich.

He wore jeans and a black turtleneck courtesy of his host, one Bui Tin, a former newspaper editor in Peking until the reign of terror of the seventies forced him to flee for his life.

Whatever gear Bolan had brought with him was lost on Mount Nicholson, though he hadn't brought much. He'd figured to have been home by now.

"I still cannot get over the loss of your father," Bui said as he shuffled between Bolan, Mao and the front door. "He was the best of us, Angela. With him gone..."

"We can't give up," Mao said, pulling the wadding through the barrel of the .44. "Father would never give up, and neither will I."

Bolan looked at Mao, at the determination on her face still scratched from her run-in with the bushes in Aberdeen. She also wore jeans and a sweater, her long black hair, wet from a shower, hanging limply.

"What exactly was your father doing?" the Executioner asked.

"Moving us around...hiding us," she replied. "The red ties have still killed a hundred of us, counting the men who died at the grave."

"How many of you are there left?"

"A hundred twenty, hundred thirty..."

"One hundred and thirty-two," Bui stated, shaking his head sadly. He was a small man, perhaps seventy years old, his hair bright white. "You have to understand, Mr. Belasko. Mao Hsing was like a god to us. His mind was brilliant, his writing...well, he won the Nobel Prize for literature in 1974."

"I didn't know," he said, then glanced at the phone near the small kitchen. Brognola was supposed to be returning his call from a secured phone.

"He had an international following," Bui continued, "and used it to write about the plight of not only the dissidents, but the egg people and the Vietnamese boat people, too. He was considered a monster on the mainland. They'd been trying to get him for a long time. He was our leader, our organizer. But now..."

"We will not give up!" Mao said loudly.

There was a gentle knock on the door. Bolan got up to hide behind the door in case he was needed. The old man walked to the red front door and opened it slightly, speaking in whispers with the man on the other side. The man entered, carrying a canvas duffel bag that appeared to be heavy.

He was young, early twenties perhaps, and his face lit up when he saw Mao. "You're all right," he said, hurrying to her. "Did they hurt you?"

"I'm fine, Shing," she said, oblivious to his affection. "Did you acquire the ordnance?"

The man smiled and dumped the contents of the bag on the floor. Boxes of shells, loaded clips and concussion grenades fell out. "We pooled our resources and bought these on the black market," he said. "Though weapons are becoming harder to come by. The mainland is cutting off the supplies."

Bolan moved to the ordnance, the young man eyeing him suspiciously as he bent down and picked up a loaded clip, then returned to the broken-down Beretta.

"Who's this, then?" he asked.

The woman didn't even look up. "Mike Belasko, meet Cho Shing. Mr. Belasko thinks that he can talk the Americans into helping us."

"Helping us die, maybe," Shing said. "America's too busy selling hamburgers to care about people like us."

Bolan oiled the mechanical pieces of the Beretta and snapped it back together. "There are good people everywhere," he said. "Even in America."

"Belasko saved me today at the funeral," Mao said. "The red ties were trying to take me away."

"Why?" the old man asked, moving to sit on a low-slung couch. "Why not just kill you like the rest of us?"

"Two reasons," Bolan said, slamming the clip into the Beretta's grip and standing. "The red ties knew Mao Hsing was at the Hilton, so they probably know I went there to meet with him. I killed two of their men at the hotel. They probably figured Angela could give up information on me."

He moved to the small dining area, took his combat harness off the back of a chair and slipped into it. "The other reason is that they knew Angela's father was leader of this movement. His pockets had been turned inside out before he died, and I caught the red ties searching the suite, maybe looking for a list of hiding places and safehouses.''

He dropped the Beretta into the holster that resided under his left arm, then moved back to the pile on the floor to stick extra clips in the bands on the back of the harness. "I actually think it's possible Mao Hsing threw himself out that window to keep from talking.''

"My father would do that," Mao agreed.

Bolan nodded, hooking several of the grenades onto the harness. "So now they want that same information from you," he said.

The Executioner reached out a hand, and Mao gave him the .44, which he slipped into the holster under his right arm. "How would they know he was leader?" he asked.

"Maybe one of the people they killed told them," Shing said.

"Yeah, but usually it works different than that. All covert operations work the same way. They look for moles, turncoats, snitches—somebody who not only can give them information, but continues to give them information. Once you find someone who's ready to talk, you don't kill him. You use him."

"No!" Mao said, her eyes flashing. "Nobody in our organization would sell us out."

"Right," Bolan returned. "You're not the first person to say that and be wrong about it. You're all in hiding, and they've still managed to ferret out a hundred of you. How?''

''I won't hear any more of this,'' she said with finality, turning her back on Bolan just as the phone rang.

The old man looked up at him with raised eyebrows. Bolan moved to the speakerphone on the small coffee table and picked it up. ''Yeah,'' he said.

''Mike?'' It was Hal Brognola's voice.

''Yeah. Thanks for making the call.''

''Have you had any luck with finding that information?''

''A little. Hal, I'm going to put this on speaker so the people with me can hear, too. It concerns them.''

''I don't like that idea.''

''Indulge me,'' Bolan said, and turned on the speaker. ''Do you know what's going on down here?''

''This has nothing to do with your mission.''

''There's a list, Hal, a dissident list. Chinese hit teams are working the island, eliminating as they go. They tell me no one will give them asylum because the People's government has told everyone not to.''

''I don't like being on the speaker,'' Brognola said. ''Can't we—?''

''Hal, Mao Hsing's daughter may have some information that could be helpful to us. All she wants is for her and her people to have political asylum in the U.S.''

''Decisions like this aren't that simple.''

''They are to me.''

"Listen—Mike and...whoever else is there with you. Believe me, I understand your plight and my heart goes out to you. But it's my hands that are tied. We've just conferred most-favored-nation trading status on China. It's an important step forward in our relations, a huge step."

"More important than these people's lives?"

There was no response on the other end, just dead air. Bolan turned to look at the others. Their heads were low, eyes downcast.

Finally Brognola spoke. "Politics is a sticky business, Mike. Officially nothing can be done. But maybe you can come up with something, some other way of helping out. I'll be blunt. We need that information. The United States has vested interests in Hong Kong that may be in jeopardy. See if there's something else you can trade for the information. On this end I'll try to work out something with a more neutral country...some sort of emergency immigration...something."

An explosion outside rattled the windows, and Bolan dropped the phone and ran to the door, the Beretta in his hand. He peered through the gap between the curtain just as another explosion burst orange and black in the sky in the distance.

He threw open the door, and everyone hurried out onto the landing. They were fifteen stories above the beach and could see that the rising fireballs were coming from a boat-refueling station at ground level. Repulse Bay was shaped like a horseshoe, and behind them upscale homes rose majestically up the surrounding hillsides.

Crowds of people were running toward the inferno several hundred yards distant, and another storage tank went up in a monstrous ball of fire. Bolan ignored the fire and began scanning the surrounding hills. He saw several black Mercedes converging on a two-story mansion farther up the hill from the firestorm.

"That house up there," he said, pointing. "Does one of yours live there?"

"No, no," Bui said. "Too ostentatious. A *hong* trader lives there."

Mao grabbed his arm. "The fire—"

"Is just a diversion," Bolan said, "meant to draw everyone down to the beach. See the house? Look, they're surrounding it."

"Red ties," Mao rasped. "What are they doing?"

"You're sure none of your people live or work in that mansion?"

"Positive," Mao replied. "What's going on?"

"A well-executed military exercise," Bolan said. "They'll be in and out of that place before anyone knows what hit them. A *hong* trader, you say?"

"Sure," Bui answered, "a big honcho with Sime Darby."

"I have an idea," Mao said. "You want my information and I want safety for my people. I think we can trade."

"Trade what?"

He turned to her, the gas fire reflecting twin lights in her intense eyes. "You know about this military stuff, we don't. We're teachers and writers and artists. If you train us to fight the red ties, I'll tell you what you want to know."

"We don't need Americans to help us," Shing said. "We'll take care of ourselves."

If Bolan didn't know better, he'd think the youth was jealous.

"Just like we've been doing, right?" Mao returned. "By hiding from the light like rats."

"How long?" Bolan asked. "How much training?"

"I trust you enough for you to say," she answered.

Bolan shook his head, feeling a sense of responsibility. "I can't make soldiers out of them," he said, "but I can teach some of the basics, maybe try to make them urban survivors."

"We have a deal, then?" the woman asked, sticking out her hand.

Bolan shook it. "Deal," he said. "Now, a question. Did your father have contacts in the investment community?"

She shrugged. "People, all kinds of people, sought out my father's friendship. He was connected all the way to the Bank of China. Why?"

Bolan watched the red-tie squad take the house, violating it through every possible entrance. This wasn't a hit. "I'm wondering if the hit list and this business with the *hong* are connected. They've been done by the same team of trained specialists. There must be some sort of connection."

"We should go in," Bui said. "It's not wise for all of us to stand out here in the open together."

"In just a minute," Bolan replied, watching the mansion. Mao was at his arm.

"What do we do now? What's the first step?"

"I want to have a meeting tomorrow with everyone on that list. And please, when you tell them, don't tell anyone that the rest of the group is coming, too. Okay?"

"No sweat."

He saw it then, the reason for the fire, the reason for the stealth attack. The red ties moved quickly and quietly out of the darkened mansion. A large man came through the front door, a woman dressed for bed slung over his shoulder, her hands and feet bound. A kidnapping.

"Where do we meet?" Mao asked.

Bolan turned and pointed up, to their right, to Victoria's Peak, the apex of Hong Kong Island. "Up there."

CHAPTER FIVE

Colonel Li Soo, wearing a business suit, sat at the large Bank of China conference table as the *hong* shuffled in, all of them unkempt and weary, their eyes full of fear and hatred for the man who had kidnapped those closest to them. Mr. Wang had insisted Li and Chao be present for the meeting for reasons of "solidarity," but Li figured he was there as a bodyguard in case any of the distinguished gentlemen forgot his manners and tried to kill the banker.

The men slouched nervously at the table, eyes darting, waiting for word, any word, that could give them a reason to hope. Londy Than wept quietly, grieving for the wife Chao had killed the previous night. The others just seemed shell-shocked.

Wang, for his part, strutted around the room, his cigarette puffing like a steam engine, a smirk of superiority etched onto his face. "I tried to work with you yesterday," he said. "I extended the hand of friendship from the People's Republic to the citizens of Hong Kong. But you berated me and behaved as if you, not the People's Republic, are in charge here. You alone bear the responsibility for what happened last night. Let us hope today's negotiations go better."

"What have you done with our families?" Than asked, his eyes puffy and red rimmed.

"They are our honored guests," Wang said, moving to the man to flick ashes on his rumpled suit. "Major Chao, will you show the gentlemen that we know how to treat people with respect?"

Chao rose silently from the table and placed a videotape he carried into a VCR that sat atop a large-screen television brought in especially for the occasion.

Li watched as the TV sprang to life with pictures of two women and five little children in a room, the children crying as the women, their clothing torn and disheveled, tried to comfort them. It wasn't a reassuring sight.

The men jumped up from the table and ran to the television, chattering in Cantonese. Occasionally a red tie with an exposed gun would wander into the frame just so there would be no doubt that Wang meant business. Li's mouth was dry, his hands gripped knuckle white on the chair arms.

This was what they'd done to him; the people on the tape all carried the same hollow-eyed expressions of fear that he'd seen in his brother's eyes on the tape in Lhasa. He knew their pain as he knew his own, knew their bondage, for it was the same as his. He felt ashamed.

"Return to your seats, gentlemen," Wang said contemptuously, savoring the horror that clung to them. He turned off the television. "Perhaps now we can get down to business. What I am prepared to offer you is very generous. Run all your holdings through the Bank of China. Do it secretly. Give us power of attorney over everything. I've done some checking, and I believe we can accomplish all the paperwork in five days. When everything is done, I will return your families to you and allow you to flee the island in any manner you choose. If you don't comply, we will grind our guests into sausage and make you eat them. Understand?''

There was, of course, no dissension.

After they had been dismissed, Wang turned triumphantly to face Li and Chao. ''I've done it,'' he said. ''China will control the flow of capital through the trading center of the world. We can use the threat of calling in notes and freezing assets to force the capitalist economies to make whatever trade and political concessions we desire. The People's Republic enters the twenty-first century as a major economic player without so much as making one investment. A great day for China!''

''A great day for Wang Wushen,'' Li said sardonically. ''Your personal power base has increased dramatically. Are you really going to free the hostages?''

''One thing at a time,'' Wang stated. ''Let's get the paperwork done first.''

''I say we kill them now,'' Chao said. ''Now that we've shown the video, we don't need them anymore. Kill them and free up manpower for other things.''

Li watched Wang's jaw tighten for just a second, his eyes flicking to the colonel—the slightest loss of control, which was quickly regained. What did it mean? "We will continue to accommodate the hostages," he said quietly, then changed the subject. "Do you have anything else on the American?"

"I have a meeting scheduled with my contact within the dissidents' organization," Li replied. "He may provide answers."

"That's not good enough," Wang said. "I want the American out of this business immediately. We drew a great deal of negative attention to ourselves with the violence of yesterday. My superiors are extraordinarily unhappy. That will translate to you, Colonel, on a very personal level."

"I'm doing everything that can be done," Li said, unable to keep the contempt from his voice. "And you'd be wise not to threaten me."

"I could say the same to you," Wang replied, walking around the table to stand beside Chao, an arm solicitously on his shoulder. "You *and* your brother hang from a very thin wire."

"You are an evil man."

"And you are a stupid one," Wang said, taking a cigarette stub out of his holder and handing it to Chao, who positioned another in its place. He lit it for Wang.

"There will come a reckoning between us," Li said, fighting back the urge to throw the man from the window. He walked to the door and threw it open.

"You are a man without honor. When you die, little children will laugh at your grave."

To make the point, Li spit on the floor and walked out, slamming the door behind him. It was a childish display but released some of the terrible pressure that was building within him.

He took the long elevator ride to ground level, then made his way to the Star Ferry. He had an appointment in Kowloon, across the bay.

HONG KONG'S MAIN POLICE station was located on Arsenal Street in the Wan Chai district, directly across from the ultramodern Academy for the Performing Arts. The building itself was Victorian, part of the British colonial structures in the center of town that were slowly being dwarfed and eaten up by modern high rises. Land was the most precious commodity imaginable.

The streets teemed with people pressed shoulder to shoulder as Mack Bolan shoved his way up the stairs guarded by a stone lion. The station was alive with noise and people as cops, their uniforms of blue and green denoting the languages they spoke, herded in and out some of the half-million illegals who snuck in daily from the mainland and formed the bulk of the criminal class.

The building was dirty and in an advanced stage of deterioration, since the Britons were unwilling to spend more money to fix something that wouldn't belong to them soon anyway. Following the signs to the

homicide division, Bolan made his way into the pha-
lanx of offices and cubicles, quickly finding a frosted-
glass door with the name Chief Inspector Crosswaithe stenciled on it. He knocked.

"Go away," came the clipped response. "I'm
busy."

Bolan turned the knob and entered. The man was
sitting at his desk drinking tea and reading the *South
China Morning Post*. The office was jammed with
framed family photos and mementos of his home-
land. He barely glanced at the Executioner. "I told
you I didn't want to see you again."

"The bad penny always turns up," Bolan said, taking a chair from the wall and scooting it up to the
desk. "We need to talk."

"Are you armed?" Crosswaithe asked, putting
down the paper. "On second thought, don't tell me. I
assume the little kill fest in the hills and Aberdeen
yesterday had something to do with you."

"You can't just abandon these people," Bolan said,
looking at him hard. "There are killers out there on
your streets right now gunning down innocents. It's
your job to do something about it."

"Are you finished?" the man asked, picking his
paper up again.

Angry, Bolan tore the newspaper from his grasp and
leaned against the desk. "You're a cop, dammit."

The man's lips tightened. "Bloody hell," he said,
"a killer with a heart. Do you sing and dance, too?"

"What does it take to reach you?" Bolan asked. "Money? Do you want money? Maybe you're already being paid by the red ties."

Crosswaithe stood and glared at Bolan, his eyes as hard as diamonds. His mustache twitched violently. "Don't ever say that again," he barked through clenched teeth. "I'll drop you where you stand."

"So there is a cop underneath it all," Bolan said, sitting back. "Now all we have to do is figure out why you're leaving this alone. Because there's no cop in the world who could stand to have the horror on his streets that you allow."

Crosswaithe sat and took a long breath, his face loose, as if all the muscles had sagged. "We were told—officially—to leave it alone," he said. "I don't know why."

"Sure you do. Somebody in the Home Secretary's Office probably decided that it was the easiest way of dealing with a sticky problem. No lingering bad publicity about turning down asylum requests if the requestors are all dead."

"God help us all," Crosswaithe said. "That's what I think too. But I'm out of it just the same."

"What if the red ties' crimes extend beyond assassination and into more... financial realms?"

"What do you mean?"

"The fire last night in Repulse Bay."

"What about it?"

"It was a diversionary tactic. I watched a unit of red ties invade one of the *hong* residences on the hills overlooking. They made off with a woman. I was too far away to do anything about it.''

Crosswaithe sat back in this chair and narrowed his eyes. ''Don't pull my chain, Yank,'' he said. ''We've got no reports of kidnappings, especially a *hong* kidnapping.''

''The whole point of a kidnapping is to *not* report it,'' Bolan said. ''I just want you to think something over. The red ties are Chinese army regulars. If they are kidnapping prominent *hong* families, it must have something to do with money. How could it not? I believe a very dangerous game is being played out here. Mao Hsing, my contact, had strong ties to the banking and investment communities.''

Crosswaithe looked at the ceiling and sighed heavily. ''Why did you come into my life?'' he asked.

''I'm the punishment for all your sins,'' Bolan said, standing. ''Are you going to check it out?''

The man thought for a moment, then nodded. ''Why not?'' he said. ''What have I got to lose?''

''Your life.''

Crosswaithe half smiled. ''Easy come, easy go.''

COLONEL LI WALKED the crowded avenues of Kowloon's Tsim Sha Tsui district, looking carefully over his shoulder, trusting no one. As a lifetime soldier he'd learned to trust only his gut feelings, and what his gut was telling him now was that he was trapped between the crush of history and the ambition of Wang

Wushen. It was the destiny of all to join their ancestors. Li Soo felt very close to them now.

Kowloon was part of the mainland, a peninsula jutting into Victoria Harbour and the home of most of Hong Kong's workers. As crowded as Hong Kong Island was, Kowloon was worse by a power of three. Government housing packed families into small, box-like rooms. Privacy was nonexistent.

Checking again to be sure he wasn't followed, Li made the turn onto Bird Street, the long, narrow alley that was the home of the bird sellers of Hong Kong.

Thousands of birds in bamboo cages chirped in unison, filling the alley with melodious cacophony. The people of Hong Kong took their birds seriously as pets to be pampered, including daily walks, their owners recording their chirps and melodies to be compared with the birds of their friends. A good songbird could cost thousands of Hong Kong dollars.

Li walked Bird Street slowly, his hands behind his back as he made his way through the always crowded city.

"Sir," came a voice from behind him.

Li stopped and turned to a cage, cooing at the yellow canary within, the thing cocking its head to stare at him. "You have something for me?"

"Yes," the man said, slipping a piece of paper discreetly into Li's hand. "Two more addresses."

"Just two?"

"They're getting more difficult to come by," the man replied. "No one trusts anyone now."

"Understandable. I'm next going to want you to begin finding me the addresses of relatives of those in hiding. Have you heard anything about an American involved with your people?"

"No, sir. But I have some other news. I was contacted by Mao Hsing's daughter. She wants me to meet with her this afternoon."

"Just you?"

"She mentioned no one else. She wants me to take the funicular to the Peak."

"The Peak," Li mused. "High ground."

"Will you take her there?"

Li glanced in the direction of his contact. "No. I'm not ready to risk your possible exposure just yet. Go to the Peak. See what she wants. Find out everything you can about the American and report back to me. What time is the meeting?"

"At noon, sir. An hour from now."

"Good. Remember, I must know of the American, understood?"

"Yes," the contact said simply, then melted into the endless crowd. Li walked in the opposite direction, slipping his information into his jacket pocket. The mole wouldn't be dependable enough to tell him what he needed to know about the American. For that he'd have to trust his own resources. The names in his pocket were the first step on that road.

In two days the American would meet his own ancestors.

CHAPTER SIX

Bolan sat with Angela Mao, Shing—the young man who'd replaced their ammo—and the old newspaper editor, Bui Tin, on the Peak Tramway, the funicular railway that went straight up thirteen hundred feet to the highest point in Hong Kong.

"How do you keep in contact with the others in your group?" Bolan asked as he watched a magnificent forest of bamboo creep by as they ascended ever higher, up the greatest railway gradient known to man. The tram dated back to 1888 and had never had a single accident, always delivering its seventy-two passengers and one driver safely on either end of the trip.

"We carry pagers," Mao said. "If I want someone, I page them to a number. They respond, either by cell phone or pay phone. When I want to call everyone, we have a phone tree where everyone calls two others."

"But there must be a master list of addresses," Bolan returned. "I assume that resides with you."

"It does," Mao said simply.

"That's probably what they were looking for when they killed your father."

"And now they'll want it from her," Shing said from the facing seat on the colorful tram, its five thousand feet of coiled steel cable creaking as it drew them higher.

"This is a bad business," Bui said, shaking his nearly bald head. "All of us together."

"It's the only way," Bolan replied. "I'll bet we'll be safe enough. The red ties are going to want information at this point, not a full-scale military operation."

"You still think they have one of us under their control," Mao said. "You are very wrong."

"Fine. It never hurts to take precautions. Where did you tell everyone to assemble?"

"On the Peak itself," she replied, smiling. "You said you wanted high ground. We can talk in the gardens of the old governor's summer house."

"What's there now?"

"Just the gardens. The Japanese destroyed the house during World War II."

"Good."

Below them the city of Hong Kong shrank to insignificance as the rest of the territories opened themselves up in a wide, magnificent vista.

They were just reaching the Lugard Road station, the highest point accessible by tram. The Peak Tower Restaurant, a landmark of Hong Kong since the railway was built, was visible to their left. But they were going higher still.

They climbed out of the tram, Bolan scanning the crush of tourists and residents for evidence of the red ties' presence. As they made their way out of the station and up Lugard Road, he noticed Mao making small, silent signs of recognition to others on the road.

It all seemed odd to him. With all the governments and all the money and all the talk of human rights in the world, it had fallen to him to train a small regiment of civilians in survival against a viciously honed fighting force of professional soldiers. They had no weapons. They were very old and very young. Many of them were women. Brognola had asked him to stay and get the information from Angela Mao, but it wasn't the Fed who was keeping him here. It was the notion that *somebody* had to be here, and he wasn't going to be the one to walk away from it. Somewhere the line had to be drawn.

Lugard Road melted into Mount Austin Road, which wound upward to the old residence, eighteen hundred feet above sea level. In the distance were the homes and haunts of the very rich, the peak of the Peak. From up here he could see Hong Kong and Aberdeen at the same time.

Others were making the walk with them, a growing number. For the most part the hunted had managed to get their families out of the country, but not all. Children were among the refugees, Bolan saw, realizing how completely vulnerable these people were. It just made him angrier and more determined to work something out.

The wind was strong up that high. The garden itself was junglelike, jammed full of ferns in infinite variety, bamboo and writhing, crawling vines. Where the house had once stood was an open area. Well over a hundred people were congregated there.

Mao took him to meet a sturdy-looking man of early middle age with long hair and dancing eyes. "This is Mr. Shinshi," she said, "our salvation."

"Pleased to meet you," Bolan said, bowing then shaking hands. "Angela tells me you have offered your home to us for the training."

"Yes, yes." He pointed to the west. "It is the only structure on the island. I have a large barn and a hangar for my plane to serve as housing."

"You realize you are putting yourself and your home into grave jeopardy by allowing us in," Bolan said.

"Mr. Belasko, all land in Hong Kong is leased. Soon it will be owned by the Red Chinese anyway. They will kill me. I am proud to be able to help."

"Good, but listen. I don't want to tell anyone where the training will take place until they arrive there."

The man bowed solemnly. "I will tell no one," he said. "I am at your complete disposal."

He looked around the lush landscape for Angela. She was talking with three older men who were bobbing their heads in agreement with whatever she said. He joined them.

"Hey, Charlie," she said, "I want you to meet the Chan brothers, my father's oldest friends on the island and his bridge partners."

The men were tiny, with laugh lines around their eyes. They could have been triplets, so similar was their appearance. Their names were Kun, Le-Chun and Wee-Gee. They had all owned a tailor shop together until they'd gone into hiding.

"These are times of great sadness, Charlie," Kun said. "Because of the red ties, we could not even attend the funeral of our beloved friend."

"You are a great man to come and help us," Wee-Gee stated.

"We are people without a country," Le-Chun added as he shook Bolan's hand. "We walk as strangers in this world. Can you change that?"

"I can only do what one man can do," Bolan said. "But I will do all that one man can do."

"That is enough for us," Wee-Gee said, nodding. "Tell us how we may help you."

"I'll work through Angela," he replied. "She'll contact you."

He turned to the woman. "Is everyone here?"

"Everyone who's going to come, I suppose," Mao answered.

"Then let's do this and move on. We're tempting fate as it is."

"It is the fate of the coconut husk to float, for the stone to sink," Le-Chun said. "Let us hope we are coconuts."

"Guess that's one way of putting it," Bolan said, bowing. Then he turned and walked to the center of the clearing. Foundation stones from the demolished house jutted out of the tangles of weeds, and a thick jungle surrounded them. The Executioner wasted no time. The English speakers in the crowd translated for those who spoke only Chinese.

"I have agreed to help you defend yourselves against the red ties," he said loudly. "That won't be an easy thing to do. They kill with professional detachment and ferocity. You are civilians who must learn to become killers. I can help you in several simple ways, but make no mistake, you are merely buying time here, trying to stay alive long enough to work out a political solution to your problems. If none presents itself, you will perish, but at least you will perish with your enemies' blood on your hands. You'll die like men. The road I lead you down will not be easy or pleasant. Those of you who cannot live with my proposal are welcome to go now...please. No one will think the less of you."

Bolan watched twenty to thirty people, mostly family units with small children, get up and quietly leave. More stayed than he thought. They'd had enough.

When the area had cleared, he spoke again. "I'll take you to a place of training, and we'll work with weapons—guns and knives. We'll learn some hand-to-hand techniques. I'll teach you to think like—" he gestured at the terrain all around them "—a jungle animal. That city below us is a jungle to you now, a jungle of stone, and you're the prey trying to survive. I'll help.

"Go home now and wait. Don't leave. Sometime in the next thirty-six hours, someone will come for you and ask you to go with them. You will follow them without question. Needless to say, security will be our number-one concern. You must tell no one that you're going or where. All of our lives depend on it. Absolute secrecy, please. Questions?''

"How long will we be gone?" a middle-aged woman asked in perfect English.

Bolan frowned. "Five days or until they find us," he answered.

A man stood. "You mentioned weapons training," he said. "Where will we get these weapons?"

"We'll buy what we can on the black market," Bolan answered, turning and looking hard at the hundred people who formed a semicircle around him. "The rest we'll take from the red ties we're going to kill."

NIGHT HAD FALLEN HARD on the island of Hong Kong. The streets were full of people searching out cheap thrills, and the air was chill with the promise of spring rains, not always an auspicious sign.

Chan Le-Chun sat hunched over in the dim light of the dingy stall and worked on the alterations on the suit he'd promised the tourist he'd make in one day, his long needle dipping expertly in and out of the fabric that would eventually be a pair of pants.

It was late, close to midnight, the time when most of the stalls and kiosks in the "Wanch," Wan Chai's late-night outdoor market, closed up shop. He'd once had a beautiful tailor shop on Hollywood Street with his brothers, but now, since they'd gone into hiding, they'd had to ply their trade in secret, under the gaudy neon glare of the hostess clubs, topless bars and whorehouses of the Wan Chai district. The chill air smelled heavily of fish and fruit from the open market.

His brothers were waiting for him now at the Chili Club on Lockhart, where they'd eat Thai food and discuss the things the American had said. So many changes. Everything happened so fast.

"You make suits?" asked a man who'd suddenly loomed into the entrance of his narrow, cloth-filled stall.

"Yes, sir," Chan said. "I'll make you a fine suit."

The man stepped into the stall and squatted to get at eye level. He was Chinese, dressed nicely in a business suit. A great sadness seemed to hang around his eyes. "Are you a good tailor?"

"Don't let my surroundings fool you," Chan replied, drawing himself up. "I am the best. Like a coconut, I float. What sort of material were you considering, sir? I must say that you'd look wonderful in silk."

"Well, where I've just come from, I would ask for wool," the man said, standing, hunched over because of the stall's low ceiling. "Where I go from here, who knows? How would I look in a shroud, Mr. Chan?"

"Y-you know my name," Chan Le-Chun said, and at that second realized his life was over.

"Yes." The man sighed and walked out of the stall.

He'd never seen a red tie in person before, but knew them instantly—the sunglasses, the dead faces, the terrible silence. Three of them jammed themselves into the stall and grabbed him.

They beat him then. He felt it at first, deep, wrenching pain, the kind of pain that had real physical damage connected to it. Then the pain went away, and he knew true fear. He could sense the blows, deep, thudding hammers, but there was no longer any sensation connected to it. Bones snapped, disks ruptured, a lung collapsed—he felt none of it. It scared him to death, as if he were already dead.

"Enough of that," came the voice that had first assailed him. Without hesitation they dumped Le-Chun on the ground, his face partially smothered in a pile of cloth samples. He wasn't dead. Why wasn't he dead?

The man spoke again. "Put a bullet in his head and let's get out of here. I want to get a night's sleep. I'm visiting the temples in Shatin tomorrow. Hurry."

"Yes, Colonel."

Chan Le-Chun lay there waiting for the inevitable. He wasn't frightened anymore; he was accepting. It was time to die. He could feel the presence of the man with the gun looming over, heard the snap of the firing mechanism of his pistol when he snapped a shell into the chamber. Then, right beside his ear, he heard the explosion of the thing as it went off. But that was for just a second. His hearing went.

But he didn't.

He lay there holding his breath, absolutely stupi-
fied. The man had missed, the bullet eating up the
material samples right beside his head.

Then they left, just like that. And he was alive.
Feeling began to return, the pain finally making him
cry out. Colonel. They had called the man "Colonel."

BOLAN AND MAO RAN down the emergency-room
corridor. The crowded waiting room was full of the
participants of a Wan Chai free-for-all between U.S.
Navymen on shore leave and one of the Triad gangs
who ran the city's illegal drug business.

"What was the room?" Mao asked, turning a corner and looking at the numbered doors.

"ER-10," Bolan said, spotting it and hurrying that
way. The red ties had left one alive. It meant something.

They hit the door, meeting a young British doctor
on the way out. The man was pulling a sterile cap off
his head. "Mr. Chan..." Mao said. "Is he all right?"

"Are you his family?" the man asked.

Bolan looked through the glass cutout in the door
to see a heavily bandaged and tractioned Chan Le-
Chun being fussed over by several nurses.

"Yes," Mao said, lying. "He's my uncle. Will he be
all right?"

"I won't lie to you," the doctor said. "They broke
him up pretty badly. We'll just have to see. We've put
him back together. He may walk again. He may eat

solid food again. It's all a question of how strong he is."

That didn't make sense to Bolan. The red ties were far more efficient than to beat an old man senseless, then let him live. He pushed through the door and moved to the bed, waving away the nurses as he did so.

The old man was heavily sedated, but he brightened when he saw his visitor, motioning from a full arm cast by wiggling two unbroken fingers.

"Hey, Charlie," he rasped weakly as Bolan approached.

"My name's not Charlie." Bolan smiled and leaned down to pat the old man's shoulder. "Your brothers are on their way here now."

Chan nodded. "I suppose I won't be going with you to train," he said lowly.

"I'll make sure you're protected here. We'll keep moving you if we have to. Why are you still alive?"

"They b-beat me up," Chan said, coughing painfully. "Then the colonel told them to put a bullet in my head."

"The colonel?"

"That's what they called him. A red tie took out a gun and shot at my head. I guess he missed."

"What else did they say?"

"The colonel told them to hurry up, that he was going to Shatin tomorrow to look at the temples."

Bolan stiffened. The whole thing stank of a setup. He turned toward the door, saw Angela push against it, her eyes wide, falling in as machine-gun fire raked the hallway outside, the doctor going down in a hail of bullets.

The woman rolled into the room, and Bolan slid the Beretta across the floor to her even as the .44 filled his other hand. Red ties poured through the door space, and Bolan banged against the bed, sliding it all the way to the side wall.

It happened in flashes, Mao firing wildly up from the floor at anything that came across the threshold as the Executioner picked his targets from the other side, everyone firing to a terrifying racket.

The first two gunners through the door went down, one pumping blood from a neck wound, his arms and legs thrashing wildly. Mao scrambled to her knees, sticking the Beretta into the belly of the third man through and blowing his intestines all over the room. Bolan took the next one out with a chest shot, the man falling back against the man behind him.

The Executioner charged the door while he had the advantage. He dived onto the falling pair, blood spurting everywhere, the living red tie banging hard against the wall as Bolan went for the AK-74 in his hands.

As they struggled for the weapon, a man in the hall tried to get a clear shot at Bolan. Rolling with his adversary, the soldier used him as a shield as the gunner opened fire. The Executioner's hand pulled on the dying gunman's fingers, forcing them to fire the Kalashnikov. The ensuing burst of rounds drilled into his accomplice, killing him.

Bolan rolled out from under, standing in the blood-slick hallway. Mao, gun at her side, joined him, her face a hard mask. The hallway reverberated with the screaming of both staff and patients.

"Le-Chun's dead," she said. "They got him after all."

"They never wanted to get him," Bolan told her.

"What?"

"Gather the weapons. Let's get out of here. We'll talk later."

As doctors and nurses hurried to assist the dead and dying, Bolan and Mao picked up as many guns as they could carry. Then he grabbed her hand and ran, shoving into the confusion of the inner lobby and into the night, his eyes scanning quickly for trouble before they moved on.

They kept to the streets, always moving. Movement was life; stopping meant death, not just to themselves, but to anyone around them, and the streets of Wan Chai were jammed with tourists and uniformed military personnel on leave.

"You said they didn't want to get Le-Chun. What did you mean?" she asked.

"They left him alive on purpose so that he could give me information."

"What sort of information?"

"He told me the red ties were led by a colonel and that the man was going to Shatin tomorrow to look at the temples. If they didn't get me here at the hospital tonight, they figure to do it tomorrow when I go to Shatin."

"You think it's a trap and still you'll go?"

"There are traps and then there are traps."

"I'm going with you. This is my fight."

He stopped walking and looked at her. "Don't lose yourself in this, Angela," he said. "There's more to life than revenge."

She stopped walking at the mouth of a dark alley and drew him into the darkness, where all he could see were her eyes dully reflecting the light from the streets. "When I was a very small child," she said, "my father took my mother and me to China. He had left after the '49 Communist revolution and became a very outspoken critic of Mao Tse-tung's regime. But your President Nixon established friendly relations with China, and my father wanted to see his family once more. That was during the so-called Cultural Revolution, where all Western influence was being purged from the land."

She stopped talking for a moment, and when she resumed her voice was husky, choked. "We went back to the village of my father's birth, but the local Party bosses incited the villagers against my father and his 'imperialist devil' of a wife. My mother was a beautiful, educated, refined woman who loved everyone. They stoned her to death on the streets like a dog. My father grabbed me and ran, saving my life.

"We came here, to Hong Kong, where my father's writings could be close to the source, his information firsthand from the refugees who swam to safety from the mainland. My life is unrest and turmoil. I will avenge my father's death and my mother's, and I will do my best to save these people just as my father did his best. I am going with you tomorrow.''

"Sure," Bolan said. "I can see where you're coming from. But we'll need a couple of things first."

CHAPTER SEVEN

"This is not right," Chan Wee-Gee whispered as Bolan led the silent line of twenty people through the back streets of Hong Kong. "I must stay. I must bury my brother."

The night was cool, drizzly, as the city watched and waited for the one thing its money couldn't fix or control—typhoons. At 4:00 a.m. the streets were dark and silent. Occasional police vehicles and the ubiquitous black Mercedes of the red ties kept the group in the shadows.

"We'll all mourn Le-Chun's death," Bolan said, looking past Wee-Gee to Chan Kun, "but to die uselessly yourselves trying to bury him does no good for anybody, especially your brother's memory."

The line of people reached the major intersection of Harcourt Street just across from the harbor and the Star Ferry pier. He sent them across singly, so as not to attract attention. He wanted to make this trip once, and quickly. Everything he had been planning for would be destroyed should their unauthorized flight in the ferry draw attention. It was a huge gamble, but should he manage to get everyone to another island, they'd be buying themselves precious days while he continued to work on Brognola and on Crosswaithe for diplomatic help.

Sticking close to the buildings, he led them down Edinburgh Street, beside the old city hall, now a museum. Headquarters for the British forces, which consisted of a small unit of Gurkha regulars from India and a ceremonial band, was a mere block away.

Mao waved to him from the pier, motioning for them to hurry.

"Come on, people," Bolan said, breaking into a trot. "The meter's running."

They hurried down the darkened pier, catching up to Mao halfway to the ferry, for most of Hong Kong's history the only transport between the island and Kowloon. Now there were underwater tunnels for both cars and trains, but the ferry still ran to full capacity seven days a week.

"Mine are already on board," she told Bolan as they hurried to the loading ramp. "The pilot is losing his nerve. A million Hong Kong dollars may not be enough to get him through this."

"We'll get him there. Any word on the Kowloon side?"

"Shing has everyone from that side prepared and at the dock. The first regular morning run begins at 6:00 a.m. I hope we've got enough time."

"We've got time," Bolan said, hustling his people up the ramp. "Did Shing manage to procure the equipment I asked for?"

"Yes. Everything's ready. He even managed to borrow a car."

"Good." Bolan and Mao followed the last of the refugees up the ramp, only to be met by the bribed pilot on deck.

"It's too late," the man said, looking small and frightened. "Everyone must leave. We don't have any time."

"Now wait a—" Mao began, but Bolan silenced her with a raised hand.

He put his arm around the pilot's shoulders and walked several paces along the deck with him. "We're going," he said quietly. "And we're going right now. Everything will be fine. We've got plenty of time if you do the job I know you can do. You've taken a lot of money from us. You will fulfill the bargain."

"You may have your money back."

"We're determined people," Bolan told him. "If you're in with us, I can trust you to keep silent. But now...I'm afraid your defection will have terrible consequences for you. We're taking the boat no matter what. As for you, would you prefer to be shot or drowned?"

The man nodded his head for several seconds. "You know," he said, "if we hurry, we might just make it."

"My sentiments exactly. You'd better hustle up to the wheelhouse."

"Yes, sir."

They were under way within a minute, slapping the dark waters of Victoria Harbour, nearby junks and sampans already coming awake for a new morning of survival. The distance to Kowloon was less than a mile, the trip made in several minutes. This was the easy leg, however. The next part was the tough one.

As they pulled into the Kowloon dock, the pier flooded with people hiding behind buildings and crates. Bolan hurried to the wheelhouse and the man who stood, shaking, before his controls.

"You're going next to Tree Island," the Executioner said, pulling the microphone jack out of the ferry's radio. "Then you'll be free of us. If you ever tell anyone about this, I'll come back and make your life hell. I hope you believe what I'm saying."

"Yes, sir. I believe you. Yes."

"Good," Bolan said, tossing the mike out of the window to sink in the harbor. "You're doing the right thing here." He patted the man on the back, then hurried out and down the gangway to the main deck, while Mao got the rest of the dissidents on board.

"Sure you want to go with me?" he asked.

"Try and stop me," she replied, hurrying down the ramp as soon as the last person had climbed aboard. Bolan ran after her, helping her pull the ramp away from the ferry. He waved up to the wheelhouse, the pilot waving back and getting under way immediately.

Bolan wasn't going to Tree Island just yet. He had a date in the New Territories.

They made their way along the darkness of the pier, the smells of drying squid and petroleum heavy in the wet air. Shing's car, a small English Ford, was already running and waiting for them on Salisbury Road.

As they approached, he jumped out of the driver's seat to open the back door for Mao. "I'm a big girl," she said, shoving him aside and opening the door herself, "all grown-up."

Bolan shook his head. "Can we work out the social arrangements later?" he asked. "Time is our enemy right now."

"Please be careful of the car," Shing said over his shoulder as he slid behind the wheel. "My cousin will be very unhappy if we don't return it in perfect condition."

He took them around the harbor on Salisbury, then headed straight north on the Princess Margaret Freeway.

"How long before the temple opens?" Bolan asked as he scanned the road, making sure they weren't being followed.

"We have a little over an hour," Shing replied, looking at his watch, "to get there and complete our business. I cannot believe that you've brought a woman along on so dangerous a job."

"She's the best fighter I've got," the Executioner responded. "What's the name of this place again?"

"Temple of Ten Thousand Buddhas," Shing replied. "Very famous."

The ride took forty minutes, leading them into what was once the peaceful fishing village of Shatin, but was now a center of government housing for one hundred thousand people.

As they approached the temple through Shatin Pass, Bolan was immediately impressed by the possibilities for successful confrontation. The Temple of Ten Thousand Buddhas sat partway up a high hillside, its only access up four hundred stairs. Farther up the hill were three other temples, including a giant statue to Quan Yuen, the bodhisattva of Mercy.

Shing parked in a public-housing project near the stairs, and they unloaded the bulky camera equipment, the young man insisting on carrying most of it himself, not allowing Mao to take anything. The most important piece of equipment lay wrapped in a blanket. Bolan took it himself, carrying it under his arm. Had anyone been looking, they'd have seen that it was very difficult to disguise the appearance of a high-powered rifle.

They climbed the stairs, Bolan continually looking back down the hill. So far, they were all right.

The temple was magnificent, a nine-story pink pagoda, its forty-five-foot-high walls angling toward the center. The walls inside were covered with twelve-inch-high Buddhas in gold and black, more than twelve thousand of them.

Incense stung the eyes and clung in the throat as the hazy light of hundreds of candles illuminated the alien atmosphere. Stairs wound around the outer walls, enabling one to climb all the way to the top for a panoramic view of the new city below.

This was to be it, the place where Bolan would throw down the gauntlet to the red ties in a very direct and intimidating manner. "There," he said, pointing to an altar containing a large golden Buddha set near the back. "That's where we'll set up the camera."

CHIEF INSPECTOR Ian Crosswaithe stood in the drizzle at the Buddhist cemetery at Tai Tam Gap and tried to ignore the pain in his leg. Five years ago he'd taken a bullet in the shin during a Wan Chai drug raid, and damp, cold weather had caused him leg pain ever since.

Londy Than, a prominent *hong* member, was burying his wife, who'd died on the same night as the fire at Repulse Bay, a night that none of the ruling *hong* had been willing to talk about with him on any level. He hated the American for dragging him into this, but, bloody hell, the man was on to something.

Crosswaithe stood back, away from the ceremony, not wanting to appear callous. After it was over and the priests had collected up their robes and incense, he quietly approached the man.

"Chief Inspector Crosswaithe, Hong Kong Police," he said, approaching the man, who ignored the hand Crosswaithe had extended.

"There's no need for any police here," the man said, his eyes cold and distant. Relatives stood nearby, and Than moved them away with a wave of his hand.

"I just wanted to offer my condolences," Crosswaithe said. "Her death was sudden. She was so young."

"A heart attack in the middle of the night. She was cold dead when I woke up."

"Is that why you didn't have her taken to the hospital?"

"There was no need. My personal physician came to the house and made out the death certificate. I took care of everything else. Now, if that's all..."

"Not quite," the inspector said, grimacing as a bolt of pain shot up his shinbone. "You have a son, I believe. But I don't see him here."

"He was too distraught," the man answered, his eyes focusing somewhere behind Crosswaithe. "I sent him to stay with some relatives on the mainland."

Crosswaithe turned quickly, looking behind him. There, twenty feet away, a red tie stood near a mausoleum, watching. He turned back, but Than had walked away.

"Sir," he called, following, "just another question."

"Can't you leave me alone in my grief?"

"I'm sorry," Crosswaithe said. "Nearly done." He pulled a notebook out of the pocket of his raincoat and flipped through several pages. "One of my men went down to your house. He said that it had been vandalized badly, everything torn to pieces."

"I went into a rage after Nela died," Than said. "I—I got carried away. So what? I can do what I want with my own property."

"Judging from your French Impressionist collection, I'd say the art lovers of the world might take exception to that statement."

"I must go now."

He started to walk off, but Crosswaithe stopped him with a hand on his arm. The man turned and stared until the inspector removed his hand. "Let me help you," he said. "I know there's more to this man—"

"Stay out of it," Than said venomously. "This is a Chinese matter. All you can do is make trouble for yourself and more trouble for me. Go home, Inspector Crosswaithe. Pack your bags and return to England. Don't think about us anymore."

With that, Londy Than turned and joined his party. As everyone filed away, the inspector walked slowly to the grave, watching the gravediggers cover the coffin with damp, cold earth. Something nasty was going on. He was convinced that if he was to dig Mrs. Than out of the ground, he'd find a hole the size of a shilling in her head.

To hell with regulations. Maybe it was time to shake the bush a little bit.

"HEY, CHARLIE," Angela Mao whispered harshly. "Time to wake up. I think we got company."

The Executioner came awake instantly, taking several deep breaths to clear his mind as he sat up. They were behind the thirty-foot-tall statue of Quan Yuen in the meditation posture, and Shing was perched high atop the deity's shoulder. They'd set up so early that Bolan had decided to rest the body while waiting for the quarry. As always, he was able to sleep anywhere and for any amount of time and still be fresh. It was an old combat trick, and one that had served him well over the years.

He stood, climbing up the back of the statue to join Shing on the stone shoulder. Several hundred yards below sat the Temple of Ten Thousand Buddhas. Small groups of men seemed to be making their way up the stairs toward it, pretending to be separate parties, but obviously weren't. Though not wearing their familiar red-tie outfits, they moved too much as a unit.

"Look at the man in front," Shing said, handing Bolan his binoculars.

The lead man was indeed interesting. Though dressed in a business suit, he looked as if he'd be more comfortable in a uniform. His bearing was regal, his nonchalant reconnoitering of his surroundings professional and detached. Could this be the colonel? The others, as they climbed closer to the temple itself, began to fan out on the surrounding hillside. It was a setup, all right. The colonel was about to find out that his quarry wasn't stupid. All the stakes would rise after this morning.

He climbed down from the statue. "Time," he said as he turned to the monitor showing a steady picture from within the temple.

"Eight-fifteen," Mao said, handing him the rifle. Shing slid down the statue's back to land in a crouch beside them.

He looked at the young man. "Did you count them?"

"Thirty. Can we take that many?"

"Don't you wish," Bolan replied. "We're not here to fight it out with them. We're here to prove a point, to get some information and to pick up some weapons."

He released the Beretta and the .44 from his combat harness and handed them out, making sure Mao had the Beretta. She'd drawn blood twice with it, twice when it had really counted. "They've got two choices when I start taking them out," he said. "Either make a hasty retreat or attack. If they attack, choose your targets carefully. They've a lot of hillside to come up and no cover. Slow and steady does it. If they retreat, they'll regroup at the bottom of the hill. We won't be able to leave that way."

"What about my borrowed car?" Shing asked.

"They don't know it's yours. Come and get it later."

"My cousin's going to be really mad at me. He saved five years for that car."

"Give me some sound inside that temple," Bolan replied, locking his mind to combat, shutting out everything else.

He reached down and broke open a box of .308 Winchester ammunition, taking out a shell. What he'd wanted was range, something that could outdistance the close-in weapons he'd seen in the possession of the red ties. They'd gotten him a German Krico 650, what they called the "Super Sniper." It was a single-shot, distance competition rifle fixed with a stubby Beeman SS-3 scope, which made him think the gun had come from Germany by way of America. It wouldn't be his first choice of rifle, but it would do quite nicely.

The sounds of the temple came through the speakers, chanting, the spinning of prayer wheels, bells. He pulled back the bolt on the Krico and dropped in a shell, slamming it home, then filled the pouch on his harness with the rest of the ammunition.

"Turn on the VCR," he said softly, then looked at Shing. "Put your male ego aside for a minute and listen to me. Angela's good with guns. She's tough and I trust her in combat. Do you understand me?"

The man nodded solemnly.

"Have you ever killed anyone, Shing?" he asked.

"No."

Bolan tightened his lips. "It's easy. You just aim and pull the trigger. The hard part is your mind. Don't think, just do. Follow Angela's lead. Don't try and protect her. She's better at this than you. Do what she says, or we all could die. We'll play the yin-yang games later, all right?"

Shing reddened, then bowed slightly to each of them in turn. "I apologize to both of you. I do not wish to jeopardize the mission with my childishness."

"Not childish," Mao said, her voice soft, "just not appropriate right now." She gave him a quick hug, then hurried to hug Bolan also just to cover up her show of affection.

Then she turned to the Executioner. "We won't let you down, Charlie," she said, then smiled wickedly. "Let's kick some butt."

Bolan moved around the side of Quan Yuen, taking in the action through the rifle scope, using a small screwdriver to adjust the cross hairs as he did. The lead man had reached the temple, hesitating slightly before moving in. His men had spread out in a wide circle around the temple itself. Apparently the colonel was expecting that Bolan would hear Le-Chun's dying words, then go to Shatin and hide in or around the temple, thinking the colonel was on his own, simply sight-seeing, and try to take him. The fact that the man had set himself up as bait was of no small interest to Bolan.

The Executioner moved around the back of the massive statue again. "He's inside," Mao said, pointing to the screen. The colonel had moved into the temple and was looking around, making himself visibly obvious.

"It's time," Shing said.

Bolan nodded. "Just listen to one thing. The man leading these troops has just set himself up as the patsy on this mission. Anything could happen."

"I don't understand," Shing told him.

"He wants to die," the Executioner replied, then cocked his head. "Interesting. The best move in war is always to deny people what they want."

The colonel had walked to within good range of the temple camera, and Mao zoomed it in slightly to get a good close-up of his face. Bolan took a long breath, then picked up his microphone, flicking it to life. "Good morning, Colonel," he said.

The man jumped, startled. "Where are you?" he asked, pulling out his handgun, a 9 mm Ruger.

"You didn't really think I'd fall into such an obvious trap, did you?" Bolan replied. "What kind of suicide mission have you set yourself up for?"

"Your government has no business becoming involved with the affairs of China and Hong Kong, Belasko... or whatever your name is."

"I'm denied the pleasure of your name, sir."

"For you, my name is *si*—death."

"Maybe, but not today, I think." Bolan watched his eyes and their horrid yearning. For what, he wondered. "And for the record, I work for no government. I'm just a guy trying to lend a helping hand to good people who deserve help. What is it you're doing?"

"Visiting the temples of Shatin, of course," the man replied, his eyes roving, freezing when he caught sight of the hidden camera.

"That's right," Bolan said. "By tonight the whole world will know who you are and the dishonorable things you do with your pitiful life."

The man drew himself up. "I am a man of honor," he said. "But you cause me to lose face. You and I may not survive together in the same plane. Where are you, coward? Come out and face me."

"Like I said, Colonel, not today."

"Then, what?"

"Well, I'm going to see how many of your men I can kill before you can get them out of here."

Bolan scrambled up the statue, the Krico strapped to his shoulder. Flinging himself over the broad shoulder to lie on his belly, he braced the rifle on a strong forearm.

He settled the sights on a man hovering behind one of the temple's outbuilding shrines. He wanted debilitation, and quickly. Breathing easily, lightly, he drew the cross hairs to the base of the brain, then squeezed smoothly. The man's head snapped back, the body going down like a rag doll. Bingo.

He swung to another target, loading quickly, no one realizing a comrade had gone down yet. This one was walking back and forth near the steps, smoking a cigarette. Bolan squeezed again, a chest shot, cigarette smoke drifting out of the wound when he went down.

The soldiers were reacting to the rifle cracks now, as Bolan expended the shell and loaded another. A man was pointing up toward their position, and Bolan shot him in the head, the corpse tumbling backward down the four hundred steps that led up to the temple.

The colonel was out in the stone yard, calling to a large man who was in the process of ordering a charge.

Two men started up, and Bolan took out the lead man, who tumbled into the man behind, both of them falling backward.

Always in the center of the action, the colonel made an inviting target, but one Bolan resisted simply because it was so inviting—the man had a death wish, and Bolan could turn that to his advantage.

The colonel was yelling through cupped hands, waving his troops back down the hillside to the town. It was a wise move. Bolan had the angle. There was no safe cover for the red ties.

Bolan still had plenty of range left in the rifle, though. He got two more before they even left the temple grounds. "Go for the weapons!" he yelled while reloading. "Shoot anything that moves!"

Mao and Shing charged down the hill toward the temple as Bolan picked off another red tie leaping down the stairs. He got him in midleap, the man tumbling forward, bouncing down the two hundred feet to the bottom of the stairs.

He jerked back the bolt, the casing flying. They were on the outside edge of his range, and Bolan loaded and fired again, his shot falling just short, kicking up dust behind the fleeing men. Working quickly with the screwdriver, he adjusted the cross hairs down slightly and reloaded, catching the slower of his adversaries in the lower back, the man crumpling in slow motion to sprawl on the stairs.

Below, Mao and Shing had reached the temple grounds and were gathering weapons and ammo, dropping them in heavy canvas bags. As they sprinted for the long stairs to get the men lying there, the Executioner readjusted his sights and prepared for a counterattack.

The red tie at the top of the stairs wasn't dead yet. Mao put a bullet in his head as he was going for a handgun, Shing staring in rapt fascination as she squatted and stripped the man of his weapons.

"Move, Shing," Bolan whispered. He was a standing target.

Shots rang out from below, and Mao hit the ground, rolling. Shing took a hit to the arm, backing up almost comically, then falling.

The red ties were coming back up the hill, trying to take it in their Mercedes. One man drove while the others crouched behind like GIs following a tank.

Six cars moved slowly up the steep incline, but Bolan doubted they could actually take the sixty-degree angle of ascent. He tried a shot at the gas tank, hitting the car but not stopping it as Mao dragged Shing to his feet and helped him out of the compound.

Reloading, the Executioner tried the same car again. This time it went up with a huge *whump*, jumping, sprouting a massive orange fireball, while burning red ties charged away from the conflagration.

It was time to move, and fast. Bolan slid down the statue and grabbed the videotape he'd made in the temple. The rest of the equipment was nothing but bulk now. They'd leave it behind.

He circled the statue, hurrying to join Mao and Shing. Hundreds of feet below, the red ties had abandoned the cars and were charging up the hill.

Shing was bleeding badly from the arm. Bolan removed his belt and made a tourniquet as the red ties began to fire from below, still out of range, not getting close. "You're going to need to move on your own, Shing," the Executioner said. "You up to it?"

Shing gritted his teeth and nodded.

"Then let's go."

They hurried up the remainder of the hillside, faced with the vast sweep of mainland China. To the northeast, a mile distant, was some sort of stadium, already filling with people.

"What is it?" Bolan asked.

"Racetrack," Shing replied.

The soldier was already running. "Crowds and doctors," he called over his shoulder. "Come on. I feel lucky today."

They crested the hill and charged headlong down the grassy slope, Bolan noting that Mao was hanging back, making sure Shing kept pace.

CHAPTER EIGHT

All the homes on Cape D'Aguilar had high walls, not so much for security as privacy. The cape was the most isolated area of Hong Kong Island, accessible only by one narrow thoroughfare, Shek O Road. Travel was discouraged on the D'Aguilar Peninsula because of the military base, Little Sai Wan, located at its head. The people who lived on the cape kept to themselves and wanted no visitors, and that was just fine with Wang Wushen.

He stood on the twenty-foot wall, watching the Mercedes carrying Li and Chao make its way along the rocky, windswept shore. A dull, overcast sky and higher-than-usual winds sent salty white spray over the rocks to splash the vehicle. The weather was turning progressively worse. It was that time of year.

Wang worked very hard on his serene exterior, but beneath the surface he seethed. While on one hand his bold move to bring the *hong* in line had paid off handsomely, the paperwork proceeding more quickly than expected, on the other hand he had the American running wild. And he had Colonel Li, who had directly confronted the American and lost face for all of them. To make matters worse, what had been a quiet, simple series of eliminations had now turned into bloody fighting on the streets, drawing attention to the red ties and hence to him.

He didn't like it. At the moment of his greatest triumph, tragedy loomed in the wings. Already Beijing had made its displeasure known, and that displeasure was falling on *his* head no matter how hard he tried to blame it on Li. He was supposed to clean it up, and quickly, before the world press got hold of the story and made it a bigger issue than it was.

The Mercedes made its way to the main gate, and Wang turned and walked down the stone stairs of the castlelike walls. The house and its environs had been leased through no fewer than three phony buyers so as to never connect it to the People's Republic. No one actually lived in the house. It had been set up as a safehouse for any espionage activity necessary before the takeover in 1997. Wang was finding it very handy now.

He hit the gate controls, and with a hydraulic whoosh the heavy iron gate creaked slowly open, the Mercedes sliding quickly in. Wang put on a smile as he loaded a cigarette into the holder and pulled open the car's back door.

Li stepped out, followed by Major Chao, the big man hurrying to light Wang's cigarette.

"So," Wang said with a false smile. "I see you've survived your encounter with the American."

Colonel Li met his gaze head-on. "I failed," he said. "You have my apologies."

"Apologies," Wang repeated, still smiling. "Shall we go inside?"

They walked to the house, a two-story, boxy stone structure that reminded Wang of a prison. He could never live here. It was too depressing. But right now it was reassuring—its concrete walls a foot thick, its windows tiny, barely large enough to look out, guard stations on top of the house and at the wall corners. Inside the place was comfortable and homey, but it was also a state-of-the-art listening post, arsenal and sometime jumping-off point for state terrorists either coming or going.

"The American has hidden the criminals somewhere... to train them," Li said.

"All together in one place?" Wang asked.

"Yes."

"Where?"

As they arrived at the front door, Dr. Werner, wearing a black body stocking, opened the door for them. He was thin, skeletal. "Hello, Soo," he said, eyes bright, glazed. "I hear our field tests are breaking down."

Wang ushered them through the door and into a sunken living room, filled completely with a circular red leather sofa and round coffee table in the center. There was a large dining area with attached kitchen beside the living room, and dormitory-style bedrooms upstairs. The rest of the rooms were filled with electronic equipment and weapons, the eavesdropping equipment manned twenty-four hours a day.

"Colonel Li was just telling me that the criminals are all together in one place," Wang said as they sat on the circular sofa. Werner rang a bell for tea.

"Whatever for?" he asked.

"Training," Li replied. "With the American."

"I'd like to meet that one," Werner said, arching an eyebrow. "He must be quite the specimen."

"We could have taken him this morning," Chao said, and everyone turned to stare at him.

"I don't recall asking for your assessment," Li stated coldly.

"No...please," Wang said, hissing out a long streamer of smoke. "Please elaborate."

"He had a single-shot rifle," Chao remarked, staring hard at Li the entire time. "Had we rushed him, he could not have gotten us all."

"He could have gotten a lot of us," Li said, shaking his head. "And are you forgetting that he had help?"

Chao grimaced. "A man and a woman...civilians. We let him slip away and have lost honor because Colonel Li is a coward."

Li was on his feet, moving toward his subordinate, who crouched to meet him. Wang found it amusing but not enlightening. "Chao...no!" he said. "Stand away from him. Now!"

Chao, smiling broadly, headed toward the dining area.

Li whirled to face Wang. "I made the proper military decisions, sir," he said, voice dripping blind rage.

"Your *major* is just a dressed-up bully, not a soldier, and certainly not an officer."

"Sit down, Colonel," Wang said pleasantly as the tea arrived, along with his caged songbird. "We must talk of many things."

At that moment shouts could be heard from upstairs, followed seconds later by a young boy charging down the stairs, heading for the door. Wang recognized the boy as Londy Than's son. In the blink of an eye, Chao had picked up a dining-room chair and thrown it across the width of the large room, hitting the boy squarely, knocking him over.

Everyone laughed except for Li, who jumped up and ran to the child, helping him to his feet, making sure he was all right.

Several red ties came down the stairs and took the boy from Li. "That boy is China's future," Wang said softly to the red ties. "I would not want to be the one who let that future slip away."

The boy was screaming and crying. "You haven't mistreated them, have you?" Li asked.

"That one seems healthy enough to me," Wang replied. "What business is it of yours?"

"The women. You haven't violated the women?"

Wang smiled at the thought of the previous evening with the wife of the head of the Inchan Syndicate. "Women were made to be violated," he said, waving away the red ties with the yelling boy. "Don't concern yourself. The situation is well in hand, as it were."

Tea was passed around, and Wang took the bird out of its cage to perch on his shoulder. "There is sadness in Beijing, Colonel Li," he said. "This entire mess is turning into an international incident. We do not want that."

"One of the reasons I did not continue the futile charge up that hill, sir," Li said.

Wang hated honorable men. They were so boringly predictable. "I have been issued orders to pass on to you. You have three days to end this madness."

"Three days?" Li repeated, his teacup poised, frozen in his fingertips. "There are still over a hundred on the list."

"Plus the specimen from America," Werner added.

"You said they were all together in one place," Wang reminded him. "You may get them all at once ... plus the American."

"Except ..."

Wang sighed deeply. "You don't know where they are, do you, Colonel?"

"No, sir, I don't. But my contact is on the inside and will get in touch with us as soon as he's able."

"And when might we expect that to be?" Wang asked.

"Any time."

"Or no time. I can't depend on your contact, Colonel. Every moment that elapses without resolution on this issue brings us closer to crisis point. We're attracting very negative attention."

"What would you have me do?" Li asked, putting down his cup and opening his hands. "We're searching. Here, Kowloon, the New Territories...we're getting to the islands. But there are a hundred of them. We're trying to chase down anyone who might have some idea, but so far, the secret has been kept."

"There is one thing you haven't tried," Wang said.

He enjoyed watching the confusion cross Li's face. "What is that?"

"Inviting them back."

"And how might I do that?"

"I think death has a way of bringing people back. I think a lot of death might bring a lot of people back."

"You're not suggesting—"

"Everyone has cousins here and in Kowloon, nieces, aunts, nephews, half brothers."

"People who have done nothing to us."

"We have three days, Colonel. We've no other choice."

Li stood, pacing quickly, shaking his head the entire time. "You're talking about simply gunning down innocent civilians for no reason. I won't do it."

"Actually I was thinking this might be more in Major Chao's area of expertise. It will free you up to concentrate completely on the American. And speaking of the American, it seems our training isn't as good as it should have been. He's taken out twenty-five of your men, Colonel."

"I know," Li said, his tone as sharp as a knife.

"What do you intend to do about it?"

Li just stared at him.

"Well," Wang said, "we've been giving this some thought also, Dr. Werner and myself."

Werner sat back on the sofa in the lotus position. He smiled, catlike. "I've been having some ideas in this area," he said softly.

"What sort of ideas?" Li asked.

"Should we show him?" Werner asked.

"I think so," Wang replied, ringing the bell again. "Colonel Li needs to understand what true dedication to a cause means. Perhaps he'll learn from it."

Two red ties came into the living room, holding between them a man struggling to free himself, alternately pleading and demanding in Cantonese. He wore only a bathing suit.

"That chair should be sufficient," Werner said, indicating one of the high-backed wooden dining-room chairs.

"Who is he?" Li asked.

"Nobody," Werner said. "The locals are always sneaking down here to swim. He was spotted on perimeter watch and brought in."

The man was thrown onto the chair, his arms and legs tightly secured.

Werner was up, a nimble skeleton in black, a syringe produced somewhere from inside his outfit.

"The brain is a gland, Soo," he said, moving up to the man, who watched wide-eyed as the needle hovered beside his head. "All our feelings, our moods, our anxieties, elations and emotional connections are all tied to brain excretions. We are living in the era of brain research, mood enhancement.''

He injected the complaining man in the base of the skull. ''What makes us human, eh?'' Werner asked Li.

''Respect,'' Li stated. ''Honor. Love. Duty.''

''No,'' Werner said. ''Chemical reactions in the brain. Change the chemistry and you change the man. We've been pumping up the notion of humanity in your red ties. Now, through brain chemistry, we're going to pump it up even more. How do they say it, more human than human.''

The man on the chair was beginning to jerk in his seat, his face twitching.

''Yes,'' Werner hissed, dancing away from the chair. ''Now, our friend is an extreme example, but this is what we envision.''

The captive man's face was dark, animallike, and he was straining at his bonds.

Wang took a long drag from his cigarette. ''The last time we played, Colonel Li, your gun was not loaded. I sincerely hope it is today.''

Li's insides turned to powdered glass as he watched the man jerk to stand, the chair smashing to pieces from the force of his movements, his bonds falling to the floor. He was growling like a wild beast. What kind of people were these?

Chao understood before Li did, so surreal was the entire scene. Screaming in rage, the man charged them, teeth bared like fangs, his hands grasping clawlike.

"Primal man in all his fury," Werner said loudly, above the animal sounds. "Beautiful, isn't it?"

Chao was already firing as Li dragged out his Ruger. He watched the nearly naked man take hit after hit, falling back but always returning, a cornered beast fighting for its life. He jumped on Chao even as his blood pumped furiously from his body. Li rushed forward to stick the Ruger's barrel in the man's ear and pulled the trigger.

The head exploded partway off, knocking the man from Chao, and still he came, turning from Chao to Li, his brain exposed, gray matter oozing down his neck.

Li's own brain was on fire now as he continued firing, round after round. The man finally gurgled loudly to a rush of blood from his mouth, then fell hard, like a tree, at Li's feet.

The pistol dropped from Li's grasp, and he stared at all of them. "You're insane. You can't ever use this."

"Oh, we can and we will," Werner said, bending to study the body. "In controlled doses, of course."

"Controlled doses? You give this to real soldiers, and there's no way anyone, even you, will control them."

"That's what we intend to find out," Wang said. "We'll just think of Hong Kong as a huge science lab ready for experimentation."

Li sat heavily on the sofa. "May the spirits of our ancestors protect us."

"Communism," Wang reminded him, "does not believe in spirits."

MACK BOLAN SAT at the phone in Mr. Shinshi's study on Tree Island. The man's computer screen glowed before him, a still-frame image of the colonel at the Temple of Ten Thousand Buddhas looking out of the screen at him.

"I've got it up now, Hal," he said.

"We're ready on this end," Brognola responded. "Go ahead and fax it."

The Executioner punched up a fax number on the keyboard and hit Enter, and the transmit light bleeped immediately as the photo was digitalized halfway around the world.

"We're rolling," Bolan said. "You have any luck finding a country to grant asylum to these people?"

"This isn't easy, you know. It's not looking good. Maybe you'd just better think about getting out of there before it gets completely out of hand."

"It's already out of hand, and if my friends here are to be left to be gunned down, believe me, Hal, I'm going to be standing here beside them."

"For once, big guy, I don't know what to tell you."

"Yeah. Who you got there with you?"

"Larry Thornton. He's Justice's resident expert on the Chinese military. He's . . . wait, the fax is coming through over here. Thornton's got it. I don't want you to stay there. This isn't why—"

"Save your breath, Hal," Bolan said. "You know me better than that. I'm committed here."

"Hold the line. Thornton wants to speak with you."

Bolan sat back heavily in the desk chair, his eyes fixed on the window behind the computer. Tree Island was aptly named, a large pine-and-fir forest eating up all the land that wasn't cleared for Shinshi's compound.

"Mr., ah, Belasko?" said an unfamiliar voice.

"Just call me Mike," Bolan said. "What have you got, Mr. Thornton?"

"You've found the diamond in the rough, Mike," the man replied excitedly. "This is a picture of none other than General Li Soo, the top-ranking military man in the People's Army bar none."

"They call him 'Colonel,' not 'General,'" Bolan said.

"The general had a brother, Li Yun. It was a night-and-day kind of deal, the general a loyal Party man, his brother a radical dissident. Their father had been killed in the '49 revolution and Li Soo had raised his brother ever since, becoming a father figure to him. Li Yun was one of the leaders of the prodemocracy group at Tiananmen Square back in '89, was arrested in the crackdown. At that point General Li just dropped off the map, punished for Yun's radicalism and, we think, for his failure to denounce his brother publicly. This is the first we've seen of him since the '89 crackdown."

"What happened to the brother?"

"Our intelligence indicates he died of malnourishment and mistreatment in prison in 1990, but I'm going to maintain deniability on that. I can't be completely sure."

"But you are sure of the man in the photo?"

"Absolutely. He's fallen a long way since being supreme commander of all their armed forces."

"Thanks," Bolan said. "Can I speak with Hal again?"

"Sure. Just a minute."

"Yeah?"

"Hal, I need you to do me a favor or two."

"You've got it."

"Why don't you make a few calls to your friends in the news media and tell them that a kind of genocide is going on here. Make some waves. Maybe if we shine the spotlight big enough on Hong Kong, the Chinese will back off."

"Why don't we hold off on that a day? Let me cash all my diplomatic chits first. I really am trying to work something out here."

"I'm working on the Britons, too," Bolan replied. "Maybe we'll get lucky. We're buying hours at this point. See you, Hal."

"I hope so. That's it from here."

Bolan cut the transmission and stood, stretching, his back still stiff from the run-in with the hurricane fence in Aberdeen. Shinshi's house was open and airy, opulent in an old-world way, with servants, and fresh flowers on all the tables. He had made his fortune producing kung fu movies for the Shangai circuit, running afoul of the People's Republic when his films became too political. He had been living a life of seclusion on Tree Island for fifteen years under an assumed name.

Bolan walked through the house, captured and purchased weapons and ammunition making a pitifully small stack in the terraced living room.

Shing was waiting for him, sitting with Shinshi on a sofa. Shing's arm was in a sling. A vet at the racetrack had repaired the damage.

"Any good news from America?" he asked, standing at the Executioner's approach.

Bolan shook his head. "Nothing much yet," he said. "They're still trying."

"Sure."

Bolan looked at Shinshi. "I gave them your number for return calls," he said.

The man nodded. "I presumed you would. What will you have us do first?"

"I want to divide the camp into age groups," Bolan said. "Those too old and young for combat in one group, everybody else in the other. Let's take a look outside."

He and Shing moved out the front door and into a wide-open yard, the hangar and the barn forming the outer perimeter. A hard-packed runway led from the hangar directly through the trees all the way down to the sea. Shinshi's small Cessna sat at the mouth of the airstrip.

The yard was full of people, and Angela Mao was leading them in the ancient rituals of t'ai chi, meant to focus their mental, physical and spiritual energies.

"May I have your attention!" Bolan called loudly, and everyone turned to face him.

"The red ties will be searching for us everywhere," he said, with Mao translating. "I have stationed junks on the waters surrounding the island to watch for suspicious activity. All of you will get your turn at perimeter watch. But you have to help me in several ways. If you hear low-flying aircraft, hide in the barn or the hangar. If that's not possible, take to the trees and find a hiding place.

"I'm going to be teaching you many things in the next few days. Be prepared to listen to them and follow my instructions exactly. We've drawn blood from the red ties. Life will become even more difficult now that they've lost face. Those of you who are below the age of fifteen and above the age of sixty will be group A and will meet in the barn. The rest of you will be Group B. Your meeting place is always the hangar.

"I'm going to be distributing the guns to you in order from the oldest to the youngest."

There were murmurs, then shouts of disapproval.

"You wonder why?" Bolan said. "I'll tell you why. We're trying to learn to survive here. The young can run. The old can't. They get the weapons training."

"We only have one question, Charlie," Mao called from the rear of the group. "We all came here on the

Star Ferry. If the red ties find us, we've got no Star
Ferry to leave on. What do we do?''

"We fight where we stand," Bolan replied, the cold
wind whistling through the camp the only sound.
"We'll either kill or be killed. Now, go to your meeting places. I'll come to each group and begin the
training."

Grumbling, everyone moved in the assigned directions, Bolan moving toward the hangar to talk to the
younger people first.

CHAPTER NINE

Bolan was tired, but the time was so short. He had stopped looking at his watch at midnight, and figured he'd go on until he dropped. Everyone was gathered in the hangar, sitting on the floor bundled up. The cold wind hadn't ceased for two days, splattering the island with intermittent patterns of rain.

"You've got to understand," he told them, one of the younger men translating, "there's one major difference between you and the people who seek to kill you—you are human. They aren't. They'll automatically kill you with whatever weapon, including their hands, that is available. They survive on their ability to be vicious and feed on your humanity. I'm asking you to give up that humanity for a little while. Those of you with weapons must commit yourselves to firing those weapons without question, killing without remorse or thought. It's the only way you'll survive. We've spent the day learning about your weapons—loading, firing, cleaning, clearing jams. Practice these things until the weapon is your friend. Believe me, it will be your best and most dependable friend before this is all over.

"Those of you without weapons must contain the human's natural inquisitiveness. At the first sign of anything unusual, simply turn and run as fast and as far as you can—traffic jams, mailmen at the door, strangers needing assistance—all of these things are to be avoided at all costs. If someone knocks on your door, don't answer.

"Always have an escape route, wherever you are. If you're staying in a house or apartment, make sure there's more than one way out. Sleep in your clothes and your shoes. Practice your escape routes. Know them in the dark.

"Compassion for you is the enemy. You must learn cruelty, not as a way of life, just as a way of survival. If you can kill a red tie, simply do it, whether you're in immediate danger or not. I know I'm challenging the values of your entire lifetime. Just remember that your enemy isn't human. Whatever part of your humanity you must give up, do it and trust that you will return from that horrible place of animal passions once this is over."

As he spoke, he saw Angela Mao standing in the hangar doorway trying frantically to get his attention. "Those of you in the first group," Bolan said, "lay out your bedrolls and get some sleep. Those in the second group, meet me in ten minutes in the barn for hand-to-hand fighting techniques."

He hurried through the hundred-foot-long hangar and met Mao in the darkness of the yard. "What is it?"

"You'd better come see," she replied, her voice shaking.

She led him quickly into the house. The big-screen television was running in the spacious living room, pictures of police cars and ambulances filling the screen. A shoot-out was in progress in the Wan Chai district.

"What's happened?" Bolan asked.

"Red ties," Shinshi replied. "Small squads have been moving through the city, indiscriminately killing anyone who is a known relative of those on the criminals list."

"Dammit," Bolan said. "They're trying to draw us back."

"As far as I'm concerned," Mao said, "they're doing a fine job of it. When everyone hears—"

"Don't tell them yet," Bolan said. "Going back now won't solve anything. The police need to start doing their job."

"It's worse than that," Shinshi said, running hands through his hair. "The killers...it's as if they're monsters of some kind, crazed. One of the reports said it took twenty bullets to bring down one of them, that he kept coming like a wild dog."

"Tiananmen Square," Bolan whispered.

"What?" Mao asked.

"When the regular army was reluctant to go into Tiananmen Square to shoot down their own people during the prodemocracy movement, there were many reports that they had been injected with something that turned them into raging beasts. Afterward the reports were downplayed and given the deep six. Maybe now we know the truth."

"We can't keep this from our people," Mao said. "It wouldn't be fair. They must be told so as to choose their own course of action."

The Executioner nodded. "You're right. But let's hold it through tonight, anyway. There's no way to transport everybody back."

"So what do we do?"

He looked hard at the woman, at the anger and determination on her face. "You want some action?" he asked.

"You bet, Charlie."

He turned to Shinshi. "That's a great speedboat you've got tied up on your dock. Mind if I borrow it for a little spin?"

The man took a long breath. "Why not? The keys are in it. I'll tell everyone you were called away."

The big man nodded. "They could use a night's sleep anyhow."

While Bolan got into his combat harness, Mao chose a nickle-plated .45 automatic they'd purchased on the black market. She stuffed it into the waistband of her jeans and covered it with a brown leather jacket.

They were out the back door in thirty seconds flat and on the dock within a minute. The boat was a beauty, black and sleek with two powerful Evinrude motors on the back.

The sea was choppy when they climbed in and started the engines, Mao untying the line as Bolan steered the craft away from the island.

"I can't believe this is happening," the woman said as they sat across from each other, the wet wind cold and biting, her hair billowing around her head.

"I think they've made a mistake that will work to our favor," Bolan shouted above the whining motors. "They want to hurry up and get this over with before it becomes an international issue. But now the Hong Kong police are involved, and the killings are reaching massive scale. This can't go on much longer."

"You considered this possibility?"

"The thought crossed my mind, but after getting the ID on General Li, I assumed things would remain quiet. Li was a good man, a real soldier."

"You were wrong."

"Maybe. There's another, more frightening possibility. Li lost face when we met in the New Territories. They may have taken the real military man out of the action and put God only knows who in charge. If what's happening is any indication, madmen are running the show."

"I've got to hand it to you, Charlie. You're the life of the party. I'm surprised you let me come."

"You know what to do with red ties," he said simply.

CHIEF INSPECTOR IAN CROSSWAITHE dived behind the overturned table as the burst of rounds from a sub-

machine gun splintered the floor just behind him. The
nightclub was dark, streaked in erotic red light that
cast a bloodlike glow over everything.

Breathing heavily, he dropped the cylinder from his
.38, punched out the shells and used a speedloader. He
was back in business within twenty seconds.

They had three red ties trapped in here. Already casualties were high with no end in sight. He wondered
if it was Hong Kong that was trapped.

Bodies lay on the floor all around him, tables and
chairs strewed everywhere, the moans and cries of the
wounded all he could hear now. They were conserv-
ing ammunition.

"Chen," he called to no response. "Chen!"

Nothing.

"Whyng! Leung!"

Nothing.

"Bloody hell," he whispered, getting up on his
knees to peer over the table. "Noonan!"

"I—I'm near the bandstand, Ian," a weak voice
replied. "But I'm down. I'm hit."

"Is it bad?"

"Yeah. Worse than bad."

Crosswaithe flinched. He'd known Dick Noonan
for twenty years. He couldn't stand the thought of him
lying there, the life oozing out of him, with nothing
being done. "We'll get you out of there as quick as we
can!" he said, the words sounding as hollow as death.

He looked through the remnants of the oldest topless dance club in Hong Kong. The floor looked like a

slaughterhouse. Maybe fifteen people lay there, not all of them dead. Most were cops. His men.

They'd gotten a call that night that whole families were being killed. He could endure it no longer. Taking everyone on duty, he sent them to the government housing projects in the Tai Hang district where the calls had originated. Most of the red ties had gotten away, but these three had been trapped in their car. They'd tried to outrun the police, but had gotten boxed in quickly, crashing their black Mercedes into a light pole on Lockhart and running into the Bottoms Up Club.

The first five cops through the doors were gunned down by automatic fire, along with anyone else who happened to be in the way. Crosswaithe had been with the second five through. They'd fared little better.

The red ties were behind the bars in the center of the room. The Bottoms Up had four hexagonally shaped bars, all connected by mirrors, which presented the mirror maze. The gunmen squatted behind the bars with perfect vision to any part of the room. On the other hand it was nearly impossible to tell where *they* were because their images were being reflected from so many surfaces. Crosswaithe knew there were only three of them. They looked like a hundred in the mirrors.

"You still with me, Dick?" he called.

"Yeah . . ."

"Just hold on."

"Inspector!" a voice called from the doorway, generating a burst of gunfire from behind the bars.

"Would you stay back!" Crosswaithe called.

"We've got custody of an armed man...an American, along with a local. He said to tell you he knew you were a cop."

Crosswaithe smiled, shaking his head. "Let him go!" he called. "He's one of us!"

ON THE OTHER SIDE of the door, Mack Bolan and Angela Mao stood with uniformed police in the bar's cloakroom with the lights out. The cops backed away from them after hearing from Crosswaithe.

"Inspector, you okay?" Bolan called.

"Peachy!" the man called back. "Come to gloat?"

"No, to join you."

"Great. I think police academy begins a new semester every three months."

"Funny man," Mao said lowly.

Bolan looked round the room, then walked outside. When he returned he was dragging two large aluminum garbage cans, filled to the top.

Mao covered her nose, while the cops backed up, gagging. "Take this," Bolan said, sliding one up to her. "Use it like a shield as you go through, then get rid of it and break right. There's a piano over there you can use as cover."

"You come up with the worst plans, Charlie," she said, hefting the trash can. "I don't know why I let you run around with me."

"Go," he said, shoving her.

He grabbed his can and was right behind. They burst through the doors into the club, the red ties standing to fire. The brief second of reaction time gave Mao a jump, and she made her position without drawing fire. It was all concentrated on Bolan.

The room exploded with white light and staccato gunfire. Bolan tossed his can at the bar and dived for the table that protected Crosswaithe, a trail of death splintering the floor just behind him.

He made the table. Set in a natural alcove behind a pillar, the spot was good defensively. He rolled up next to Crosswaithe and jerked the Beretta out of the harness, snapping a round into the chamber.

"You smell like garbage," Crosswaithe told him. "And you know I don't want to know about those guns of yours. You're putting me in a very compromising position."

"You got some kind of plan here, Inspector?"

The man frowned. "The place is surrounded," he said. "They've no way out. Normally I'd wait for more backup, gas the hell out of the place and flush them out. But as you can see, we've got people hurt everywhere. I've got men, good men, down."

"You're ready to do it, aren't you?"

"Yeah . . . if you are. But how?"

"I've got something else you don't want to know about," the Executioner said, reaching into his jacket. "Angela!" he called across the room.

"What's the story, Charlie?"

"Come up firing when you hear the pop," he said. "Don't stop firing until you're out of ammo or I tell you different."

"Don't worry! Hey, I got some live people back here with me."

Bolan pulled two concussion grenades from the clips of his harness. "Tell them to take it easy," he called back. "We'll be done in a minute."

He turned to Crosswaithe. "I suppose you gave them the chance to surrender already?"

"We thought the roadblocks and the 'Halt! Police!' probably sufficed in that area," he answered, an eyebrow arched at the grenades.

Bolan handed one to him. "You ever play cricket, Ian?"

"Of course."

"Well, I want you to lob this up into that bar pit."

"Listen," Crosswaithe said. "We just can't—"

"Now!" Bolan yelled, pulling the pin and throwing his grenade, Crosswaithe right with him.

The *whump*s went off almost simultaneously, glass shattering like the sound of a million bells. Bolan popped up from cover immediately, the Beretta stiff armed in front of him.

Most of the bar was demolished. One red tie emerged from the dust cloud, his clothing in shreds, blood pouring from his body, shards of glass embedded all over him. He had a MAC-10 in each hand, and pulled the triggers on full-auto, the dust flashing to daylight as Bolan, Crosswaithe and Angela Mao fired controlled, single shots at him.

The man was stumbling as the second red tie came through the dust, an arm missing, still firing his weapon. Bolan emptied the Beretta, then drew the .44, working on head shots. It was the only way to bring them down.

The first man was on his knees, still trying to fire guns he'd already emptied as he coughed blood and growled.

The one-armed man went down hard as the third gunner came at them without weapons, charging, snarling, an enraged beast.

"Try and take him!" Bolan yelled, both he and Mao running for him at the same time. She took him low, at the ankles, as the soldier vaulted an overturned table and hit the man at shoulder level, taking them all to the floor.

The man kicked out, Mao flying across the room as Crosswaithe yelled for more help and cops came pouring through the door.

The red tie's sunglasses had come off in the fall, and Bolan was staring into bloodred eyes with pupils like pennies. The man growled low and took the Executioner by the shoulders, flinging him aside as several more police piled onto the man. The cops were thrown off the red tie as quickly as they could jump on him. Incredibly the man stood, dragging a half dozen of them as he moved relentlessly to the door.

Bolan jumped on his back, pinching his carotid artery as hard and as long as he could, cutting the blood flow to the brain. The man threw the police off his arms and reached back, but he was weakening, his arms without strength, his legs wobbly.

He passed out, Bolan jumping from him as he crumpled to the floor. "Chain him up," he ordered.

"Heavy chains," Crosswaithe added. "I want him in a cell before he comes around."

He turned toward the door. "We need medical personnel and stretchers in here now!"

Bolan watched as Crosswaithe ran to kneel beside a plainclothes policeman lying near the bandstand, taking the man's hand. The inspector held the hand for a moment, then placed it on the man's chest, crying quietly as he did so.

Then he took a deep breath, wiped at his eyes, stood and returned to Bolan. "They're going to pay for this," he vowed. "I don't care what it takes."

TWO HOURS LATER Bolan, Mao and Crosswaithe looked through the one-way into the interrogation room where the red tie was chained to a chair bolted to the ground. When he'd regained consciousness, however, his mood had changed. Gone was the animal insanity; now he simply sat stoically, his eyes myopic, as he listened without response to the questions the interrogators were asking him. Meanwhile two nurses were tending his wounds, swathing him in bandages.

"I feel like I'm staring into the face of the devil," Crosswaithe said.

"How long on those blood tests do you think?" Bolan asked.

"Better be soon," the inspector replied. "I want to show this man to the world and tell them what he'd been pumped full of. I want every human on this planet to see the horror that is about to become Hong Kong." He slammed a hand on the wall. "Dammit, I sound like a politician."

The phone on the table buzzed, almost as a response to the pounding on the wall. Crosswaithe picked it up. "This had better be the lab," he said.

"No, sir," came the reply. "Governor Purdy is here with another gentleman and wants to speak with you."

"Send them here to me," he said softly, and hung up the phone.

"What is it?" Mao asked.

"We're about to see the power of the People's Republic, I think," Bolan answered.

"The governor of Hong Kong is coming into this room in a moment," Crosswaithe said. "The highest British official for the protectorate, whom I've never met, is coming to see me...with a Chinese gentleman."

There was a tapping on the door, then a tall, distinguished man in a gray suit walking in first. It had to be Purdy. Bolan could tell a politician a mile away. They all had the bearing of responsibility and station. Most were, unfortunately, as empty and full of hot air as an inflatable love doll. He was followed through the door by a Chinese man in a silk suit done in the palest of greens. He was aloof and somewhat prissy, gazing at them all through the haze of a cigarette smoldering in an ebony holder.

"I presume you're Inspector Crosswaithe," the man in the gray suit said.

"Lord Purdy," he replied, bowing slightly. "To what do I owe the—"

"Stow it, Inspector," Purdy said, moving to stare at Bolan. "And who might you be?"

"My name's Belasko. I'm an American citizen who's not particularly disposed to people addressing me in that tone, regardless of their station in life."

"Belasko," the Chinese man said, smiling slightly. He walked up to Bolan, looking him up and down like a prized stallion.

"I don't believe I've had the pleasure."

"This is Wang Wushen," Purdy said. "Director of the Bank of China."

"Killers," Mao snapped.

"Hong Kong youth," Wang stated, blowing a streamer of cigarette smoke at her. "No respect for their elders. That will all change soon, young woman."

"My name is Angela Mao, daughter of Mao Hsing. You can kill me, but you cannot break my will or the will of the free people of Hong Kong."

Wang laughed. "So political," he said, but his eyes had drifted back to Bolan. "You're a large man, Mr. Belasko. Physically imposing."

"And you're pretty smooth, Wang," Bolan replied. "Why don't you tell us what you want?"

Purdy moved to look through the one-way glass at the bandaged red tie. "We had a great deal of trouble on our streets tonight, Inspector," he said, still facing the window.

"Sir, there are assassination squads running loose in our city right now, I—"

"Let me repeat myself," Purdy interrupted, turning angrily to face the inspector. "We had a great deal of trouble on our streets tonight. It is your job, your *duty* to avoid such problems. We thrive on tourism and the even flow of capital. Such actions as you and your men performed tonight affect both of those areas."

"Five of my men are dead," Crosswaithe told him, then pointed through the window, "because of him and the other red ties."

"I did not come here to argue with you," Purdy said. "That man you're holding is here under a People's Republic diplomatic visa."

"I've seen no such visa."

"You're being insubordinate," Purdy said loudly. "That man and the men you killed have diplomatic immunity in Hong Kong. You must release your prisoner immediately while I use every bit of protocol at my command to apologize for the ones you killed."

"My job is to keep order in this city," Crosswaithe said. "How can you expect—?"

"Your job is dangling by a string right now."

"If you want my damned job back, I'll—"

"Wait," Bolan said. "No reason to be hasty. If the man has diplomatic immunity, he has diplomatic immunity."

The Executioner walked up to face the governor, eye to eye. "If this gentleman has the power and the desire to set mass murderers free on the streets, I suppose that's the way it'll be. When I speak to the press, I'll explain that to them."

"I'm liking you less all the time, Belasko," Purdy said.

"And I'm fascinated," Wang told him. "What, Mr. Belasko, has an American to do with any of this?"

"Think of me as a citizen of the world. And if you blow smoke in my face, I'm going to shove that cigarette holder right down your throat. How much blood is on *your* hands?"

"So impetuous," Wang said. "That's what I've always liked about you Americans. That indomitable spirit—win, win, win. Good for you. Governor Purdy, may we have that poor man released now so that I may get him proper medical attention?"

A young Chinese man charged up to the open doorway, sliding on the hall floor, grabbing the door frame to stop himself. "Ian," he said, hurrying in. "The lab tests, I . . . Excuse me, I didn't know—"

"This is Governor Purdy, Lok," Crosswaithe said, breathing deeply, "and Mr. Wang."

"Your Lordship," Lok said, bowing to both men. "I'll come back later."

"No, no," Crosswaithe said. "Not at all. Give me the results of the test."

The young man shook his head, his glasses sliding down his nose. "He was injected with something, all right, something strange that interacted with his brain receptors. Some sort of endorphin compound. That man had enough adrenaline pumping through him to fire up a hundred men." He turned to stare through the window. "It looks like it's worked its way through his system now. I'm telling you, people pumped up like that are living on a plane far beyond anything human."

"Still want to let him loose, Your Lordship?" Crosswaithe asked.

"I have my responsibilities. I must uphold our international agreements."

"And is this the man who dictates what those international agreements are?" Bolan asked quietly, pointing a finger at Wang.

"Oh, there was something else," Lok said. "Auto theft wanted me to tell you that all those black Mercedes you carted in are registered to the Bank of China."

Crosswaithe jerked to Wang, whose expression never wavered. Bolan realized the guy thought he was smarter, better than all the rest of them.

"How do you explain that?" the inspector asked Wang.

"Stolen," the man said. "A whole fleet of them, twenty-five in all."

"Did you report the theft?"

Wang smiled. "As a matter of fact, I did. About a year ago. It made the papers...even the English-language papers."

"You're part of this, Wang. You're up to your elbows in blood, partner. And you don't even care," Bolan said.

"Our man really needs to be freed now," Wang said to the governor.

Bolan laid a hand on the interrogation window. "I fought with that man in there," he told the governor. "He was flying high on something...had the strength of a lion, and the rage. I literally watched him throw a grown man across a room."

Purdy ignored the Executioner. "Release him now!"

Crosswaithe started to speak, but Bolan got his attention and shook his head. The inspector, looking quizzical, walked out the door.

"You really should go back to your country, Mr. Belasko," Wang said. "This is no longer a place of welcome for Americans."

"Maybe I'll just do that," Bolan replied amiably, winking at Mao as Lok took the opportunity to get out of the room and walk down the hall. "I'll put it on my list of things to do, right behind attending your funeral. You're in this now."

"You are a foolish man."

"No," Bolan replied. "Methodical."

Through the window he could see Crosswaithe walk into the interrogation room and talk with protesting police, who helped up the red tie, now wearing striped prison pajamas, since his own clothes had been shredded by flying glass.

They all walked into the hall to meet Crosswaithe, coming out with his charge. The prisoner was supported by the two cops, who transferred him to Wang and Purdy.

"There will be no more incidents like this, Inspector," Purdy called over his shoulder as they walked the prisoner out. "The red ties are free in Hong Kong."

"Free to kill?" Crosswaithe asked, incredulous.

"Free!" Purdy returned.

As soon as they disappeared into the confusion of the lobby, Crosswaithe turned to Bolan, confused. "Why did you let me take all the heat?" he asked. "You wanted audience with higher-ups, you wanted to save these people, yet you let them walk out of here without a sound."

"Yeah," Bolan said easily.

"Why, Charlie?" Mao asked.

"Well," the big man said, "first thing is that Purdy was already set. There was nothing to talk to him about. Second I wanted that red tie set free."

"Why?" Crosswaithe asked in exasperation.

"I expected nothing good to come of this process," he said, indicating their environs with a shrug, "so I took the liberty of planting a bug on our boy's shoe when we took him at the Bottoms Up. From now on we'll know where he goes, who he talks to and *exactly* what he's talking about. I think we made an interesting trade-off."

"You're the only man I know," Crosswaithe said, "who can make the word *interesting* sound scary."

CHAPTER TEN

The sun was rising to another day of overcast, cold, intermittent rain and strong winds as Bolan and Mao made their way in Shinshi's speedboat around Lantau Island and the new Hong Kong airport, which was still under construction. They ate dim sum and tried to pretend they weren't dead tired.

"It seems so hopeless, Charlie," she said, picking up a steamed dumpling with her chopsticks, then holding it before her mouth. "Even if we find some way to deal with the red ties, Beijing will just send more to take their place."

"Aristotle says that hope is a waking dream," Bolan replied from the tiller of the duel outboards. "Don't stop dreaming, Angela. I haven't. You saw what happened in Wan Chai last night. How long can this stay quiet? Once the world finds out about all this—"

"What happens then?" she interrupted. "You think the world cares about us here on a little island in the middle of nowhere?"

"I've got to believe the world cares," he returned. "That's what keeps me going."

"You're a good man," she said, turning to stare over the bow. They were swinging around the Sha

Chau island group, Tree Island barely visible as a small dot two miles farther on. "You're strong like my father."

"I'm strong like you," he said.

She turned back around, giving him a tired smile. "What's going to happen to Crosswaithe?"

"If he doesn't keep quiet, I give him two, maybe three more days before he's suddenly and mysteriously called back to London. We need him. I wanted him stirred up, but now that he's lost men, he'll become a bulldog. The powers that be won't tolerate that for long."

"Will he keep fighting the red ties?"

"They'll have to cut off his head to make him stop at this point."

They approached their loose outer perimeter of fishing junks. Bolan passed within twenty feet of one, using the flashlight to give them two quick flashes, which were immediately returned. Several men and women on the junk's deck came to the rail and waved as they passed.

The island loomed larger before them, a densely tree-covered emerald in a sea of gray. "You think your bug will do any good?"

"Can't hurt," Bolan said, swinging wide around the island to come in from the other side. "It's only going to range out between two and three miles, but the inspector's watching it himself. Hong Kong's a small place. We may get lucky. Our best shot right now is Wang."

"Your financial theory."

"Yeah. Why is it that the director of the Bank of China comes in to pick up a crazed killer from the Wan Chai jail? This is all going to come down to money before it's finished, trust me. And that snake in the silk suit is stuck right in the middle of it."

"What are you going to do?"

"I'm not sure yet, but in my country we have a saying—if you can dish it out, you'd better be able to take it."

She smiled. "I like that saying," she replied. "I think I'd like to jam the barrel of my gun down Wang's throat."

"Well, maybe if you're a good little girl, I'll invite you along to the party."

"I'm good at being bad," she said.

Bolan nodded. "Fair enough. Get the line."

He cut the motors, letting the boat glide up to the forty-foot dock. Mao threw a line over the piling near the ladder, then pulled them up tight. She was as good on the water as she was on the land. Bolan pulled the handset from the boat's radio and moved to the ladder.

Chan Wee-Gee hurried down the dock, waving his arms as they climbed. "Hurry!" he said. "There's trouble, big trouble. We saw it on the television. Everybody wants to go home."

Bolan nodded tiredly. He'd been halfway expecting this. It was their lives to do with as they chose. He hoped they'd listen to him before making any rash decisions.

They walked the long, heavily forested path to the compound, people running out of the hangar and the barn as he moved through the yard. All of them were calling to him.

"You're a popular man today," Mao commented.

"Right. Now I know how Mussolini felt when they came to take him away."

An avalanche of voices assaulted him, Cantonese, English, all talking at the same time, surrounding Bolan and Mao, pressing close.

The Executioner put up his hands for silence. "We need to talk! But not all of us. Pick ten to represent you. We'll meet in fifteen minutes inside the house."

With that he turned from them, walked onto the porch of the ranch-style dwelling, then into the house. Shinshi stood smiling on the threshold, holding a shot glass full of bourbon out in front of him.

"It'll take the chill off," he said.

Bolan downed the shot, the warmth spreading through his chest immediately.

"Have you kept the phones locked up?" the big man asked, giving the glass back.

"Locked tight. I'm sorry about everyone finding out about last night. Apparently someone had a small radio."

Bolan shrugged it off and sat on the edge of the couch. He didn't want to lean back and get too comfortable. There was too much to do. "It needed to be dealt with. Now's as good a time as any. Do me a favor, though, would you? Call the police station in Wan Chai district and ask for Inspector Crosswaithe. Give him this number and ask if there's anything he needs to tell me. Tell him not to call on a cell phone. They may be scanning him.''

''You got it,'' Shinshi said, walking off.

The representatives of the group straggled in one at a time, Bolan taking them to the large dining table whose chandelier was a movie spotlight.

They sat. No time was wasted. ''We must return to the island,'' a gray-haired man said. ''Our relatives are being killed in our place. Our joss has run out. We must return and prepare to meet our ancestors.''

''What you're saying,'' Bolan replied, ''is that you are returning to Hong Kong to die. Is that everyone's feeling?''

There was affirmation around the table, but not a resounding mandate. Good. ''Give me another day,'' Bolan said. ''Perhaps we can end this madness without sacrificing ourselves.''

''Every minute that passes is a death sentence for one of our relatives,'' the same man replied. ''Our camp is already full of grief. The horror has no end.''

''One more day,'' Bolan urged. ''I want to make you better prepared to fight, not submit. I want Mr. Shinshi to start using all his media contacts to get international coverage for Hong Kong. I want to choose my own hit squad to take the fight to the red ties. The

Hong Kong police are now actively on our side. Let's give that a chance to work."

"Words," the gray-haired man said. "Just words."

"Hey, Mike," Shinshi called, running from the den, which contained the phone and computer, "Inspector Crosswaithe says he must speak with you right away. He's still on the line."

"Give me one minute," the Executioner said to the representatives, standing quickly and hurrying out of the room.

He reached the den and picked up the phone. "What's up, Inspector?"

"Your bug is working perfectly," the man said, excited. "After you left, I heard a conversation about going to the Vicky Rose, one of the floating restaurants in Aberdeen, and killing some cousins of one of your dissidents."

"And?"

"I called every harbor boat in the damned islands and posted them around Vicky Rose. We saw the red ties. They went by in a yacht, took one look at the police protection and slid by. Not a shot fired."

"Good. Listen for anything that might give a clue as to where they congregate, where they live. Write anything down that sounds even the least bit interesting."

"You've got it, mate. It's great to be on the winning side for once."

"Don't break out the champagne yet," Bolan said, "but this is the first positive step we've taken. You're a good man, Inspector. Angela Mao says so."

"Sometimes it just takes us a while to remember who we are, that's all," the man returned. "Keep me posted."

"You got it."

Bolan hung up with a surge of confidence. It wasn't impossible. They could lick this thing. He returned to the dining room.

"I just got off the phone with Inspector Crosswaithe," he said. "Because of some surveillance steps we've taken, he was able to repel a hit squad bound for the Vicky Rose."

"My cousin's family all works at the Vicky Rose," one of the men at the table said.

"Everyone is safe," Bolan replied. "The police did their job. We're not helpless. We're not finished."

"How were the police able to know about the Vicky Rose?" asked Chan Wee-Gee. Both he and his brother, Kun, had chosen to sit on the delegation.

"Surveillance," Bolan said, avoiding an answer. "We have our own ways of—"

"We're all in this together," Mao said. "They have a right to know. Charlie planted a listening device on a red tie who was arrested and later released. We are getting firsthand information from the enemy."

There was general jubilation around the table, a drop of water to parched throats. Bolan frowned at Mao, who stuck her tongue out at him, but she may have been right about giving out the details of their wire. Everyone seemed in much better spirits once they'd discovered the red ties were as human as anyone else—and as capable of making a mistake.

"Just give me one more day," Bolan said. "Already many of you are becoming familiar with the weapons that can save your lives. There are other notions, other methods of self-protection, I can teach you. When we return, it will be as a unit with a chain of command and a game plan for survival. The red ties won't bother your relatives. They'll have their hands full with you."

"Shall we take a vote?" Mao said. "Home now and death, or a chance to win with Charlie?"

The war council voted unanimously to back Bolan's plan.

IT WAS LATE, sometime past midnight, as Bolan sat huddled in a blanket on the straw-covered floor of the barn, his newly formed staff of twenty recruits gathered around him on the floor and above on the small loft. Two horses shared the barn with them, along with assorted chickens and guinea hens.

The recruits were young and in good physical shape, seventeen men and three women, including Angela Mao and Shing. Their purpose was to take the fight to the enemy. He wanted to do exactly what the red ties were doing: isolate a small group, then attack it with a large force. If they could ambush red ties, keep them off their guard, the resulting confusion would hopefully stop the machinelike nature of their assassinations. They could acquire more guns, too, the greatest necessity at the moment.

The recruits had been divided into two squads of ten each, Mao in command of one, Shing of the other, with Bolan to act as CO.

"So," the Executioner said, "you turn around and a red tie is standing right in front of you. What do you do?"

"Jam his nose up into his brain," Shing said, indicating the flat of his hand and the shoving motion it would take to drive the cartilage upward.

"The eyes," a young woman said, "preferably with my house keys between my fingers."

"Good," Bolan said. "What else?"

"The throat," someone added, "crush the larynx."

"The testicles," a young man called, "or the spray bottle of ammonia in the face."

"The ammonia's important," Bolan said. "You don't have to carry a large spray bottle, a little goes a long way. Gut them straight across the stomach if you can get your knife out. Don't waste the effort of raising the blade. Go in straight at the waist, push hard, then pull. If he's dead, get his gun. If he isn't...run."

Bolan heard his name being called softly and looked up to see Shinshi at the barn door, motioning him forward.

The big man stood, pulling his blanket a little tighter around him. The weather was getting progressively worse, the wind nearly frigid. "Your elbow can be your greatest weapon," he told the recruits. "Practice the exercises we learned earlier today. Work in teams. I'll be right back."

He moved through the young people, their eyes so bright, their lives just getting started. He wanted them to have that chance at life. As they paired off, one sneaking up on the other, the victim coming straight back with a hard elbow to the face or the solar plexus, the Executioner walked up to speak with Shinshi.

"Trouble?" he asked.

"Of a kind. In the movie business we'd call it the monster shot."

"The weather?"

"A typhoon. It has just passed Guam, building strength and intensity, and is heading this way."

The Executioner shrugged. "It'll be just as tough on the enemy," he said. "How long before it gets here?"

"They move slowly. Maybe two...three more days. We'll all want to be off the island by then. It's possible the water surge could submerge Tree Island for a time. It has happened before."

"Okay. We'll let everybody get a good night's sleep, then we'll start trying to arrange safe transport to the mainland or Hong Kong Island."

As they spoke, making plans for the transportation of the dissidents, neither man saw the figure slip out of the shadows of the compound yard and into the house Shinshi had just vacated. The person moved slowly through the darkened house, listening for movement of any kind, making for the locked den and the telephone within.

The door opened easily, the result of a piece of tape placed there this afternoon that kept the lock from engaging. With shaking, sweaty hands, the figure moved to the phone and picked it up, punching in a number long committed to memory.

It rang five times before it was answered. "Yes?"

"Colonel Li," the person whispered, "I have a great deal of information to impart to you."

CHAPTER ELEVEN

Bolan sat, holding the telephone, in front of Shinshi's big-screen television and watched the Singapore newscaster reporting from the Bottoms Up Club. "Look, Hal," he said, "I'm doing the best I can on this end, but Eurasian newscasts aren't going to get a thing done for us. I need international reporting. You have to help us."

"How?"

Bolan sat back on the couch, the room alive around him. People moved in and out with supplies to get breakfast to those in the barn, as the Chans cooked in the kitchen, the two old men turning out to be surprisingly good chefs. Several of the women sat at the dining-room table, sharpening kitchen knives and spoon handles, turning household items into deadly weapons. Angela Mao sat sullenly beside him on the couch, watching Shinshi's contacts do their inadequate best at news reporting.

"The Chinese are moving into the world market in a big way," he said. "GATT is opening them up like nothing in their history. They're not going to want the bad publicity that international coverage of this thing would bring. They'd lose too much face with their new partners in commerce."

"You may have a point."

"After you hang up, pick up your telephone and leak this thing to the American press."

"The administration—"

"The hell with the administration. Leak it, Hal. The press will love a story like this."

"I've got to think about this."

"Well, maybe I can make it a bit easier for you. Either you do it or I will."

"Okay, okay...."

"I'll be in contact," Bolan said, then hung up. The phone rang immediately.

He jerked it to his mouth. "Yeah?"

"It's Ian Crosswaithe, Mr. Belasko."

"I don't like the tone of your voice. What happened?"

"Your wire's off," the man replied. "I'd kept twenty-four-hour surveillance on the plant. About an hour ago our subject got a call telling him to report immediately to headquarters. He was staying in Wan Chai and we had a tail on him. He got in one of those black Mercedes and headed to the other side of the island. We followed but lost him—and the bug—somewhere on the D'Aguilar Peninsula."

"They knew."

"That would be my guess also."

"What's happening?" Mao asked from beside him.

He waved her off. "There's more, isn't there?"

"I'm afraid so, old chap. The Vicky Rose was torched during the night. Old wooden ship, not fireproofed. It went up like a box of matches and burned straight down to the waterline."

"Anybody hurt?"

"You don't want to know."

Bolan grimaced. There was no end to it. "You lost the bug an hour ago?"

"Give or take a few minutes."

"Then we don't have much time. You ready to put it on the line?"

"Just name it. I'm in my office."

"We've got to evacuate this island quickly. There's nowhere to run from here. Get over to the Star Ferry. I'll meet you there in a few minutes."

"That quickly?"

"Hurry. I've got a plane to catch."

He hung up and looked at Mao. "The bug's gone. We've got a traitor."

She frowned. "The plant was bound to be discovered. That doesn't mean—"

"You've got a lot to learn," he said, standing and walking to the den door. He reached into his pocket and pulled out the key, unlocking the door. Only Bolan and Shinshi had keys. The room itself looked undisturbed. He bent to examine the door as Mao moved up beside him.

"Here," he said, pulling the remnants of a piece of tape from the door-locking mechanism. He showed her the tape. "Someone managed to get to this door while it was opened. He taped down the lock so it wouldn't engage, then returned, probably sometime during the night."

"This is just a tiny piece of tape, Charlie," she said. "You can't reach those conclusions just because of a small piece of tape."

"Why won't you get it through your head that one of us can't be trusted?" he asked, exasperated.

She shook her head. "These people have been like family to me all my life," she said. "I—I just can't let myself...I just can't."

He took her by the arms, staring hard. "You're not capable of making a rational judgment on this issue. Do you understand me?"

She nodded, gulping.

"Listen to me, it's very important. Tell nothing to anyone. No one, not even Shing."

"But Shing is—"

"No one!" Bolan said. "At this moment you're the only person on this island I know I can trust. You need to look at life the same way. If there's any telling to be done, let me do it."

"All right, Charlie," she said, looking at the ground and pulling away from him. "I don't agree with you, but you are right in that I'm too emotionally caught up to make solid value judgments on this issue. I will honor your request."

"Good girl," he said. "Now. I want you to get everyone together and down to the pier. I'm going for the Star Ferry to get us out of here. It may get dicey."

"You can count on me."

"I know I can," Bolan said, moving away from her and back into the living room.

"Mr. Shinshi!"

"I'm coming," the man replied, running into the living room in a silk bathrobe and house slippers. "You people get up too early."

"We need to take your plane to the mainland right now," Bolan said, taking him by the arm and leading him toward the door.

"But I'm not dressed, I—"

"You've got five minutes."

Shinshi scurried away and returned several minutes later, fully clothed.

"Can you deal with the wind?" Bolan asked.

"Let's see."

They walked out onto the porch. The yard was filled with people doing t'ai chi. The sky was dark, the wind swirling heavily as the typhoon moved inexorably closer to Hong Kong. Paper and trash danced in the air, borne on the wind that gusted up to thirty miles per hour.

"What do you think?" the Executioner asked.

"An hour from now, I'd say no," Shinshi replied. "But now...we can make it."

"Then let's go," Bolan said.

Both men strode immediately into the yard, breaking into a trot as they approached the hangar. The Executioner left his combat harness behind, unwilling to deal with Kowloon airport officials if he arrived armed.

The twenty-year-old Cessna sat off to one side of the hangar to make room for the people who slept there. The airplane was painted in shades of white and blue, a star-field pattern scattered on the fuselage. It looked almost like a flag. Shinshi pulled the blocks out from under the wheels, then climbed into the cockpit to run the preflight check.

Bolan climbed into the copilot's seat, noticing the inside of the plane smelled like jasmine incense. "Is it gassed up?" he asked.

Shinshi nodded, his eyes scanning the instrument panel as he flipped on toggles. "Ever since the red ties came to Hong Kong, my plane has been fueled and ready to go."

"What do you think?"

The man shrugged. "Let's go. The sooner the better in this wind."

He toggled on the engine contacts and hit the throttle, the engine coughing as the prop half turned, then again. On the third try they got contact, the prop spinning to a blur as Shinshi taxied them out of the hangar and onto the small runway.

"Here we go," Shinshi said, kicking up the throttle, Bolan strapping in as the plane picked up speed on the runway. He could feel the wind buffeting them as their ground speed increased, surging for escape velocity.

The water rushed up quickly at them, then they were suddenly airborne.

The runway had taken them east, away from Hong Kong. Shinshi made a long, slow turn that put them on a five-minute course to Kowloon. When they came out of the turn, however, the man was no longer smiling.

"What's wrong?" Bolan asked.

"She's not responding well. Something's wrong with the vertical stabilizer. It's slow to respond. Look out your door. Tell me if you see any kind of fluid leak."

Bolan opened his door and leaned out of the aircraft. Reddish orange fluid was sputtering from the bottom of the aircraft to coat the bird's fuselage. He closed the door and sat back heavily in his seat, readjusting his seat belt.

"It's leaking, isn't it?" Shinshi asked.

"Like a cut artery," Bolan said.

"So we can't turn the plane. And we have to wonder who cut the lubrication lines. We've been sabotaged, Mike. Put your feet on the rudder pedals and take the wheel."

Bolan put his feet on the two pedals before him and grabbed his control column. "Got it."

"Okay," the man replied. The wind was beginning to buffet the plane, the trip getting rougher. Below, the islands and their thousands of junks and sampans lay mired in high seas, whitecaps on the dark waves. "Now, on my signal, I want you to turn right on the wheel while pushing down the left rudder pedal as hard as you can. Ready?"

"Ready."

"Go."

The two men worked the rudder, the mechanism frozen in place without lubrication. They strained at the wheel, barely inching the plane to the right. After a minute of struggle, Shinshi sat back and turned to the Executioner.

"It's no good," he said. "It's locked up tight."

"What now?"

"We're going to have to ditch in the harbor," the man said matter-of-factly. "You have my apologies. If our joss is very, very good, we will survive. Hitting water at a couple of hundred miles per hour is a lot like hitting concrete at the same speed. I'm going to cut the engines and try and catch as much headwind as possible, but we run the risk of flipping over."

"What do you need me to do?"

"Pray to your ancestors. That's what I'm doing."

The man reached out and cut the engine, the prop jerking and coughing, then simply freewheeling. The plane dropped as Shinshi fought to keep the nose up.

Victoria Harbour loomed before them from fifty feet in the air. Shinshi had found somewhat of an open corridor between the harbor commerce where they could crash without taking others out with them, and he was struggling to maintain a level target as they dropped to thirty feet.

"I just want to tell you," Shinshi said, "that whatever happens I am grateful to you. I had come here to escape many years ago and have stayed hidden like a frightened child every since. You have put the fight back into me . . . made me a man again."

The cockpit was shuddering in the winds now, the instrument panel shaking crazily as Shinshi fought to hold control. "We'll talk about it later, over a drink," Bolan said, taking the wheel to try to help the man. They had dropped to twenty feet.

"Okay, Mike," Shinshi said. "Whatever you say."

They were just above the water, still moving too fast, when a breaker caught the landing gear, tilting them in Shinshi's direction, his wing dipping too low as all hell broke loose.

The wing was torn from the plane, and they hit nose first. Bolan jerked hard against his harness as Shinshi's entire seat broke free, the man meeting the ocean at the windshield. The craft kept tumbling, and Bolan held on as water filled the compartment.

The plane stopped tumbling with its nose in the air, the tail section already heavy with water, dragging it down into the dark harbor. With shaking hands, Bolan unclamped from the harness. He took one look at the pilot's seat and the blood and tissue left behind. Shinshi's ancestors were already greeting him. The soldier turned to push at his door, but it was gone. He slipped into the cold water just as the plane slid away beneath him.

He swam out several feet, then turned to look back. Nothing remained except a small oil slick. He turned toward the harbor proper, landfall several hundreds of yards away, and continued on.

Bolan's head hurt, and his chest ached from where he'd been jerked against his restraint. The waves were so high he could barely keep his head above water. But he was still alive, and that was good enough for now.

He managed to make his way to a nearby junk and traded them his watch for a quicker trip to the docks. They wrapped him in a comforter and putted toward the Star Ferry pier, Bolan sitting astern and looking furtively for any sign that Shinshi might possibly have made it. There was none.

They arrived at the pier at the same time the Star Ferry was arriving from the Kowloon side. Crosswaithe stood on the dock to reach out a hand to help him up from the boat.

"Dramatic arrival," the man commented as Bolan handed the comforter back to the people on the junk, thanking them.

"Too dramatic," Bolan replied without mirth, then nodded toward the ferry and its disembarking passengers. "I need that boat."

Crosswaithe agreed without hesitation. "I'll commandeer it in the name of Her Majesty's government," he said. "No sweat."

He turned and walked down the pier toward the ferry. "We'll need a pilot, too," Bolan called.

"No, we don't," Crosswaithe said. "When I was a lot younger, I put myself through school piloting the ferry between Dover and Calais."

CHAPTER TWELVE

Bolan stood in the wheelhouse beside Ian Cross-waithe, who was piloting the ferry as if he were born to do it.

"It's like riding a bicycle," the inspector said. "Once you've got the hang of it, you don't forget."

Right now he was running a bull's-eye between Lantau Island and the New Territories, having cleared a path through the harbor with a bullhorn and his badge.

Bolan wasn't as jubilant. Binoculars up to his eyes, he continued to do full-circle sweeps, scanning for any sign of the red ties. "How long has it been?" Bolan asked.

The inspector looked at his watch. "One hour and forty-five minutes since we lost contact with your bug."

The Executioner shook his head. "Time enough for them to organize."

"What makes you think they'd come to Tree Island?" Crosswaithe asked. "The MO has previously been to isolate and assassinate, not confront."

"They've never had everybody all together before. And believe me, Tree Island *is* isolated. They also, I'm sure, are now under some pressure to bring this to a swift conclusion. Even the Eurasian telecasts are exerting pull." They should have been coming into view of his own forward warning posts, the junks, but they weren't there. He hoped that meant Angela had already sent them scattering.

"But more important," Bolan said, "strategically Tree Island would be the best place to meet in battle from the Chinese point of view. General Li cut his teeth in the jungles of northern Vietnam and Cambodia. It would seem perfect to him. I know this man, Inspector. I feel I can sense what he's up to. He'll be here. And soon."

"Well, let's hope we're faster," Crosswaithe replied. "I'm sorry I couldn't bring more people with me. I run homicide, but I've got a superintendent who's been told to keep a close eye on me, I'm afraid. Commandeering the ferry wasn't high on his priority list."

"We'll have to get to him, too, then," Bolan stated, pulling the binoculars from his eyes and gazing over the bow. They were coming up on the island, mere moments from it, his warrior's senses telling him there'd be nothing easy about the evacuation.

"The pier's on the northwestern side of the island," he said, pointing. "Are you going to be able to get that close?"

"Ferries are flat bottomed," Crosswaithe replied. "I'll get her in."

As they closed on the island, the Executioner could see the hurried preparations for departure as the trees bent under the relentless swirl of the tropical winds. He reached up and pulled the chain on the compressed-air horn, blasting a warning to those not yet prepared.

The inspector took them around to the northwest side, several large waves washing up over the lower, second-class deck. The pier came into view, and people were lined up and waiting, Shing working crowd control. The man waved to them as Crosswaithe cut the engines, backwatered, then slid up to easily bump the dock. Shing jumped on deck to secure the lines.

"We're going to have company," Bolan said, the binoculars to his face again. Two miles in the distance he could see a line of speedboats plowing the South China Sea, bumping over the waves to slam on the other side, barely touching down before they were airborne again.

The red ties had arrived.

"How many of them?"

"A lot," Bolan said. "Maybe all of them."

"God," Crosswaithe whispered.

Bolan put a hand on the man's shoulder. "You handle it here. Get these people on the boat, and fast. I'll hustle the rest out of the compound."

"Hurry," the inspector urged, the binoculars now glued to his face.

Bolan was out of the wheelhouse and down the companionway to deck one. Shing was already helping people aboard. "They're coming," the Executioner told him. "Get the weapons aboard first. It's going to be messy."

"Yes, sir."

The soldier jumped to the deck and ran, shouting as he did so. "Be prepared to fight! The red ties are right behind us!"

He charged up the pathway to the house, hurrying along anyone he met. The last few stragglers were leaving the compound yard as he reached it, Mao at the door of Shinshi's house, locking it.

"Don't!" he called. "It doesn't matter."

"Shinshi?" she said, her eyes wide.

"Gone," Bolan replied, moving into the house to retrieve his combat harness. He could hear the distant crack of small-arms fire. It had begun.

He slipped into the harness, then moved to a living-room window, tearing down the curtain and giving it to Mao. "Next to the hangar is a huge fuel tank for Shinshi's plane and boat. Open the top and dip the curtain in. I'll be right out."

As she nodded, turned and ran, Bolan moved into the bedroom and grabbed a lighter from beside the king-size bed. He ignited the bedding, the mattress catching quickly, then the curtains.

The bedroom was engulfed in flames as he hurried out, running back to the kitchen to grab the propane tank that ran the hot-water heater and the stove. The tank was as tall as Bolan and heavy—full. He knocked the cylindrical tank over, then rolled it to the bedroom, shoving it on a throw rug to slide across the polished wood floors and into the flames.

Then he got out. Mao was already dipping the curtain into the five-hundred-gallon tank when he got there, shouts and more gunfire coming from the dock area.

"Good," he yelled, shoving her away from the tank and grabbing the curtain. "Run! Get to the ship!"

"I'm staying with you!"

"Then don't get in my way when *I* start running!"

The drenched curtain came out of the tank like a giant candle wick. He let it drape over the tank and down to the ground, the last bit still inside.

"Ready?" he asked, stepping several paces from the curtain, his lighter out and burning.

"Ready."

He tossed the lighter at the material. "Run!" he yelled, shoving her in front of him down the path. There were several seconds of silence, then the house and the fuel tank exploded at the same time in a monstrous conflagration, a huge yellow-white fire flower erupting from the center of Tree Island, its concussion throwing both Bolan and Mao to the ground. The heat from the fireball singed their hair and the clothing on their backs.

They got to their feet, and charged down the path. Behind them the high winds were already whipping the flames into a mighty fire, encompassing even the trees, smoke swirling eerily through the evergreens. It would give them some cover, and Bolan hoped it would be enough.

They reached the landing, wispy smoke already making the area look like a fog bank. People lay wounded all around the pier, the whine of the speedboats the only clue the red ties were there. The swirling smoke was cutting them off.

He leaned down and grabbed a man who'd been shot in both legs, hefting him over a shoulder. "Help the wounded!" he yelled. "This fire won't last forever!"

Several people rushed forward out of hiding and helped the wounded onto the ferry, Bolan and Mao bringing up the rear. Occasional gunfire still flared, but it was distant and undirected.

As the man was taken from Bolan's shoulder and pulled onto the boat, Mao removed the tie lines. "Inspector, let's get the hell out of here," the Executioner called, jumping aboard just as Mao did, the ferry already on the move. The island disappeared into the smoke within seconds.

The people aboard the boat were nearly hysterical, fearing for their lives.

"It gets worse from here!" Bolan yelled. "Calm down and listen to me. This is going to be the longest thirty minutes of your life. To survive, you're going to have to control yourselves and remember your training. You chose this path. Now you have to see it to resolution."

He stared, frowning, until both decks quieted, then said calmly, "Arm yourselves with the weapons that you trained with. Don't waste ammunition. We don't have it to spare. Pick only targets you think you can hit. Now, there are several doctors aboard. Come tend to the wounded. If there are any nurses, help them. If not, the doctors may pick assistants. Move the wounded to the more interior areas of the ship.

"Control things down here," Bolan told Mao, then moved to the outer companionway and up to the wheelhouse.

"Bloody hell," Crosswaithe said. "I can't see a damned thing."

"You're going to have to kick it up full throttle, Inspector," the Executioner said, "whether you can see or not. Listen. It's quiet. Their motors are shut down. They're listening for us and waiting for the smoke to dissipate. If we wait, they'll find us."

"I've got no sense of direction here. I'm liable to run us right into something."

"Well, we've got to take our chances. Let's go."

Bolan looked back in the direction of the island, a glowing fireball in the midst of dirty smoke. Thank God for the wind. Smoke was everywhere. The red ties had to have heard their engines kicking up. The whine of the speedboats began again, following the sound of the ferry. But they had to be slow and careful, lest they run into one another. It would be all right as long as they had smoke cover.

"I hope we're going in the right direction," Crosswaithe said, leaning over the wheel, squinting into the smoke. "My eyes are starting to burn."

"Shh." Bolan had a finger to his lips. "Listen."

They quieted, listening to the pinging whine of a speedboat engine coming closer. "There," the soldier said, drawing the .44 and priming it as a wraithlike shadow crossed the bow. "It's one of them. They'll circle us and come back. Bring us hard to port!"

Crosswaithe spun the wheel without question, the ferry pulling left as Bolan leaned out the wheelhouse window. He braced himself, the vessel plowing into the speedboat a second later, cutting it in two as the red ties jumped into the water. The Executioner saw a head bob like an apple and took the man out with a precision shot from the Desert Eagle. Gunfire erupted on deck, short, staccato. Then all was quiet in the water.

"Get us back on course," Bolan said.

"And what course might that be?" Crosswaithe asked. "I don't even know what direction I'm going right now."

A large aluminum fire extinguisher was fixed to the wheelhouse wall. Bolan took it down and smashed the glass of the wheelhouse windows. Then he climbed through one of the cutouts and stood on the frame, looking back over the top of the boat. He could still see the fireball the island had become, glowing like a lantern directly behind them. He climbed back into the wheelhouse.

"Okay, so far," he said.

The man shook his head. "I never thought I'd see worse than London fog," he said, rubbing his eyes. "But this... Oh-oh."

Bolan followed his gaze. Ahead the smoke was dissipating rapidly, barely hanging above water level. He suddenly had visibility. Grabbing the bullhorn from the chart table, he stuck his head out of the window space. "Get ready! Remember your training."

They ran out of smoke as they passed between the brother islands of Tai Mo To and Siu Mo To. Crosswaithe steered toward the small channel of Kap Shui Mun, near the construction of the new airport, hoping to lose their pursuers in the confusion of traffic in the narrow inlet. Then came a five-mile run to Victoria Harbour. That stretch would be the place of confrontation.

"I'll be back," Bolan said, moving out of the wheelhouse and down the short gangway that led to the top deck. Everyone stared through the windows, watching red-tie speedboats breaking from the smoke a half mile behind them.

"Break this glass out," Bolan said, "or you're going to be dealing with it in your face. Use whatever's handy. Smash out the glass and clear the rough edges. You may have to get out of here the quick way."

He walked the deck, his presence reassuring, the calm he exhibited emulated by those around him. The sounds of shattering glass filled the air, the upper deck immediately becoming cold as the swirling winds blew through the now-open deck.

They were suddenly surrounded by river traffic, barges carrying building materials and junks filled with workmen. The red ties caught up slowly, content to wait out the congestion, then take them in the open sea.

Top deck calmed, he hurried down the interior companionway to the lower deck, where most of the weapons were being manned. Those with guns crouched near the deck to shoot over the outer rails while everyone else huddled in the interior.

He moved among the dissidents, patting them on the shoulder as he passed, the young people of Bolan's personal squad, plus old men and women, all equally intent and equally motivated. "You'll do fine. Their boats are much faster than ours, but they won't be able to shoot well with all the bouncing. Spare no one. Choose your shots. Always try for the boat's pilot first."

The red ties were closing on them slowly in the channel traffic, and ahead was open sea. Mao and Shing sat side by side, their backs against the gunwale as the Executioner approached. She was checking the clip on the nickle-plated .45 she'd grabbed the day before as he spoke softly to her, occasionally taking a peek over the gunwale to look at the dozen black powerboats in pursuit. Men in black swerved the vessels through the congestion, vying for position, stalking them on the water.

The Executioner looked at the .45. "Only for close in," he said, then turned to shake his head at the Remington 12-gauge pump shotgun leaning against the rail between them.

"No," he said to Shing. "Use that only if they're boarding. Here—" he moved the Beretta from his harness and handed it to the man "—take this for now. And I want you upstairs, commanding the upper deck."

"Separating us, huh?" Mao said, smiling.

"I can't afford to have both of you dying at the same time," Bolan replied and her smile faded immediately.

"We've got a surprise for you, too, Charlie," she said, reaching behind them to slide out the Krico 650 he'd used at the Temple of Ten Thousand Buddhas. Shing handed him the remnants of the box of shells. "We thought you could do some early work."

"Good," he said. "I'll try it from upstairs. Come on, Shing. Keep your head down, Angela."

"You, too," the woman told him.

Bolan stood and hurried to the outer steps. They reached the upper deck, Shing stopping in front of him.

"I hope I will not dishonor your trust in me," he said, still favoring his injured arm.

Bolan just smiled, hugging the man quickly. "You really like Angela, don't you?"

"Like her? She can cook a six-course meal, fix the engine of your car and teach you the pressure points on a person's hand. What a woman!'' The young man looked to the floor. ''I hope we live to know one another,'' he said.

''You'll do fine,'' Bolan replied, nodding toward the deck. ''Make sure your people stay alert.''

Shing nodded and hurried off, the Executioner moving to a quiet spot amidships and centering his concentration as he loaded a Winchester shell into the breech and slammed home the bolt. He raised the rifle to his shoulder and adjusted the scope.

There was excitement all around caused by the fire and smoke of Tree Island. But in the midst of it, the red ties were picking their way closer, tightening the noose, the closest boat no more than fifty yards from them.

They were passing through a series of pylons meant to serve as the supports for the railroad trestle being built across the strait to service the new airport, when Bolan focused on a speedboat that had broken free of the traffic constraints and was in open water.

It was time. Without hesitation, he lowered the sights onto the boat's pilot and set the cross hairs right between his eyes. With the practiced ease of a hardened warrior, he squeezed the trigger immediately on sighting, the Krico barely recoiling. He was already reloading and picking another target as the boat he'd just shot at veered sharply and smashed into a pair of pylons. There was a rending of fiberglass and steel, the boat torn immediately to pieces, bodies and boat parts flying in all directions.

Bolan heard Crosswaithe's voice loudly through the bullhorn from the wheelhouse. "Look alive, chaps. We've just crossed over into open water."

"Over here!" Shing called, pointing, just as Bolan's second target disappeared behind a huge barge loaded with sand dredged from the strait.

The Executioner hurried to the port side. One of the speedboats several hundred yards distant had also broken into open sea, angling toward them at breakneck speed.

He tried to line up the pilot, but the speedboat bounced a wave as he shot, the boat's bow blocking the hit. He ejected the shell and tried again. This time his shot took out the pilot at the neck, the man slumping. Remarkably the red tie beside him was able to get control of the boat and continued onward, two in the back seat opening up with AK-74s, bullets pinging, whapping into the wood of the deck. A man yelled, grabbed his chest and went down, then another.

"If they have weapons, take them!" Bolan yelled. "If they're alive, get them downstairs. Everybody on the port side, listen up! Fire at will on the approaching boat. Take it out!"

Gunfire rattled from the port side of the ferry, the men on the boat returning fire.

The boat came on. A red tie fell from the stern into the water as his chest exploded, then the second pilot was hit, the boat still coming, locked on a collision course.

"Keep firing!"

Screams and shots erupted from the starboard side, but Bolan was locked in deadly concentration on the boat racing toward him. There was no stopping it now.

The vessel hit them seconds later to loud splintering after skimming high over the ferry's wake. The bow crashed into the side of the ship five feet above the waterline, punching through halfway and sticking, its inboard motors still whining. It dangled from the port side, three dead men awkwardly jumbled within.

The Executioner turned to starboard as the gunfire got serious. Mao, below, walked the deck and directed her gunners. The red-tie boats were closing in. They were everywhere and quickly overtaking the ferry.

"Shing!" Bolan called, pointing to the man, who nodded in return. He rallied his riflemen to the starboard stern as the big American turned and hurried back down the gangway to the wheelhouse.

"There you are," Crosswaithe said from where he squatted, the entire wheelhouse splintered by gunfire. He was trying to run the helm from beneath the windows. "Could you do something to get these bloody bastards off me?"

The red ties were swarming like flies, emptying entire magazines at a burst, the bullet hits continuous, like woodpeckers.

Bolan fell to a crouch, crabwalking fore, getting just below the window line. Then he jumped up, filling the window space, the .44 stiff armed in front of him, leaning on the window ledge for support.

Two boats were pulling in front of them, criss-crossing at the bow, their gunmen aiming up at the wheelhouse. The Executioner found the first pilot, firing three times from the Desert Eagle. The man collapsed bloody as the boat crossed the wake of its counterpart and went high in the air, flipping over. The ferry slammed into the dead hulk, shoving it aside. The other boat trailed out wide and turned for another pass.

Below, the fighting was intense, the speedboats dipping in close, exchanging horror for horror with the guns on deck, the wail from the wounded and dying below now a constant dirge.

The battle was evenly met so far only because of the rough seas, and Bolan knew it. Hong Kong Island loomed in the distance, so near—taunting—and yet so far away.

The lead boat had made its wide, sweeping turn and was heading back for them, and Bolan saw the bulky grenade launchers being brought out.

"Hold on to your hat, Inspector," Bolan muttered as the speedboat came right at them like cars playing chicken on a deserted highway.

Two men stood in the back of the speedboat and fired their launchers methodically, one charge right behind the next. Several seconds later the first bomb hit, orange fire and black smoke rising before the wheelhouse, then other, more jarring explosions all over the ferry.

Bolan heard the sizzle, then knocked Crosswaithe to the floor just as the grenade hit the wheelhouse exterior, blowing half of it to hell with a deafening roar, both men taking wooden shrapnel in the back and legs.

"Fire!" Crosswaithe, yelled.

The Executioner rolled painfully off the man to grab the extinguisher he'd used to break the glass out of the windows. Half the wheelhouse was simply gone, and the rough edges left behind were blazing furiously.

He jumped up, aiming the small hose and pulling down on the hand clamp, CO_2 spray smothering the leaping flames. He turned to the inspector, who was bleeding and black with soot.

"Can you still pilot?" he yelled above the motors and the screaming.

"I'd like to see somebody try and stop me!" Crosswaithe replied regaining his feet and hunching over the wheel.

"I've got to check battle damage! I'll be back!"

"Go! Go!"

Bolan ran through the gangway, the outer stairs no longer in existence. The aft end of the upper deck was in flames, black smoke pumping furiously into the sky. Shing still directed the defense as the dead and dying lay all around, the speedboats still on the attack outside, moving in ever closer.

Bolan ran aft in a crouch, coming up to smother the fire with the hissing CO_2. It went out just as the canister ran dry. As Bolan dropped the extinguisher, a speedboat pulled alongside at a breech in the port defenses, men scurrying to try to board.

"Shotgun!" Bolan called, and Shing tossed him the Remington.

The Executioner pumped a shell into the chamber and jumped through the hole in the upper cabin, landing on the aft deck.

He raced to the rail as three red ties were pulling themselves aboard. Without a word, Bolan pulled the trigger and pumped again.

The first shot had knocked two of the three men off the ferry. The remaining red tie charged with an animal growl, Bolan taking the man's head off with his second shot from five feet.

He approached the rail, pumping as he did, and took out the pilot of the boat as he tried to drift away, the vessel floating dead in the water, rolling with the wake and with the waves.

He pumped the shotgun and ran starboard as another speedboat pulled up close. He fired at the motors—once, twice. The second shot hit the gas tank, exploding the back of the boat, tearing it up, burning men jumping into the South China Sea.

The soldier turned fore to see bodies all over the deck and screaming people, the doctors working furiously over the wounded as Angela Mao kept walking the line, holding the defenders in place with her sheer presence.

Fires burned everywhere, the blazing ferry filling the sky with black smoke. Bolan looked through the smoke over the bow. They were within minutes of the confusion of Victoria Harbour.

"Hold on!" he called. "Courage! We're almost home!"

Mao jerked to face him from ten feet. "We're low on ammo!" she called.

"Choose your shots carefully!" Bolan said loudly but with absolute calm. "Conserve your ammunition."

The Executioner then turned and ran the interior stairs to the upper deck, hurrying back to the wheelhouse.

"Look!" Crosswaithe said, pointing fore. "Pumpers!"

Bolan looked out over the bow. Bright yellow pumper boats, surrounded by harbor patrol boats, were steaming toward them.

Within twenty seconds the pumpers were hitting the ferry with drenching sprays of cold salt water, the black boats halfheartedly making one more pass, then backing off as harbor patrol surrounded them.

"I guess my chief isn't so bad after all," Crosswaithe said, picking a long wood splinter out of his thigh.

"Score one for our side," Bolan replied wearily, leaning the Remington against what was left of the wheelhouse wall and reloading the .44 as the man-made rain fell on them from twenty different water cannons.

.They'd made safe harbor. "I'm going to check below," he said, both men knowing he was going to make a casualty count but not wanting to say it.

As he cleared the gangway, the living were already helping the wounded to medical treatment below, harbor patrol boats taking them right over the side to hurry them to the hospital.

"Status?" Bolan asked as Shing directed the activity.

"Ten dead up here," the man replied, "another fifteen hurt. Could have been worse, Charlie."

"Yeah. And it could have been better." Bolan found similar conditions on the lower deck, a quick head count coming up with twenty-five dead out of one hundred fifteen. Many were in a bad way, though, and after what had happened to Chan Le-Chun in the hospital, taking people there might be like taking them to a morgue. This had to be stopped, and the only way to do it was to take the fight to the red ties.

Fires doused, Crosswaithe took the ferry into her berth at the Star Ferry pier. Company administrators were running outside, screaming when they saw what had happened to their ship.

Bolan walked off the vessel with the other passengers still on their feet, ambulances already on hand for the dead and injured.

"Scatter, people!" he called. "Change hideouts. We'll be in touch tonight."

"I'll get us a taxi," Mao said, hurrying ahead.

"Good," the Executioner replied.

A young American man in a Hong Kong suit and a baby-smooth face approached Bolan as he headed toward the taxi, a cameraman in tow. "Sir," he said, "I'm Joel Stanley, Asian Bureau, World Cable News. We got a call from our Washington Bureau... something about a major, breaking story here at the docks, I—"

Brognola had come through. Good. "These people," Bolan said, watching Mao waylay a cab half a block away, "have the story of a lifetime for you. Tell the world, son. Maybe you'll win a prize or something."

He started to walk about, but the newsman cut him off. "I'd like to interview you first."

Bolan stared hard at him. "I'm not the story," he replied. "Now get over there and do your job."

He walked off then, not responding when the man called after him, and climbed in the back of the cab beside Mao. "Where we going, Charlie?"

Bolan leaned across the seat to the driver. "Bank of China," he stated.

CHAPTER THIRTEEN

As the taxi slid away from the docks, Mao stared at him, openmouthed. "Why are we going to the Bank of China?" she asked.

"I'm going to take out a loan," Bolan replied, settling back in the seat. The central money district of Hong Kong Island was active, people filling the streets as if the world weren't coming down around them. Everyone was doing business, talking on their cell phones, planning for a tomorrow that could possibly be as dark as the typhoon clouds rolling in.

"You're a crazy man," she said. "You'll get yourself killed in Bank of China."

"Maybe. It's been my experience that people who have others do their dirty work for them usually aren't prepared to deal with it themselves. We'll see, won't we?"

She sat back and shook her head. "What am I going to do with you, Charlie?"

"Keep your promise about giving me the information I'm seeking."

"You remember that, huh?"

"I'm beginning to think that information might be far more important to you than it is to me," he said. "Everything that's happening here is tied together.

Your father died to protect a secret he hoped would save all your lives. That's why I think he wanted to meet in person—to hold that information back until he could get immunity for everyone. So in a sense, Angela, his last words were meant for you, not me.''

She leaned over and hugged him. ''True or not,'' she replied, ''I thank you for saying that.''

''Bank of China,'' the driver said, stopping halfway up the block, Victoria Park and the Hilton on the right, the bank building looming vulturelike on the left.

''Wait for me,'' Bolan told the driver as he climbed out.

''No can do,'' the man replied. ''Very busy day. Very busy.''

Bolan reached up under his jacket and pulled several thousand Hong Kong dollars out of his harness pouch. He stuffed them in the driver's hand. ''Wait for me,'' he repeated.

''No problem.''

Bolan looked at Mao. ''If I don't make it back, get hold of Hal Brognola, Department of Justice, Washington, D.C., and negotiate with him until you get what you want. Understand?''

''I want to come with you.''

He shook his head. ''Stay here for thirty minutes, then get the hell out.'' Bolan shut the taxi door and walked off, his clothing ripped, black with soot and dried blood, his face smeared with grime.

The interior of the bank was drab and gloomy. It was almost as if the Chinese existed in a kind of fear-laden ennui, putting in their days, hoping no one would punish them for real or imagined infractions. Happiness was nowhere in the equation. Duty was the only driving force.

The lobby was spacious and quiet. He walked up to an information desk, approaching a young woman whose eyes got huge when she saw him. "Do you speak English?" he asked.

"I speak English, Mandarin and Cantonese," she replied, her eyes now narrowing suspiciously. "How may I help you?"

"Well," he said, "I've got an appointment with Mr. Wang. Where might I find his office?"

"Seventy-fourth floor," she said, reaching for a telephone. "I will call and let them—"

"That won't be necessary," Bolan stated. He placed his hand, full of several hundred Hong Kong dollars, on top of hers. "I'll just drop in."

She turned her hand up, the money transferring to her without anyone else seeing. She looked up at him, the barest twinkle in her eyes. "I hope you and Mr. Wang will have a very pleasant visit."

"Thank you." He moved to the bank of elevators, nodding at all those around him. He stepped into the car, a security guard who'd been watching him striding in his direction just as the doors closed. Too late for the party.

It was a long ride up, many people getting on and off while he continued his ascent. Everyone watched him, but no one interfered. They'd all look at the lighted dial of the 74 on the number plate and smile. It told him all he needed to know about Wang Wushen.

After the last of his passengers got off at 63, Bolan settled in the posture, hoping he could trust the twinkle in the receptionist's eyes. By the time the doors slid open on 74, he was ready.

Walking swiftly, he immediately discerned his direction. A large conference room sat to his left, with several other bank officials to the right with their own secretaries. But straight ahead sat a stern-looking Chinese woman—Wang's secretary.

He strode quickly up to her. "Is he in?" he asked.

She responded in Mandarin, and Bolan walked past her. "I'll just announce myself," he said, shrugging the woman off when she jumped up to try to intercept him.

Wang's door was open. Bolan strode right in, slamming the door hard to close it. The man sat at a huge desk, playing with a yellow songbird that was jumping from one of his fingers to the next and back again.

"Convince me not to kill you right now," Bolan said, reaching into his jacket and coming out with the .44.

The man jumped, the bird squawking and flying off as he reached into his own jacket.

"I don't think so," the Executioner growled, hurrying around the desk to stick the .44 in the man's face. He pulled Wang's hand from the silk sports jacket and stripped him of the .22 he'd been reaching for.

The secretary came charging in, yelling loudly.

"Tell her to go away," Bolan ordered. "We need to take a meeting."

Wang spoke rapidly in Mandarin, Bolan picking up the name Soo and smiling. "That's good. We'll invite Li. He needs to be in on this."

"What do you want from me?" Wang asked as his secretary hurried out.

Bolan pushed him back in the chair and sat on the edge of the desk to look down at him.

"What would you think I'd want from you?"

Wang seemed to relax in his seat. He settled back, folding his hands on his lap. "Why have you come to my country, Mr. Belasko?"

"I'm a tourist in Hong Kong, Mr. Wang. And it's not your country, not yet." He hefted the .22, then stuck it in his pocket. "You got any more ammo for this gun? We used up an awful lot on your boys a while ago."

The man reached out and pulled open the top drawer of his desk. A box of shells sat within. Bolan took them, sticking them in the pocket with the gun.

"Assassins use .22s a lot, Mr. Wang. Did you know that?" Bolan asked. "They're good close-range weapons, and their report is easily silenced. I could probably put a pillow on your face and pop a couple of these into you, and the boys in the other offices wouldn't even hear it.''

"What do you want?" Wang asked.

"I want the killing to stop now. I want the red ties to go home. This is all bound to end soon anyway. American newscasts are covering the fight for Tree Island. It's bad publicity for China and will cease regardless. I want it to stop now, before anyone else gets hurt. If that happens, you'll get to stay alive. If not, I'm going to kill you."

"I am but a cog in a giant wheel," Wang explained.

"Yeah, a big cog. From what I can tell, you're the honcho around here. My proposition is extraordinarily simple and direct. Will you implement it?"

"Would you believe me if I said yes?" the man asked.

"Probably not," Bolan replied, "but it's worth the try."

"You're an American spy."

"American tourist."

At that moment the door burst open. Colonel Li plus several other red ties shoved their way in as Bolan moved behind Wang's chair, grabbing the man in a headlock and sticking the .44 in his ear.

"The gang's all here," the Executioner said. "Good. Welcome, Colonel. Sorry about your demotion. Guess that's what comes from free thinking."

Li pulled a 9 mm Ruger from inside his jacket and pointed it in Bolan's general direction. "You seem to know a great deal about me, Mr. Belasko. You have me at a disadvantage."

"We kicked your boys' butts this morning," Bolan said.

"It was impressive," Li replied. "You have a great deal of combat experience."

"I've been around. I thought you had me in Aberdeen."

"Yes, well, what exactly is our present situation here?"

The red ties had moved into the room, spreading out. There were five of them. Bolan kept his eyes moving as he spoke. "I was just explaining to Mr. Wang that I would kill him if he didn't stop this madness at once. American newscasts are already doing stories on these killings. It's pointless to go on."

"I'm just a soldier doing what I'm told," Li answered.

"Sorry, buddy. The Nuremberg option doesn't cut it with me. You're killing innocent civilians. It's not honorable."

The man's eyes flashed. "What do you know of honor?"

"I know the same things you do," Bolan said simply.

"Would you get this scum off me!" Wang shouted.

Bolan tilted the .44 and pulled the trigger, blowing off part of Wang's ear.

The man screamed, a hand going to his head, Bolan realizing Wang's surprise that someone would actually shoot him.

Bolan jerked the profusely bleeding man by the neck until he was standing, whimpering like a baby. He used him as a shield, moving toward the door, the red ties automatically surrounding him at a distance of five feet.

"You get on the horn to the butchers in Beijing, Colonel," Bolan said, "and tell them it's all unraveling and is going to come out into the open. Tell them they're going to lose face before the entire world."

"It strikes me," Li said as Bolan made the door and dragged Wang into the waiting room, "that if I can just kill you now, a lot of those problems might just go away."

"Try it and your boss here goes first," the Executioner stated, moving to the elevator and pushing the button. The door opened immediately.

"What an exciting eventuality," Li said, jumping into the elevator with Bolan just before the doors closed.

The two men stood facing each, a softly crying Wang between them. Li's Ruger was still in his hand, its barrel sticking in Wang's belly. Both men were pointing their guns at the same person.

"This man's death would give me nothing but satisfaction," Li said.

"Please, Soo," Wang said in English. "Please don't let him kill me."

"It would be for the good of the People's Republic," Li said. "Your death would also be destroying an enemy of the collective. It would be a hero's death. I'd tell them you sacrificed yourself bravely for the good of all."

"On the graves of my ancestors," Wang cried, reaching out to hug himself to a disgusted Li, "I implore you not to kill me."

The car had stopped many times, the elevator doors opening and closing—but no one got on.

"Why are you doing this?" Bolan asked Li. The man looked up, locking eyes with him. The Executioner saw vulnerability there.

"You...can't know of my motivations," Li replied.

"How can you work with them after what they did to your brother?"

The elevator reached the ground floor, and Bolan dragged Wang across the polished floor, a trail of blood following.

"What of my brother?" Li asked, following him, the Ruger still in his hand. "Is there news?"

"Your brother died in Huairoun Prison two years ago. Li Yun starved to death, Colonel."

"Lies!" Li roared as another elevator disgorged the other red ties, who hurried to catch up to their commander. "My brother lives! He is the reason I'm here."

"I'm sorry," Bolan said, taking in the situation immediately. His arm tightened on Wang's neck enough to make the man gag. "You've been listening to the wrong people. I understand everything now. They're all using you."

"It's a lie," Wang gasped. "Yun is alive, Soo. I swear it."

Bolan had made the front doors and pushed out of them, into the cold afternoon. Li was still behind him, his eyes dark and brooding. Now the bank's security force joined the red ties stalking the Executioner. "I have no reason to lie to you," he told Li while letting his eyes drift to Wang. "Does *he?*"

"Soo...please," Wang begged.

Li leveled his Ruger on Wang's chest. "Gentlemen," he said, "ready your weapons!"

"No!" Wang yelled.

Bolan heard the screech of tires from Garden Street and turned just enough to see the taxi containing Angela Mao bouncing over the curb and speeding across the mall toward him.

Twenty weapons were drawn down on Bolan and Wang. Li addressed the men. "We will have to shoot *through* Mr. Wang in order to take out Mr. Belasko. Should we do that? Chao? Would you like the first shot?"

A big man lowered his weapon, others following suit. Li shrugged. "The will of the people," he said, lowering his own weapon. There were no smiles now, though. "It looks as if we'll have to deprive Mr. Wang of the opportunity of being a hero today."

The cab skidded loudly and came to a stop right behind Bolan. Mao opened the back door. "Get in, Charlie," she said from the driver's seat. The driver was nowhere to be seen.

"Remember what I said," Bolan told Li. "There's no more point to this assassination team. Leave these people alone."

"I'll remember," the colonel said, his eyes roving Bolan's face, looking for truth. "One more question before you leave. Why did you not shoot me at the Temple of Ten Thousand Buddhas when you had me at your mercy?"

"I didn't shoot you because you wanted me to," Bolan said. "Besides, a man like you needs to go down in an honest fight. You've just got to know who you're fighting is all."

He shoved Wang at them, then jumped into the back of the taxi. The vehicle squealed out of there, burning rubber on the bank's paving stones.

LI SOO WATCHED the American drive away, waving down his men when they raised their guns to fire at the fleeing taxi. They had enough problems without adding a massacre on Garden Street to them. Wang groveled on the pavement in front of him, hunched on the ground, his hands covering his head. "You may get up now, our hero," the colonel said. "He is gone."

As the man looked around tentatively, Li noticed how natural he looked slithering. Then Wang stood, his fear abating. "I need a doctor!" he yelled.

"An ambulance has already been called, sir," Chao said with authority.

Wang jerked a clean linen handkerchief from his jacket, putting it to the ragged remnants of his right ear. "I want that man dead," he said to Chao. "I don't care what it takes."

"He made some very good points," Li replied. "Perhaps we should share them with Beijing."

"No," Wang replied. "I've been given the responsibility of seeing this through to the end. We just have to jump up the schedule. Even with publicity, if they're dead, they're dead. No show, nobody to cry over. Nothing to be done about it." He looked at the men standing around him. "Get out! Go back to your jobs!"

"In case you're not aware of it," Li said, watching the security guards and the red ties, except Chao, drift away, "they've got guns now and have had training in their use. We killed many in the harbor today, but they also killed many of us. This is no longer quiet assassination, Mr. Wang. We've reached open, public warfare."

"You," Wang said, pointing to him, "nearly got me killed."

"You were never in danger." Li smiled, but his mind was churning other thoughts, darker thoughts that he'd save for a few minutes.

Wang moved up to him, invading his space, the man's cheeks still shiny with his own tears. "You're off this," he stated. "I'm putting Chao in command."

"You are not part of my strict command authority," Li replied. "You will have to clear things through your commanders in Beijing. Do you wish to make the call together? We'll explain the situation."

Wang stared at him. "Later," he said as a small man with wire-rim glasses hurried out of the bank, a stack of papers in his hands.

"Mr. Wang," he called, hurrying to them. "Mr. Wang!"

"Go away. I'm dying here."

"I believe I hear the ambulance now," Li said.

"But sir," the man continued, "you told me to inform you of the progress of your... business transaction."

"You have news?" Wang asked.

"Everyone has been working around the clock," the man said, bowing slightly. "It gives me great pleasure to inform you that all the paperwork will be done sometime late tonight, four days ahead of schedule."

Wang smiled, his teeth stained red from his own blood. "Call the *hong*," he said. "I will meet with them at precisely 7:00 a.m. tomorrow morning. We will sign the paperwork."

He turned to gaze haughtily at Colonel Li. "Success is more than possible."

The ambulance bumped over the curb and rushed the Bank of China entrance as the cab had done, attendants jumping out to strap their honored patient into a gurney and load him into the van.

The colonel turned to Chao. "For the moment, Major, don't do anything. I'm going to the hospital with Mr. Wang to make sure of his condition."

Chao just stared at him as he climbed into the ambulance and the attendant closed the back doors. Li sat on the ledge beside the gurney, one of the attendants looking at Wang's shredded ear as the other drove away.

"Do you speak English?" the colonel asked the attendant. The man replied with a string of Cantonese. Good.

"You caused me to lose face," Wang said, his voice raspy.

"You caused yourself to lose face," Li replied as the attendant gave the banker a shot for the pain. "Now, tell me about my brother."

"Your brother's alive," Wang stated. "The American agent was simply trying to bring dissension to our ranks."

"I want proof."

"What . . . another videotape?"

"That would be acceptable. I want it by tomorrow. In it I want my brother to say the time and the date. That will be enough."

"You could place a call to Pei. I'm sure he—"

"The videotape will be sufficient. More than sufficient."

"And what about *your* job, Colonel?" Wang asked, relaxing under the medication. "When are you going to do *your* job?"

"I had word from my informant just before being called to your office. He is now part of the American's entourage. We'll get all the ringleaders together. The rest will fall apart quickly at that point."

"I want results tonight, before the typhoon."

"You will have your results," Li promised, "one way or the other."

CHAPTER FOURTEEN

Even Victoria Park looked foreboding. As Bolan and Crosswaithe sat on the park bench watching Mao go through t'ai chi moves, led by an older woman with a wooden sword, the park's trees bent malevolently under the relentless winds while paper trash rushed past them. Very few people were in the park that afternoon as Hong Kong began taking serious notice of the impending storm, its citizens busy with what small amount could be done to protect themselves from harm.

"When's it supposed to hit?" Bolan asked.

"Sometime late tomorrow," the inspector said. Bandages on his face and hands covered wounds from the firefight on the ferry. "I've been through a lot of them in the twenty years I've been here, and they're all ugly. Water surges flood the harbor area, winds blow over trees and throw things through windows. People die."

The Executioner stretched out tired legs. It had already been a long day, and the afternoon was still young. He had showered and changed at Bui Tin's apartment at Repulse Bay, temporary headquarters for him and his squad, then made it back to the park to meet with Crosswaithe. "Remember the Chinese curse . . . may you live in interesting times?"

"Yeah," Crosswaithe said. "Well, it's about as interesting as I want it to get. We heard from the U.K. this morning, a personal call from Downing Street. The red ties all have diplomatic immunity and we're to leave them alone."

Bolan let his head fall back but found himself staring through the trees at the top ten stories of the Bank of China. He looked at the inspector. "The publicity hasn't caught up yet. Why are politicians such cowards?"

"It's not fear, it's expediency. In government, human life figures very low in the equation."

"What does that make us?" Bolan said.

"Expendable. You know, they won't keep me here long. The Star Ferry fiasco has pretty well sealed my administrative fate in law enforcement."

"Yeah. Well, don't expect me to apologize, because you did the right thing."

The t'ai chi gathering broke up. Mao hugged everyone who exercised with her.

Crosswaithe laughed. "I wasn't looking for an apology," he said. "I'm just sorry that I can't do more. I spoke with my chief, who is with us in spirit but is unable to help me officially without losing *his* job. But I have managed to get promises out of about fifty officers who are ready to follow me in an unofficial capacity. They will also guard your wounded in hospital. These are men who care about Hong Kong. They will follow you, die with you, if they have to."

Bolan turned and stared at him, a good man. "We need ammo."

The inspector nodded. "We confiscate tons of guns and ammunition and store them in the British forces headquarters building down by the docks," he said. "Make up a list of what you'll need. I'll steal it for you if I have to."

"Thanks, Ian."

"As I said, old chap. I'm sorry I can't do more. In the meantime I'm going to hunt red ties. If my men see them on the streets, they'll stop them. If they're carrying guns, they'll be arrested. If they fight, we'll fight them. All unofficial."

Mao sat down next to Bolan, her flawless face coated with a fine sheen of sweat. "So," she said, "have the great minds worked out all the political problems of the world yet?"

"Not yet," Bolan said. "But it's time for your great mind to stop playing games with me and tell me where your father hid his information."

She smiled. "Okay, Charlie. You've backed me into a corner, huh?"

"Let's just cut to the chase. I'm getting old sitting here."

She nodded, and Bolan realized she was afraid he'd leave them as soon as he got what he wanted.

"I'm here for the duration," he reassured her. "Don't worry."

She smiled then. "My father was a very religious man. He spent a great deal of time at the temple over on Hollywood Street, especially if he was troubled about something or needing guidance."

"The Man-Mo Temple?" Crosswaithe asked. Mao nodded as he began to laugh.

"What's funny?" Bolan asked.

"The Man-Mo temple," Crosswaithe said, "is a dual temple to Man, the god of literature, and Mo, the god of war, the two notions existing side by side. Man-Mo is the policemen's temple. Many of my coworkers do observances there."

Bolan was thoughtful. "And you think that your father would have left his message at the temple?" he asked Angela.

"Has to be, Charlie. He spent a lot of time there. It would have been his first thought."

"Well, what are we waiting for?" Bolan asked, starting to rise.

"No," she said, putting a hand on his arm. "Tonight. After it's closed. We'll go tonight."

COLONEL LI WENT into the office he occupied on the fortieth floor of the Bank of China building and locked the door.

He would have no more lies.

It was a ghost office, empty except for a desk and phone, perfect for him. His mind spun possibilities, hatreds and deceits into a web of great complexity and adhesion. He struggled against the web. There was only one way to relieve the horrible pressure on his brain, and the answer was so simplistic that it was a tribute to bullheaded rationalization that he'd never thought of it before.

He sat behind the desk and picked up the phone. He had a target, and the phone would be his weapon.

Using his rank and his commanding presence, he dialed through the miasma of Hong Kong phone traffic to the mainland, finally reaching his destination—Huairoun Prison, just outside Beijing. Huairoun was a bread-and-water subsistence hole for political prisoners, the place where his brother had been singled out for special attention.

Pretending to be from Pei's staff, Li bypassed anyone of authority, opting instead to speak to someone in the records department, a woman with an incongruously sweet voice. "May I help you, please?"

"My name is Chang Lin," the colonel said. "I am running the clerical department in Under Secretary Pei's offices and am trying to straighten out our books on a number of political prisoners."

"Yes?"

"I'm showing a man on my records by the name of... Li. Li Yun. We show him going into your facility in 1989 after Tiananmen Square, but have no notice of disposition on my files. Has he been released? And if so, what's the date?"

"Did you say the name was Li Yun?" the woman asked.

"Yes. I'm sorry for bringing any work to you."

"That's all right...just let me check the files. Hold, please."

Li sat shaking, his hands sweaty, his knuckles cramping from holding the phone so hard. The woman was gone for an interminable length of time before returning.

"I've got the file here," she said happily. "Just let me...ah, here it is. That prisoner died two years ago, Mr. Chang. We sent the paperwork. Check the back of your files. You may still find—"

The phone was dead, and the colonel looked down to find that he'd jerked the line right out of the machine. A darkness covered his eyes, and the receiver broke in two under the power of his hands.

Truth. He could have had it any time but had chosen to be ignorant and allowed himself to be humiliated while his brother lay dying.

How much honor could a man lose and still stay alive? He looked up to see his own reflection in the window glass and had the answer to his question.

But all bills were ultimately paid, all stories eventually reaching a conclusion. And so it would be for the stories of Li Soo and his brother Yun.

MACK BOLAN STOOD on the porch of Bui Tin's apartment, looking out over Repulse Bay as the darkness of afternoon slowly gave way to the darkness of night. He'd eaten, had even gotten some sleep and now was itching to get on the road.

The sea looked angry, and the beach people were all gone. Repulse Bay was deserted and forlorn, the air heavy with the threat of rain.

He looked farther up the mountain, at the home where he'd seen the military operation take away the woman. All the lights were blazing brightly, as if a great deal of activity was taking place inside. He briefly thought about taking a little walk up there and finding out for himself, but decided that he'd better attend to one thing at a time, and this night's thing was the Man-Mo Temple. He was already dressed and ready in jeans and black turtleneck, an oxblood-stained leather jacket covering his combat harness. It was time.

As if in response to his thoughts, Angela Mao walked out to join him, standing beside him at the rail, leaning against it on stiff arms. "The weather's like a giant beast trying to swallow us," she said. "Maybe this time it will succeed."

"Cheery thought," he said. "Are you about ready to go?"

She nodded. "We'll take Shing for a lookout, just in case, okay?"

"Sure. Did he ever get his cousin's car back from the New Territories?"

"About an hour ago," she replied smiling. "That's what we're taking to Man-Mo."

"Talked him into it?"

She arched an eyebrow and almost smiled. "His cousin's mad at him anyway. I just asked him what difference one more day would make."

"I see," Bolan said, turning toward the door. "Well, let's get Shing and take a drive on the Eastern Corridor Highway."

He walked back into the apartment, the place thick with cigarette smoke and people moving furniture, piling it so there'd be places for their bedrolls. In the kitchen the Chan brothers cooked vegetables in a wok, aprons tied around their middles. Shing was back in the bedroom, loading the Remington pump he seemed to like so much.

Mao walked through the front doors, heading directly to the dining table to retrieve her .45. She stuck it into the waistband of her jeans, then pulled the bulky sweater she wore over it. Her fanny pack with the extra ammo clips sat on the service bar to the kitchen, and she went to put it on. Kun was there, holding out two platters of steaming vegetables.

"You mind?" he asked.

"Of course not." She took the platters and put them on the table, and six people reached with chopsticks immediately. When she turned back to Kun, his face was grave.

"What are you going to do?" he asked.

"Nothing," she said, hooking on the fanny pack. "I'm going out for a while with Shing and Charlie."

"With guns," Kun said, shaking his head. "Your father wouldn't want you to do these things. I feel responsible. That American is a very violent man. You could be killed. I absolutely forbid it."

She leaned over the bar and kissed him on the cheek, then whispered, "Don't worry. We're just going to Man-Mo Temple. We won't be long. But don't tell anybody. Security."

"Security," he replied, nodding expansively. He then whispered, "If you're going to Man-Mo, our shop is only two blocks away from—"

"I'll go by your shop and make sure it's all right," she said, turning as Bolan and Shing walked back into the room on a trajectory for the door. She hurried to join them.

"Ladies and gentlemen," Bolan said, standing with his hand on the knob, "if we aren't back by morning," he said, "I have left written instructions for you with Mr. Bui. Read them."

With that he opened the door and disappeared into the night.

HOLLYWOOD STREET WAS one way heading east, so Shing brought them into Central District on Queen's Road, then doubled back where it intersected Hollywood, traveling the three blocks east to Man-Mo on the corner of Ladder Street.

Hollywood was the street of antiques, rattan and curio shops, small stores jammed together, full of merchandise. This was also the place of death rituals, sellers of coffins, wreaths and burial wear. But this night the shops were empty, boarded up against nature, the owners at home with their families lest the typhoon strike during the night.

"We've been very lucky with the car so far," Shing said. "We mustn't scratch or dent it. My cousin will kill me if we hurt his car. It is his status symbol."

"We're not going to hurt your silly car," Mao replied from beside him in the front seat. Bolan sat in the back, feeling uneasy and not sure why.

They passed the ornate temple, the oldest and largest in Hong Kong, dating back to 1842. Shing parked half a block away.

"Lock your doors," Shing instructed as he climbed out.

"No," Bolan said. "Leave the doors open and the key in the ignition."

"Somebody might steal it!" Shing protested.

"Believe me," Bolan said. "If somebody wants your car, they'll get it whether the key's there or not. Do what I say. And Shing, leave the window open."

"You're the boss." Shing pulled the lock button to the open position, cranking down the driver's window and closing his door. The three of them walked quickly to the temple, Shing walking backward, watching the car.

The temple sat right beside Ladder Street, a steep runway of concrete jammed with shops and stalls, deserted like Hollywood Street. When the temple had been built, Ladder Street was a dirt footpath leading up out of Central to Man-Mo.

"The door should be open," Mao stated, moving past the statues of the eight immortals who guarded the entry. She pulled on the heavy wooden doors, which creaked open immediately.

"Shing," she said, "you stay by the door. Keep watch and tell us if anyone comes."

Shing agreed. It would give him the opportunity of keeping an eye on his cousin's status symbol.

Bolan followed Mao inside, the odor of heavy perfume hitting him just inside the door. He had walked into a fever dream. There were no direct lights other than hundreds of burning candles and thousands of joss sticks that puffed large incense clouds that roiled slowly through the building as the candlelight glinted brightly from gold-and-brass fixtures. Monstrous spirals of incense hung down from the high ceiling, burning slowly.

"This way," Mao said, leading him past the two three-foot-tall solid brass deer in the entryway, a symbol of longevity. They continued into the inner chambers, where tiny lanterns hanging amid the incense coils added rich yellow light to the ornate rooms.

Small altars with brass-and-procelain appointments were scattered throughout the temple, but the main altar dominated the room. It was large, perhaps fifteen feet long, and was raised a half-dozen steps from the room itself. It was marble and was sensuously carved out and attended by ornately crafted gold filigree. Burning candles filled the altar, the images of the gods standing beside, one on each end.

Mao moved up the stairs with a casualness that bespoke countless trips to the temple. She spoke softly and lit a number of incense sticks, as if the place didn't have enough going already. "This is Mo," she said, pointing to a three-foot statue of a Chinese in Mandarin robes sitting on a pedestal, "the god of martial arts. He was born Kuan Yue in A.D. 160."

Bolan walked to the statue on the other side of the altar. "And this must be Man," he said, looking at the stately carved deity with the long mustache.

She stood beside him. "Born Cheung Ah Tse in 287. But where do we find the message?"

Bolan walked around the statue, checking it from all angles, then checked the pedestal it stood on to no avail. "Your father said, 'Under Man,'" the Executioner replied. "So..."

He moved up to the statue itself, reaching out for it.

"What are you doing, Charlie?" she asked. "That's a sacred object."

"Objects aren't sacred," Bolan said, taking hold of the statue's shoulders and pulling. "The things they represent are. When I get this tilted back, look beneath the base."

She grunted but didn't say anything. Bolan pulled hard on the heavy statue, just barely able to tilt it back on its base. "Oh, my," Mao said, reaching and snatching a manila envelope from beneath the statue. Bolan rocked the god of literature back to his accustomed place.

He moved beside her, the woman's hands shaking as she held the letter, tears in her eyes. There was Chinese writing on the outside of the envelope. "What does it say?" he asked.

"It says, 'If I die, please give this to my daughter, Angela,'" she replied sadly, then held out the envelope to him. "This is yours, I believe."

He was just reaching for the envelope when Shing ran into the main room. "Red ties!" he said sharply. "A lot of them."

"Where?" Mao asked.

"Here!" the man said.

Bolan grabbed the envelope and thrust it into his combat harness under the jacket.

"Is there a back door?" he asked.

"How the hell should I know?" Mao replied. A burst of gunfire from the doorway raked the altar, driving them to the floor. Shing swung around with his Remington and took out the first man in, then crawled madly through the haze of incense to try to reach their position.

The red ties piled through the door, then spread out, laying out a wide pattern of firing, the sound deafening in the enclosed space. Bolan and Mao quickly retreated behind the marble altar, bullets pinging off brass canisters and incense holders as large segments of the spiral incense started dropping to the floor.

"Where's Shing?" Mao yelled above the noise.

"Don't shoot!" Shing yelled, diving over the altar, coming up with his shirt on fire. Bolan and Angela slapped it out.

"Okay," the big man said, priming the Desert Eagle, "there's a glass case on your side with a couple of sedan chairs in it."

She nodded. "They used to parade the statues on them."

"There's two of them hiding behind that. Shing's going to drive them out with the shotgun, then you're going to nail them."

"And what are you going to be doing?"

"Just take care of your side," he said. "Ready? Go!"

Shing jumped up and pumped several rounds into the glass case as Mao curled around her side of the altar, firing as the flying glass brought the men hiding there into the open. Bolan dived the other way, firing from behind the god who'd protected Mao Hsing's secrets.

He took the open doorway, taking out two red ties before they got inside the front doors that swung shut at that moment. But they were already swarming inside the temple. Sometimes discretion *was* the better part of valor. He rolled back behind the altar. "Cover me," he said. "I'm going to look for a way out."

They nodded, and Shing jumped up to fire again as Bolan charged behind the curtains forming the backdrop to the altar. The way things were coming down, he'd have about a minute to get them out of there before it would be impossible to escape.

He found himself in a storage room, long and narrow, filled with extra spiral incense sticks taller than two men, candles, joss sticks and priestly vestments. A back door slammed open thirty feet from him.

He brought up the .44 and took out the first man through chest high, the second tripping over the body of the first and falling. Bolan took him out with a head shot before he could jump up.

The door slammed closed again, and the Executioner put three rounds into the door itself, hoping to take out someone on the other side. Dead end.

He hurried back into the fighting near the altar, the red ties creeping slowly closer, using subsidiary altars and pedestals for cover. They were trapped.

Then he saw it, the tall steel ladder bolted right into the walls and leading high into the rafters, no doubt the way the spirals were replaced. At the top of the ladder he saw a small window, barely large enough for a human being to fit through. Any port in the storm.

"Cover me up the ladder!" he yelled above the din. "Then I'll cover you!"

Without hesitation he jumped to his feet, then ran for the ladder as Shing and Mao laid down covering fire. At full speed he jumped at the ladder, reaching high. He hit hard, slamming into the wall but grabbing a rung ten feet off the ground and scrambling up into the haze as quickly as he could, bullets punching holes through the wooden walls beneath his feet.

He climbed high into the darkness, above the reach of the lights, protected by clouds of incense and candle smoke. In the rafters he had protection and high ground. Through the haze he picked out forms below, forms in motion. He fired, one of the forms crumpling to the floor.

"Come on!" he yelled, and turned to the window. It was opaque glass, meant only to let in a touch of sunshine. It would be a squeeze, but he could fit. He poked the gun barrel at the window, which shattered, raining glass. He cleared the frame of jagged remnants and turned to look down just as Mao reached the ladder and climbed quickly, Shing still firing below.

"Would you get in gear?" Bolan yelled down to him as he drew a bead on a man charging the altar. He hit him in the neck, the red tie going down untidily.

"I can't climb!" Shing yelled back. "My arm's still weak!"

"Charlie!" Mao yelled, then fired right beside his head.

Bolan's left ear went deaf immediately as a red tie's body collapsed at the bottom of the ladder.

"Cover us!" Bolan said, then scrambled back down the ladder, jumping to the ground as soon as his incense-smoke cover dissipated.

He ran to the altar, firing on a red tie charging to intercept him. The man took three hits in the chest before jumping into the air backward and crashing down flat on his back, dead before he hit the floor.

He ran to a still-firing Shing. "Go!" the man yelled.
"I'll keep them off you!"

"No way!" Bolan yelled. He holstered the .44, then
grabbed Shing, physically throwing the man over his
shoulder. He turned and charged the ladder again,
Mao emptying her clip in an attempt to keep the enemy at bay.

Bolan strained with the weight of the man he carried, but still hustled up the ladder. Mao was already
climbing out the window space when he arrived,
reaching back in to help Shing shinny through.

They were rushing the altar below from both sides
as Bolan dropped his last grenade straight down and
squeezed into the window space.

Halfway through he got stuck.

"Damn!"

He was looking out into the Hong Kong night.
Shing and Mao straddled a sloping roof of slate that
dropped off another ten feet to the top of the building next door.

"What's wrong?" she called to him.

"I'm stuck!" he yelled, hearing the muffled sound
of the grenade going off below him.

As he struggled to get through, imagining men with
guns drawing down on him from below, the two pre-
cariously made their way back to try to pull him out.

Mao got there first, grabbing one of his hands and
pulling hard. He felt some movement.

"Come on, Charlie, I—" Her eyes got wide as she lost her grip and fell, sliding down the slate roof and falling to the next building.

Shing had him then, every second seeming like fifty years, leaning back fully, all his weight tugging on Bolan. The big man slithered through, and both of them slid down the roof.

Bolan felt the cold wind whipping his face, then he was in open air, falling headfirst and twisting to break his fall. He and Shing hit hard beside Mao, the roof giving way, all of them taking the ride down into the showroom of the coffin shop next to the temple.

They hit real ground then, coffins flying everywhere, followed by a rain of plaster that turned them as white as ghosts.

Bolan was up, shaking off the back pain as he ran to the storefront window, peering between the boards to look out. Mercedes were all over the streets, blocking them at the nearest intersections as red ties piled into the temple next door.

"Let's go," he said as Shing picked himself up from the remnants of a coffin.

"Go where?" Shing asked, trying to dust himself off, then giving up as Mao dropped the clip from her .45 and reloaded from her battered fanny pack.

"Out of here," the Executioner replied as he moved to the door and pulled on the boards that were nailed up to protect against the impending storm. "Anywhere. We'll take the car."

"The car?" Shing said, running to him. "Not the car, Charlie."

Bolan drew the Beretta, leaving the depleted .44 in its holster. "I'll drive," he said, and threw open the door. He and Mao rushed out into the street, Shing dejectedly pumping the Remington to an expended cartridge, then hurrying after them.

The Executioner hit the street running, preferring better odds in a firefight, Mao right on his heels. They raced toward the Ford a half block away, empty Mercedes parked all around it. Twenty feet from the car, he heard shouting behind them, then the first shots.

"Keep moving!" he yelled, bullets ricocheting off the cobbled streets around them.

They reached the car, Bolan going for the driver's side and pulling the door open. Using the door as a shield, he crouched and aimed through the open window space at the red ties who were turning from the doors of the temple to give chase.

He chose the lead stalker and aimed at the chest as Mao and Shing jumped into the car. He fired once, and the man stumbled forward before pitching headfirst to the ground. Then Bolan took out the next closest the same way, the rest of them diving for cover behind a fleet of Mercedes.

The Executioner jumped into the Ford, turning the key immediately and kicking the vehicle into gear. The return fire began as he popped the clutch and turned a precarious three-sixty. He tromped the accelerator as his windshield shattered, gunfire now coming from behind them, farther down at the blocked intersection. They were caught in a cross fire.

"The car!" Shing screamed when the windshield went. His eyes were wide in horror as the metal thunk of bullets hitting the car cleared all thoughts from his head of ever driving again.

The back windshield went as black smoke oozed thickly from the engine. The smoke blinded Bolan, but also provided cover from the shooters behind them as they picked up speed, the Executioner trying to steer through the smoke and around the vehicles that jammed Hollywood Street.

He rammed his fist through the shattered windshield, knocking it out of the car, then cut hard right, bashing the front end of a Mercedes, the impact throwing them several feet. The Executioner steered hard left to pull them out of the skid.

"That's it," Shing said from the back seat. "My life is over." He thrust the barrel of the Remington through the back window and fired, then pumped again quickly, firing immediately. "Bastards!"

"Pick your shots!" Bolan yelled.

Mao hung halfway out the other window as he slid into another car sideways, a hive of red ties jumping out from behind the vehicle, Shing taking them out of play.

They passed the temple, slipping between two cars at fifty miles per hour. "Get down!" Bolan yelled as concentrated fire tore at them, a front tire going flat.

Cars were in motion in front of him, moving to block any attempted escape. There was only Ladder Street, so Bolan hit a hard left and took Ladder upward, the downward incline already blocked.

The angle was steep, close to seventy degrees, the street narrow, barely wide enough for a car. Empty stalls sat chained to the buildings. Those he couldn't avoid. He smashed into one, then another as gunfire erupted at the bottom of the hill.

He'd had some speed up when he'd hit Ladder, but it was dropping, even though his foot was to the floor. They'd never make it.

"This hill is too steep, Charlie," Mao stated, reloading. The red ties, a hundred feet behind, were gaining.

"Thanks for the insight," Bolan said.

The car jerked as it hit another kiosk. A ten-gallon tub of peanut oil broke open on the hood, then bouncing over the top of the vehicle after dumping its contents through the open windshield space, drenching the occupants.

"Damn," Mao said, her dripping arms dangling in front of her. "It can't get any worse."

Then it started to rain.

The car stopped moving forward and rolled backward.

Bolan jammed both feet on the brakes and pulled the emergency brake. "Out the top!" he yelled. "Quick!"

He reached up and cranked open the sunroof as the car decided whether it wanted to roll backward or stay put. They were beginning to slide, brakes and all. He turned the wheel hard left to put them into a building, but the wheel was dead; the car's trip on the blown tire's rim had bent the axle.

"Out! Out!"

Mao climbed onto the back of her seat and achieved the top of the car as Bolan picked up the Beretta from the seat to turn and cover Shing's exit.

He fired at the mob fifty feet behind, dropping one. The others scrambled for cover behind the remnants of the carts he had destroyed. He heard Mao hit the hood then roll off the front fender as Shing scurried up over the seat, using his bad arm from the elbow up to pry himself out.

Bolan fired again, hitting an exposed thigh, the man writhing into the center of the street, where the Executioner finished him with a head shot. Shing hit the hood as the car started rolling backward.

He gave it over then, sliding out from behind the wheel as the car picked up speed, drifting toward the building facades. He holstered the Beretta, then climbed through the open sunroof, looking back the way they'd come.

The red ties were running back down the hill as the car scraped the buildings to an explosion of sparks at the contact, then drifted toward the other side of the street, bouncing over the body of the man he'd just killed.

Bolan tested the space, knowing from recent experience that he wouldn't fit through. He crouched. They were picking up speed, Mao and Shing more distant now.

The car hit a runner who'd tripped and fallen and was just getting back up, the impact throwing him over the trunk and into the back seat. Bolan gauged the windshield space—small but adequate.

He stretched out his arms and sprang as the Ford hit the gas-tank side of the street to more sparks, another runner grinding beneath the wheels, the red tie in the back seat moaning.

Bolan broke free of the window and slid across the hood, grabbing the front grillwork to propel himself the rest of the way.

The gas tank went up in the sparks, a huge explosion, as Bolan hit the ground in a roll. The fireball was hot, nearly igniting his clothes, as the out-of-control car turned into an out-of-control fireball. He got to his feet and charged back up the hill, waving off Mao and Shing, who were running toward him.

The Executioner chanced a look over his shoulder. The flaming car slid quickly into Hollywood, smashing into the Mercedes that blocked further entrance onto Ladder. It turned into a fireball, too, flinging burning fuel in all directions, setting fire, blocking entry onto their section of Ladder Street.

For the moment they were safe.

Bolan reached his companions.

"What now?" Mao asked.

He turned back to the fire again, light rain streaming his face. "We get the hell out of here," he said, "then call Ian Crosswaithe. For once I've got something real to show him."

He broke into a trot, and the others followed as the wind howled and the rain spit, the three of them melting into the obscurity only a major metropolis could provide.

CHAPTER FIFTEEN

Bolan sat in the dark booth wiping his face with one of the towels Crosswaithe had brought with him, working at the oil without much success. They sat in the Kara Karaoke, a karaoke bar in the New Harbour View Hotel. Mao and Shing sat on the other side of the table, using the towels on each other's hair while the inspector intently read the papers Bolan had brought from the Man-Mo Temple while sipping on a gin and tonic. Bolan drank coffee.

Mao pouted, staring at him as she rubbed Shing's hair on both sides with the towel.

"What do you mean?" she asked.

"I meant just what I asked," he said. "Who did you tell? There was only one way for the red ties to know we were at the temple—somebody told them. Who knew?"

"Not me," Shing said. "You never told me until we were on the road."

"I knew," Crosswaithe said. "I told no one."

"Neither did I," Bolan stated, looking pointedly at Mao. "Be honest. You've never bought into this notion. You told somebody, didn't you?"

"Maybe they just saw us on the streets and chased us," she suggested.

"Angela..."

She took a long breath, then let it out. "I told only Chan Kun," she said.

"Kun?" Shing repeated.

"He's like an uncle to me. And he was so worried that we'd run into trouble tonight."

"No doubt," Bolan returned.

"It doesn't seem possible," Shing said.

"Anything's possible in war," Bolan told him, then looked again at Mao. "We're going to have to confront him. One way or the other."

She nodded. "I may be a fool," she said, eyes tearing, "but I'm not a blind fool."

"I'm sorry," Bolan told her.

"If we prove it," she said, "let me be the one to... handle the situation."

"You know what you're asking?"

She nodded.

"This is beyond belief," Crosswaithe said, sitting back from the letter. "According to Mao Hsing, the Bank of China is planning to take over the money of the *hong* by—" he bent over and read again from page two "—any means necessary, including hostage taking."

"Which explains the death of Londy Than's wife," Bolan said, "and the things I saw at Repulse Bay that same night."

The inspector sat back again, folding his arms. "Which means it would be happening soon," he said.

"Yeah . . . like now," Mao said, then mouthed a silent *I'm sorry* across the table that Bolan shook off. She'd learned. Finally.

Crosswaithe shook his head. "Then he indicates a safehouse on Cape D'Aguilar that he says is a Red Army headquarters and contains computers holding the proof of the takeover."

"Isn't that near where you lost the wire?" Bolan asked.

The man nodded. "I'll get a chopper in the air while the weather's still cooperating," he said. "We'll get some pictures from up there."

"We don't have the time," Bolan said. "I say we send my squad down to the peninsula in cars while we direct them in ourselves from the chopper. That way we handle everything right now, have this operation bagged by the morning. Then you can go to your government with proof instead of theories. Deal?"

"Deal," Crosswaithe agreed, sticking out his hand to shake across the table, then pulling it back when he saw the peanut oil still clinging to the Executioner's hands.

"Waitress!" Crosswaithe said, pointing to the table. "I need some coffee over here!"

"Me, too!" Bolan called, holding his cup up.

It was going to be a long night.

BOLAN STOOD TO ADDRESS his squad in Bui Tin's living room. A head taller than most of them in the crowded room, he could see everyone's face. It was two in the morning, the rain, sporadic for the past several hours, had picked up in intensity, now becoming a factor in anything they might do.

"We're taking the battle to the enemy tonight for the first time. We're taking charge of our own destinies. I don't know how many of the red ties will be where we're going, only that there will be some. I can guarantee you that. The other thing I can guarantee is that some of you won't come back. Don't be a casualty. Put away your emotions and think through what you are doing. You were chosen for two reasons. You were either the strongest and best qualified or you were single and would leave no family behind. The hopes of everyone ride on our shoulders. The hope isn't misplaced."

He looked at his watch. "It's time. Go to your assigned transport. We'll contact you from the air. Good luck to all of us."

Mao threw open the door, and the squad quickly and silently sifted out, leaving behind only Bui, Shing, Mao and the Chan brothers, who were busily cleaning up the kitchen.

"Kun," Mao called, a frown etching into her face.

The man turned, smiling wide as he dried one of the woks. "Yes?"

"Come over here," Bolan said, his voice less gentle than Mao's.

The man's brows narrowed suspiciously as he set down the wok and rag, then moved into the empty living room, wiping his hands on his apron.

"We have a slight problem," Mao told the old man. "It has to do with where we were tonight."

"Did you see my shop?" Kun asked. "Is it all right? I wish I could board up the—"

"Enough," Bolan said, shaking his head at Angela. "Let me."

He walked up to Chan Kun, staring fire down at the man. "How many of us have you killed?" he asked.

"K-killed?" Kun repeated, eyes frightened. "I have killed no one, I—"

"No more lies," Bolan growled. "You're the only one who could have told the red ties we were at the temple tonight. Admit it. Things just get harder from here."

Confusion filled Kun's face, the man looking frantically at all of them. "Red ties . . . I—I've told no red ties. I swear to you on my ancestors'—"

Bolan shook him. "Who did you tell? How much blood is on your hands?"

Chan looked at the floor, shaking his head. "I . . . told no one!"

"Liar!" Bolan shook him again, the man falling to his knees.

"P-please believe me. I told no one, no one."

Bolan reached down to drag him to his feet.

"Enough."

He released Kun, all eyes turning to his brother, Wee-Gee, who walked slowly out of the kitchen, his face a mask of horror. "The only person Kun told of your journey was me. He wanted to reassure me that

Angela would check on our shop." The man took a long breath, then let it out with resolve. "I called the red ties."

"You?" Shing said. "But why?"

"They found me early on. Kun and Le-Chun were in Kowloon buying fabric that day. They hurt me and then stuck a gun in my mouth. They wanted names and addresses. I gave them names and addresses."

"No!" Kun said, moving to hug his brother, who was sobbing loudly now, his shoulders shaking. "My brother didn't do this. It was me."

"It's over," Wee-Gee said. "I want it to be over. I'm such a coward. I helped them under force, then helped them so they'd like me. I don't know why."

"Once you've sold yourself out," Bolan said, "the rest is easy. You cut the lube lines on Mr. Shinshi's plane?"

The man nodded, unable to look at them now.

Kun moved away from Wee-Gee. "And our brother," he said. "Did you tell them where his stall was?"

"Yes," Wee-Gee cried. "I was so scared. At first it was easy. I gave them addresses of people I didn't know well or like very much. When we all went into hiding, everyone kept strong contacts with one another, but the more people died, the more secretive the living became. They wanted more names and I had no more."

"And so you killed your own flesh and blood?" Kun asked.

"I was always the weakest, brother," Wee-Gee said. "You know that. When we were children, you and Le-Chun always protected me. When I'd lie, you'd cover for me. I didn't want to die. I couldn't handle this. I'm so sorry. Please forgive me."

"Forgive you?" Mao asked, and Bolan could see in her eyes every bit of the betrayal she felt. "How many are dead because of you? How many of your close friends now live with their ancestors? Tonight you wanted to kill me and Shing."

"I never wanted to kill anybody," the man said softly, the tears flowing freely down his face. "I swear to you."

"She asked you how many," Kun said furiously.

Wee-Gee lowered his head, covering his face with his hands. "Only three or four had died when they came to our shop," he whispered.

"Everyone," Kun said. "You killed everyone, including Mao Hsing, the best of all of us. You killed the man who saved your life by smuggling you here."

"I killed no one," Wee-Gee said. "I only made telephone calls."

"And you're going to make one more," the Executioner said.

The man looked up suddenly, as if the typhoon had disappeared and the sun had risen. "Yes, yes. Anything. I want to make amends for what I've done."

Bolan strode forward to take him by the arm and lead him to the telephone on the dining table. He put the man into the chair and handed him the receiver.

"Call your number," he said. "Tell them that we are all leaving tomorrow night at dark from the government pier in Central. Tell them that a U.S. destroyer is going to be anchored just south of Lamma Island to take all the dissidents secretly to the United States. Do it now."

They all gathered around as Chan Wee-Gee made the call. He whispered with urgency and swore he was telling the truth. The call took no longer than a minute. It was familiar and easy, and Bolan tried to imagine what it had to be like to sell out everything in life that meant anything to you. Chan Wee-Gee's humanity was gone. He had died that day in his tailor shop when they'd stuck the gun in his mouth just as surely as if they'd pulled the trigger.

The man stood from the table and asked, "What happens now?"

"Now you and I have to have a private talk," Mao said. "Will you come with me into the bathroom for a moment?"

"The bathroom?"

The woman nodded and led him away as Bolan sat at the table thinking. Amazingly enough, his invented phone call had started him down a line of imagining that made sense. The envelope containing Mao Hsing's detective work lay before him on the table. It was hot, important to America because it involved America's money. He looked at his watch. It was well after two in the morning, which put it after one in the afternoon in D.C. Hal Brognola would be in his office.

Bolan dialed his number, going through a complicated security procedure before reaching the man.

"Striker," the big Fed said. "Am I glad to hear from you. Things are happening here. The American newscasts have got everyone talking. Congress is shouting about it, the administration promising to not let human-rights violations go by the boards while we suck up to China. In a few days, I'll bet—"

"We don't have a few days, Hal," the Executioner said. "I've got the information Mao Hsing had for us, and it's hot. You tell the administration they need to see it right away because they'll have to make some quick decisions."

"What is it?"

"I'm not going to tell you. But I will make a trade."

"Striker..."

"Here are my terms. Write them down and I'll get back with you in a few hours."

"God, no wonder I'm turning gray."

"Just write, Hal."

ANGELA MAO WALKED back to the bathroom, located between the living and sleeping quarters, with Chan Wee-Gee. It was large for an apartment, done all in pale blues with gold fixtures on the sink and tub. She'd never noticed things in such detail before, probably because she was focusing her mind away from the task at hand.

"What you want to talk about, Angela?" the old man asked in English as she closed the door.

She fought back childhood memories of laughter, bridge games and huge dinner parties at her father's home, a home she'd been on the run from since the red ties. She fought back the memories of the Chan brothers swinging her around, tossing her from one of them to the other, everyone laughing, one of her first real memories.

"You killed my father," she said, taking off the long trench coat she wore.

"Not actually. I tried to protect him as long as I could, believe me. I told them he was on the streets that day. Someone at the hotel said where he was."

"Only because you didn't know where he was going."

"I'll make up for it, I promise you. When this is over—"

"Would you step into the bathtub please?" she asked.

"Why?"

She unzipped the fanny pack on her hip and removed the small .22 that the American had taken from Wang Wushen. She snapped a round into the chamber and pointed it at him. "Get into the tub, Uncle."

He put his hands up and backed slowly until he bumped into the tub. He tried to smile, but it got stuck at the grimace stage. "You wouldn't shoot me," he said. "I didn't mean any harm, I—"

"The tub!" she ordered, venting her anger now.

The man stepped into the tub reluctantly, his hands shaking in front of his face. "Don't hurt me, Angela. I used to change your diapers when you were a baby."

"Lie down, please," she said, taking several paces toward him.

"Why? I can stand, I . . . maybe I can help you. Get information from the red ties. I meet with the colonel sometimes on Bird Street. Maybe I can help you. Spy for you."

"Lie down! You disgust me. You're like a cat that eats its own babies."

He crouched, then slowly sat in the tub. "Maybe I can find out where they live. You can go there—"

"Down!"

He lay down, crying again, trying to talk but getting nothing but incoherence. Mao walked to stare down into the tub as she wrapped the trench coat around her wrist and hand, completely covering the gun.

"You have dishonored yourself and your name," she said coldly. "You are a traitor to your own people. But no more."

She leaned close as if to kiss him, immediately firing two shots at point-blank range into his head, blood spurting but staying in the tub.

Then she turned quickly, putting it behind her. This night she had put away the things of childhood and grown up completely. It was painful and confusing. She wanted no more of it, though more there would be.

BOLAN HUNG UP THE PHONE, hoping his game would play out right. Everything was such a crapshoot. He heard two small pops from the bathroom, then watched Mao walk out, unwrapping a coat from her gun hand, the smell of gunpowder permeating the air. She was carrying Wang's .22, the right weapon for the job. It was unfortunate that she would bear this moment for the rest of her life, but he could understand her need for vengeance. He'd been there.

Chan Kun approached her, the two staring at each other, then dissolving into an embrace—the ragged beginning of healing.

"Listen," Shing said. "Chopper."

He threw open the door, and the Executioner followed him out onto the porch to find a Hong Kong harbor-patrol chopper setting down on the white sand of Repulse Bay beach.

He turned back into the room. "This is it," he said to Mao. "Get your gear. It's time."

COLONEL LI SAT at a desk in the fortieth-floor office suite, telephone to his ear, watching the winds blow the waves of Victoria Harbour from halfway up the Bank of China's monstrous glass tree. His men were bivouacked all over the city, but this was his place, close to Wang. He and an even dozen of his men lived here, the elevator fixed to not even stop on the fortieth floor.

The phone was dead in his ear, a dial tone replacing the silence quickly enough. He'd just gotten a call from his contact, the tone indicating to him that the man had been ferreted out.

He smiled, rising. He could smell the American's hand in this.

The lights were out in the offices, most of his men asleep on the reception area's floors. He thought of Yun. His brother would have liked this place: the pace, the excitement—the freedom. But he'd never experience it now.

Looking at the phone once more, he hung it up. The American was here to answer his dreams, presenting him with a trap similar to the one Li had presented the American at the Temple of Ten Thousand Buddhas. Hong Kong was a city of glass and mirrors. Fitting. His and the American's reflections were jumbling, looking back at each other through the same eyes.

It had taken the American to make Li Soo appreciate the beauty and simplicity of truth. And he appreciated it now.

He walked out of the office to find Major Chao sitting awake at a desk, drinking tea and staring soporifically at the pornographic picture clicking past on the gently glowing computer screen before him.

"What was the call?" the man asked.

"Our contact," Li replied. Only the greatest of fools would fall into the American's trap, a fool or maybe a man to whom life meant nothing anymore. "He says we can take the rest of the dissidents all at once tomorrow night.''

''Good,'' Chao said.

''Exceptional,'' the colonel replied. His soul felt lighter already.

CHAPTER SIXTEEN

Wang Wushen tentatively brought the Australian wine to his lips and took a sip. It was dry and in perfect keeping with the theory he'd been developing—that cheap, regional red wines were the best taste for the money anywhere in the world. He thought a lot about money. And wine. And other countries. His right ear was heavily bandaged, its mangled remnants needing to be put back together in some fashion. Soon. His hearing loss could also be permanent. There was no pain, though. He had taken many pain pills.

Pei Chai sat across from him, newly arrived from the mainland. The two of them were scheming in the Australian-pub atmosphere of the Stoned Crow, one of two Aussie restaurants in Hong Kong. It was smoky and loud, dart boards and modern music keeping everything in motion. Mr. Wang didn't imagine the outback was like this.

"What does one eat in an establishment of this type?" Pei asked, frowning at the menu.

"You have no sense of adventure, Chai," Wang said as he loaded his cigarette holder and bent over the menu open on the table. "I've been told to avoid the meat pies here. What are you in the mood for?"

"What's a vegemite?" the man asked.

"Some sort of grub, I think," Wang said. "Decadence, I believe, begins with steak."

"Why the obsession with foreign restaurants?" Pei asked, closing the menu and sitting back to pick up his own wine. "I don't understand."

"We're about to become men of the world," Wang explained. "We will visit and live in many places. I'm getting a head start on the ones I want to go to. Imagine spending an amount of time in a country whose food you find inedible."

Pei looked around and leaned up close, a small bead of sweat working its way down his temple. "Is this really going to work?" he whispered.

"My dear Mr. Pei, at 7:00 a.m. tomorrow morning, the Bank of China will have possession of everything of value left in the territories. The moment the paperwork goes through the computers, I, acting as chief account executive and investment coordinator under *your* authority, will transfer two billion American dollars' worth of liquidity into two numbered bank accounts in Geneva. By tomorrow afternoon you and I will be billionaires. By tomorrow night we'll be flying to the South of France—which I hear is very nice this time of year—under forged Japanese passports. We'll live there comfortably for several months, mulling over the possibilities. This will, of course, leave Colonel Li here as the only ranking official involved in this operation left to take the blame for it."

"What about Dr. Werner?"

"Werner's a wanted fugitive already... a killer and sexual deviant. Need I say more? All he can do is run."

Pei raised his glass of wine. "There were times I doubted you, Wushen. Times when this goal seemed very far away. To you."

The men clinked glasses. It was definitely a steak night. "I told you we could make this happen," Wang said, taking a long drink. He felt good. Wonderful.

Pei nodded, smiling. "All the way from assistant under secretary of banking and finance to billionaire in one leap."

They drank again, and the waitress, a big Aussie girl named Domino, arrived to take the steak and wine orders. They settled back to finish their drinks, Wang at ease, confident as he languidly sucked on his cigarette.

"The beauty of your plan," Pei said, "is that it leaves us no loose ends."

"When you run away and change your name," Wang said, "there are no ends, only beginnings. I don't care what happens here once we're gone. Speaking of that, the American told Li this morning that his brother was dead."

Pei came out of his chair. "What?"

Wang smiled, motioning him down. "Sit, please. I don't think he believed the man. We're supposed to produce another videotape, though, to prove he's alive." He raised his eyebrows. "Another loose end not to worry about."

"This one I do worry about," Pei said, sitting again, slumping. "I was ordered to shut down his operation and send him home. What if he causes us trouble before we're able to get away?"

"No problem. Just don't tell him. I negotiated with Chao and made a deal to kill Li either on my command or when he deems necessary. He is sticking close by the colonel's side from now on, ready to execute him if necessary."

Pei looked puzzled. "You negotiated with him? What did he want?"

"One thousand Hong Kong dollars," Wang said, his eyes mischievous. "And to keep the rest of Li's gear."

"I have to ask you this. Did he want payment in advance?"

Wang shook his head. "No. After."

Both men broke out laughing. They laughed all the way through dinner. The total bill was five hundred Hong Kong dollars with a large tip to Domino.

BOLAN LOOKED through the ruby haze of the infrared binoculars at the two-story villa several hundred feet below. Not one but two Rolls-Royces sat in the driveway, a man putting tarps over them. People were running around outside, making preparations for the coming storm, several children among them. "No," he said into his helmet mike as he lowered the binoculars. "That's not it, either. What have we got?"

Crosswaithe, jammed into the small space between Bolan and the Chinese pilot, crossed out a house on the penlit area map he held, then pushed it at the Executioner's face, the penlight attached by a clip. "We've been through the most densely settled regions, but there's still a few places down on the cape. It'll be rough seas down there, though."

Bolan looked at the map, a photo recon picture that showed the peninsula and its roads and houses. His eyes were struck by a large house right on the waterfront. "Look at this one," he said into the mike, which was necessary to be heard over the rotors.

"Is that a perimeter wall?" the inspector asked, pointing to a circle around the house.

"A big one," Bolan said. "And look how the house sits right in the center like a bull's-eye. They've got this huge lawn, but look, it's bare, not a shrub, not a rosebush. Why put the walls so far from the house if you don't intend to put in a garden?"

"Why, indeed?" Crosswaithe agreed, taking the map and holding it before the pilot while pointing to the house they wanted to reconnoiter.

The pilot, named Sing, gave them the thumbs-up and banked slightly, sweeping south.

"Hey, Charlie!" Mao's voice said, breaking into their frequency. She sat behind a partition in the passenger compartment of the chopper. It had been decided that she would conduct the squad contact in Chinese so that everyone would understand exactly what was being said.

"Yeah."

"I've got the ground party on Shek O Road. The damn peninsula's only six miles long. They don't want to be seen driving up and down the roads, you know?"

"Tell them to head south," the Executioner said, taking the map from the pilot and studying it. He rolled with the feeling. It was time. "They are to proceed to within a mile of the residence that is noted in section G-9 on their maps and await my further orders."

"Yes, sir."

He gave the map back to Sing and turned to Crosswaithe, who was sitting atop an open packing crate that extended back into the passenger compartment. A metallic tubular object was nestled squarely in the packing materials.

"What's in the box, Ian?"

"Some sort of hand-held missile launcher that we confiscated a number of years ago," the man replied. "I found it in the armory."

Bolan checked inside the box. "It's an old Stinger. Surface to air. Haven't seen one of these in a while. If we tried to shoot that from in here, it'd vaporize us with the backflash." The Executioner smiled. "Uncrate it anyway."

"Sir," the pilot said, his voice excited over the headphones, "the house you wanted is just ahead."

"Try and stay in the clouds as much as you can," Bolan ordered, picking up the binoculars and keying the infrared. Below, the waves slammed hard against rocky shores, the water level rising already, flooding much of this section of Shek O. It was going to be tough to get the cars in there.

And then they reached the compound, blowing in with the swirling clouds, hoping no one would hear the noise of the rotors. It lay below him, coming in and out of view through the clouds.

"This is it," Bolan said almost immediately.

"Black Mercedes?" Crosswaithe asked.

"Four or five of them," he answered, feeling the adrenaline rush pumping him up. "The walls are high and stone, and it looks like the corners have guard towers of some kind set into the walls. I'd say most of the interior compound yard is mined. Let's stick to the road that leads up to the house. There's sophisticated communications equipment on top of the place."

They slid past, droning out to sea. "Bring it around again," Bolan said, and the pilot banked immediately. The Executioner focused on the heavy-looking iron gate. So much for taking the road in.

"We're not going to get through that gate," he said. "We'll have to take a wall out."

"A wall?" Crosswaithe queried.

"Charlie," Mao cut in, "they're in position."

"Okay," Bolan said, swinging the binoculars back north, picking up his three vehicles on the ground parked by the island side of Shek O. The other side was under water.

"Ask them if they see the telephone poles just east of them."

"I'll see." She blipped out of the conversation.

"You say we're going to take out a wall?" Crosswaithe said, looking at the missile he was sitting upon.

"You made an inspirational choice of weapons," Bolan told him.

Mao cut in again. "They see the poles," she said.

"Tell them to get the best climber to shinny up the closest pole and cut the phone line going into that house, okay? When they've done that, meet us northeast of the property on that clearing marked Country Park on their maps."

"Got it."

"What's the point of taking out the island's phone lines when they've got all the communications gear on top of the place?" the Inspector asked.

"*We're* going to take those out," Bolan said, leaning over in the cockpit darkness to tap the pilot on the shoulder, then pointing through his open doorway at the clearing below.

The man nodded and pulled away from the house but not dropping out of the clouds until the last minute. He set them down gently a mile from the northeast corner of the enemy compound with no indication from the house that they had been seen.

Bolan climbed out of the chopper, pulling off his helmet and sticking it under his arm. He stepped into ankle-deep mud, the rain falling heavily as the three cars pulled up without their headlights.

His squad jumped out of the vehicles, two Toyotas and a beat-up Honda, and moved to surround him in the pouring rain. He could hear the inspector cursing back at the chopper as the man tried to assemble the Stinger.

"They have the mother of all gates guarding their main entry," he said, Mao translating for the non-English-speakers. "I think we'll have better luck taking out a wall."

"How do we take out a wall, Charlie?" Mao asked.

Bolan turned and pointed toward the chopper and the inspector, working in its open bay. "With the help of the General Dynamics XFIM-92A Stinger, a shoulder-fired surface-to-air missile."

They all just stared at him.

"So, you have a better idea?" he asked.

"What do you want us to do?" Shing asked.

"Just follow us in," Bolan replied, already turning to walk back to the chopper. "But watch the yard. It may be mined. Stick close to the walls and work your way around to the front drive. If you see them on the grounds, assume there are no mines. Remember your training."

Mao and Shing joined him as he reached the chopper to watch the inspector. "I'll need you two with the squad," he told them. "We're going to try to knock out the communications gear on the roof."

"You got specific orders?" Shing asked.

"Yeah," Bolan said. "Take the house. Kill everyone who tries to kill you."

Mao dropped the clip from the butt of her .45 to check the load as Shing pumped a live round into the chamber of his Remington.

"Give them hell, Charlie," she said, turning immediately in the downpour and walking back to the cars. "I'm going to have to sit on somebody's lap! Why didn't we bring another car?"

"Our other car blew up!" Shing called back to her. "And my cousin's gonna kill me."

Bolan watched Crosswaithe as he fit the control board onto the launcher. The Stinger looked like a five-foot-long bazooka with a video camera stuck on the front, but the smooth-case fragmentation warhead it carried punched harder than any bazooka he'd ever seen. "We have to go," he said.

Crosswaithe hit the juice key, and the whole control panel lit up bleeping reds and greens, Christmas in May. He reached back into the crate, removing one of the ten-inch warheads residing there. "You ever fired one of these?" he asked.

"Do you really want the answer to that?"

"No, I don't suppose I do." He slid a warhead into the tube to lock into place snugly against its rear electrical connection.

"Stay back with the missile," Bolan said, twirling his hand in the door space, the pilot starting up the rotors. "When we set it down, be ready to jump out with the SAM!"

Crosswaithe gave the thumbs-up, scooting back in the bay of the old Huey Cobra as Bolan put on his helmet and climbed back in the copilot's seat, pointing up. The bird rose immediately, hovering.

The Executioner cued his microphone onto Sing's frequency. "How low can you fly this thing?" he asked.

"To be safe...ten feet above the surface, either treetops or ground."

"What about not being safe?"

"Five feet. That what you want?"

"Yeah. Make your way through the trees and try to not lose the cars. I'll tell you when to stop."

The helicopter angled off immediately, hugging rocky, volcanic ground dotted with occasional stands of bamboo trees. The slow speed kept the bird unsteady as it drifted in the harsh winds, just above the ground. Bolan concentrated on the Stinger. It had been some time since he'd last fired one, but some things you never forgot.

"Get ready," he told the pilot, who was doing an amazing job of keeping them on course as they slowly buffeted above dark, rolling earth toward their destination. They were two hundred feet from the wall and closing. It filled Bolan's vision. "Ready..."

At one hundred feet from the twenty-foot-high wall, Bolan said, "Now. Take it down."

They bumped ground a second later, he and Crosswaithe both out of the chopper, Bolan carrying the penlight as the cars skidded on the mud behind them. The inspector cradled the Stinger, a satchel at his feet bulging with four other rockets, their entire arsenal.

The Executioner moved to him, turning the penlight to the control panel as he heard voices on the wall. There had to be a hundred separate controls. He scanned them quickly, then activated the arming and sighting mechanisms.

"I think we need to hurry, old chap," Crosswaithe said casually as a shot cracked from the wall, thudding in the ground a yard from the Executioner. He pulled away from the chopper to more shots, metal ricochets. They were zeroing in on the Huey.

"There," he said, hoisting the thirty-pound launcher onto his shoulder and looking through the viewfinder on the sighting mechanism. The message ARMED was flashing in the viewfinder, but that was it. It had no infrared. He was aiming at blackness.

"Get back, Ian," he ordered.

They were yelling on the wall now, then the area lit with spotlights everywhere. Perfect. He could see the wall and raised the sighting into alignment. There were more shots, and Crosswaithe grunted in pain.

"The bastards shot my little finger off," he growled, grabbing a handkerchief from his pocket and wrapping it around his left hand.

Bolan took a breath and squeezed the trigger. The warhead whooshed from the tube at supersonic speed, the Cape lighting to daylight less than a second later as a bottom section of the wall went up in a fiery flower of bright white, its glowing tentacles reaching all the way back to their position.

The smoke cleared quickly in the high wind.

"It's still standing," Crosswaithe told him.

"Reload," Bolan said. "Quickly." The wall was indeed still standing, a large gouge scarring its front.

He heard the rocket snap into the tube, then felt Crosswaithe tapping him on the side of the helmet. He aimed and fired again, quickly, hitting close to the same section to similar results.

The wall remained standing, just a tiny section ten feet off the ground punched through to the other side.

"Reload," Bolan said, a burst of gunfire pinging loudly off the chopper, the pilot moaning.

"I'm hit."

"Hang on," the Executioner told him as the warhead snapped into the tube. He turned to a helmetless Crosswaithe. "Your man's been hit."

They both charged back to the helicopter, Bolan, still hefting the Stinger, leaning in the door with the penlight. "Sing, are you conscious?" he asked, looking at a growing pool of red that was soaking the right side of the man's uniform.

"Yes."

"Alert?"

"So far."

"Can you fly?"

"Affirmative."

"Take us up to twenty feet and run that wall!" Bolan yelled.

Sing worked the throttle, the aircraft rising.

The Executioner, still out of the bird, wrapped his legs and free arm around the skid support and held on tight as he leaned away from the bird, sighting the wall through the Stinger, the cars roaring to life behind them.

Sing opened them up full, leaning sideways as bullets sprayed the windows, shattering them. And they were fifty feet from the compound.

Bolan fired, the round aimed below the damage he'd just done. Gratification was instantaneous, as the back blast stopped them in midair before losing its force, the aircraft fighting back its control as it reached the wall. A ten-foot section had totally collapsed.

They rose quickly, Bolan's foot touching the top of the wall as they just cleared it, the gunfire right on them. "The roof!" he yelled into the teeth of the storm and its manmade thunder.

Sing angled up, but something was wrong. Gray smoke was leaking from the side of the helicopter, gray and turning darker, the rotors coughing, sputtering above him.

The two-story house was tiered like a wedding cake. They had just topped the second roof when the engine shut down, the bird dropping like a stone. Bolan pushed himself from the skid, jumping away from the chopper as it fell atop the communications equipment and died with a primal scream of metal on metal, the rotors snapping on contact with the building, slicing the air. The Executioner dived out of the way of a ten-foot section that would have cut him in two.

And then the fire started.

Bolan ran to the bird, helmet and launcher gone, even as his people charged over the debris of the wall a hundred feet distant, a firefight already in progress. Crosswaithe came rolling out of the bay and staggered, a hand to his head.

The fire was small, some fuel that had pooled beside an electrical terminal in the microwave gear, but it had potential. He checked Sing. The man was dead, hanging out of the chopper, only his seat belt holding him in.

"Come on, Ian," Bolan said, taking the dazed man by the arm as the body of the chopper caught fire all at once with a polite *whump*. "We've got to get out of here before that whole thing blows!"

"I say," Crosswaithe said, turning to watch the fire.

"Come on!" Bolan urged, grabbing the man and running, dragging him. They reached the end of the roof, and he shoved Crosswaithe over the edge. He jumped right behind him as the chopper exploded, loud this time, all orange and yellow, the fireball hanging in midair above Bolan as he hit the first floor and rolled onto his back on the flat roof.

He heard gunfire below, bullets from inside the house tearing straight up beside him, streamers of light pulsing through the holes. "Roll to the chimney, Ian!" he yelled as the roof blasted out beside him.

The chimney sat in the center of the roof but was undoubtedly set into a wall. The bullets chased him as he rolled, the Executioner jumping up as soon as he bumped the chimney and pulling both guns from his harness. He fired them immediately, stiff armed, emptying the clips right through the roof into the room below.

There was no return fire.

He ran to the northeast edge of the roof, dropping the clips as he ran. Red ties held wall positions a hundred feet away as Mao led the dissidents through the ruins, firing up at them.

An explosion went up in the yard—a mine had been tripped, driving the dissidents tighter against the wall and its rubble, halting their advance. Gunfire blazed from the house.

"You okay, Ian?" he said, shoving a clip into the Beretta, then holstering it.

"I lost my bloody finger," he said, moving up beside Bolan, gun drawn. "Of course I'm not all right. Is Sing dead?"

"Yeah."

"A good man."

"Stay here," Bolan said, then turned, charging back toward the second story at full speed, using an air-conditioning unit as a jumping point to throw himself at the second-story roof. He caught the ledge with his fingertips, digging in, hoisting himself up.

The last he'd seen of the launcher was when he'd thrown himself from the chopper before the crash. The roof was in flames. He searched for the Stinger amid the burning wreckage. The roof had collapsed beneath the weight of the chopper and the force of the explosion. Only half of it remained intact, and that was on fire.

He found the Stinger beneath a section of sheet-metal hull so hot he had to wrap his hands in his jacket to move it aside. It seemed to be all right.

He ran back, dodging fires, as another mine went up, people screaming. The red ties were silent as they chose their targets from above.

He jumped to the lower level and rejoined Crosswaithe. "You're what they call the number-three man, buddy. Load me."

Crosswaithe took a missile out of the satchel, sliding it home to lock in place. It took Bolan exactly one second to aim. There was a cluster of red ties bunched up in a guard shack at the top of the wall, having the time of their lives as they shot down at his people. He zeroed in on them and clicked the trigger, the missile whooshing from the tube.

The top of the wall disappeared in a magnificent flash, the squad members covering their heads as stone debris rained upon them. Then they jumped up and poured through the rift, running along the wall.

"It's too bright," Crosswaithe said, and both he and Bolan immediately shot at any hard light that faced them. Within a minute the light was cut by half, much of the wall itself shrouded by darkness.

"Let's get below," the Executioner said, reloading even as he lowered himself to the roof and peered over its edge. Intense but minimal light slanted into the darkness, barely illuminating the outside.

He stood. "They must have tiny windows. It's a decent enough defensive measure but has real drawbacks. Come on."

The men quietly lowered themselves from the roof and dropped to the ground. At the sound of gunfire Bolan looked up to see a gun barrel sticking through a rectangular window cutout the size of a postcard. They were set at various heights along the length of the wall.

The Executioner pulled the .44, primed it, stuck it into the cutout right next to the other gun and pulled the trigger. A body thudded on the other side. "Quickly," he said, turning and running the other way as guns angled down, firing where they'd been standing.

They charged around the side of the house away from the action, making the complete turn, stopping at the corner where the front door was and peering around. A dozen red ties, held in reserve, guarded the door.

"Sticky," Crosswaithe said.

"How about you reach into the satchel and lob that rocket the way you did the grenade the other night?"

"You that good?" the man asked.

"Only if I don't think about it," Bolan replied. The squad had fought its way to near the front gates, the reserves bringing their weapons to bear. "So let's get it over with."

The men's eyes met, Bolan nodding. Crosswaithe stepped around the corner and tossed the missile, diving back in as it made a wide, slow arc. The Executioner didn't breathe as he tracked it with the .44 to the peak of its ascent, then led it gently, waiting for it to come to him, squeezing . . . now!

It was impossible to tell where the gunshot left off and the explosion began. They were simultaneous events, the blast blowing the Executioner ten feet from where he'd fired, an arm raised before his eyes to save his sight. Disoriented, he struggled to rise on his elbows and look. The reserves were gone. That part of the house had disappeared, a smoking, charred ruin as Mao led her people on a charge at the now-unprotected entry to the house.

Crosswaithe was tugging on him, pulling him to his feet. "Good show!"

Bolan shook his head, clearing some of the cobwebs. "Let's get inside," he said, moving in that direction, the .44 still clutched tightly in his hand.

The squad had momentum right now, and Bolan's hope was that they'd be able to sweep through the building in the confusion of fires and explosions and roll over the red ties. If that didn't happen, the odds got longer. Untrained civilians could be no match for battle-hardened killers.

He reached the charred remnants of the front doorway, heavy rain sizzling the still-burning boards that poked their way out of the huge hole.

An intense firefight rocked the house, and the Executioner picked his way through rubble and the bodies of friend and foe to reach the living room, where all the action was centered.

The area was wide open, including living and dining rooms. A lone set of stairs ran to the second story, smoke oozing down from there to fog the living areas. Heavy firing was coming from the kitchen with less-intense pockets of resistance bunched behind overturned furniture in the living room. Bodies lay everywhere in the drifting smoke.

"Make your way into the living room," Bolan told the inspector. "Organize what's left of the squad to attack that nest of them behind the furniture in the far corner. That spot commands a view of the whole room. Take it, and we can catch most of the rest of them in a cross fire and finish it in here. I'll draw their fire."

"Naturally." Crosswaithe tossed aside his empty .38 and pried an AK-74 from the dead fingers of a red tie.

Bolan dived, rolling into the room, making a target of himself as he tried to make the overturned dining table Mao used as cover.

Death hissed past his ears and ate the furniture around him as he slithered through a maze of chairs and end tables, piled there by the red ties. It had been their first battle line, the squad's onslaught having forced them to secondary positions.

So far, he hadn't seen Colonel Li. He'd been hoping to end it here, but the absence of the colonel meant troops were still in the city.

He heard Crosswaithe yell "Come on, chaps!" just as he jumped up to try to run the five feet of open space separating his present position and the over-turned dining table. He had the barest edge in reaction time, hearing the report of automatic fire just as he dived behind the table, bullets thudding all around, tearing up the walls and splintering the walnut appointments.

"Hello, Charlie," Mao said as he pulled in near her. She was sitting, cradling the dead body of one of the middle-aged squad members, a slight, gray-haired woman.

"You know her?" the big man asked as the battle for the living room intensified around them with Crosswaithe's charge. It would either work or not.

"She taught French," Mao replied, "and ate dinner many times at our home. My father called her Silk Voice because she had a wonderful, throaty speech."

"Are you all right?" he asked as a cheer went up from the squad. The inspector had overwhelmed the nest and set up the cross fire.

"I don't want . . . this anymore," she said, looking up at him with deep, sad eyes. "I've seen too much. I'm tired."

"Yeah, me too," Bolan said, staring hard at her. "So what? Get your ass in gear or everybody in this house is going to end up dead."

"Sometimes you're not a very nice man."

"I know," he replied. "This tabletop is slate."

"Yeah," she said. "Heavy."

He stood, taking it by the legs and standing it with him on its short side. Mao stood also. "I think it would look better in the kitchen. What do you think?"

"Only one way to find out," she said, and squeezed his arm hard, nodding.

They both hoisted the table and charged the kitchen entry, its slate shielding them as five automatics opened up, ricochets loud amid the noise of battle.

They slammed hard into two men, then turned back to the room, blasting with their side arms. Bolan took out three with chest shots, then turned and finished off Mao's second as she swiveled back to one of the men they'd hit with the table, blowing him away at point-blank range.

It was over in ten seconds.

The battle still raged in the living room, so the two of them hurried back out, Bolan wanting to wrap it up before sustaining more casualties.

An unbelievable scene greeted them in the living room. His squad was engaged in hand-to-hand fighting with several men who'd come from upstairs. They were growling monsters, tossing people aside like rag dolls, bullet holes pocking their bodies.

"It's like those guys at the Bottoms Up," he said. "They're hopped up, out of their minds."

"Head shots," Mao said, ripping another clip out of her fanny pack and slamming it home.

"Right."

They charged the action, four of the drugged red ties rampaging through the living room, dragging squad members with them, their drool tinged with blood.

Bolan charged at full speed, jumping on the closest man's back and immediately sticking the .44 into the base of the cranium at the spinal cord and pulling the trigger.

The man fell like a tree, all motor functions gone, Bolan jumping off. "Their heads!" he yelled to the squad members. "Take them out with heat shots!"

There was more firing, and suddenly the living room was deathly quiet. All of them looked at the surrounding carnage, their faces set hard in the warrior mode. They'd proved themselves.

The silence lasted for several seconds, only to be shattered by a roar. A red tie was charging down the stairs.

"Aim at the head!" Bolan yelled, every weapon in the place firing at once and at the same target. The man's head disintegrated in bloody froth as the still-flailing body stumbled to fall down the stairs.

Several more seconds of silence were followed by another red tie on the stairs, this one running the steps, howling. They cut him down four steps into the living room, the body jerking wildly on the ground, flopping like a fish. They ignored it, watching the stairs.

No one else came, and the seconds dragged by.

"Cover me!" Mao said, running to the stairs.

"No!" Bolan shouted to no avail. She disappeared into the billowy smoke at the top.

The .44 at the ready, Bolan moved to the stairs, all quiet except for the whimpering of the wounded and dying. He started up the stairs.

"No...don't," Mao warned quietly, moving into view again. Her eyes were fearful. "You're going to have to stay back."

Another form slid up beside her, jamming the barrel of a .45 into her neck.

A non-Chinese man stood looking down at them, his arm tightly wound around Mao's waist, pulling her to him as he started her down the stairs. "You will stand aside now," he said in a European accent. "I'm going to be leaving. Thank you."

"Let her go," Bolan said. "I really don't think you want to die, and that's exactly what's going to happen if you don't give up right now. Angela's expendable, and you're history."

The man smiled widely. "I don't think so."

"Why?"

"I've seven excellent reasons," the man said, taking another step, a cluster of petrified women and children folding around him as he slowly walked the stairs.

He had the hostages.

CHAPTER SEVENTEEN

Everything stopped.

As if the whole house were suddenly frozen solid, the combatants stood transfixed, staring in horror as a madman slowly walked a group of women and little children down a staircase slippery with blood and brain matter.

The Executioner felt his stomach knot. "Nobody move," he said softly. "Let him pass."

"Listen to the man," the European said, smiling, pulling Mao closer to him as he used his free hand to wave his gun over the children's heads. Hers was stuck in the waistband of his tight black pants. "My odds are extremely bad here. It won't matter to me if I have to eliminate several of the little ones, eh?"

He jerked Mao tight against him again, leaning down to kiss her on the neck, the woman jumping in revulsion.

Bolan felt Shing move next to him.

"Don't," he whispered, raising an arm to stop the man. "This isn't the time."

The strange entourage reached ground level, the hostages staring in shock at the carnage all around them, at the red tie who still flopped like a grounded fish on the landing.

"I'm going to go out the front door," the European said, "and climb into one of those cars with my friends here. Then we are going to leave, all of us together. Stand clear."

The remnants of the squad backed slowly way, opening a large space for the man to walk through. The children were chained together, the final few links wrapped around the man's arm. They were bunched tightly around him, all of them on the edge of hysteria.

The small crowd inched toward the door, the European looking all around, making sure nothing was happening. His eyes fell on to Bolan.

"Mr. Belasko," he said. "We meet at last. My name is Oskar Werner. You have been an extremely tough opponent. Perhaps you and I should work together sometime."

"Let the hostages go," Bolan said. "Take me in their place."

"Killers make rotten hostages, Mr. Belasko. Nobody cares, you see? Besides," he said, his eyes dancing to Shing, then looking down at Mao, "I've become quite attached to this young lady."

He kissed her on the neck again, his hand moving to explore her body more intimately.

"No!" Shing yelled, charging the man.

Werner raised his Austrian Glock and fired twice, hitting Shing square in the chest with both shots.

With a strangled cry Shing went down and lay still, his body twisted grotesquely.

"Shing!" Mao screamed as Bolan bent to the man.

"No!" Werner yelled. "Leave him. Everyone back up. Give me room!"

The younger children were crying, the women trying to quiet them as Werner made the bombed-out section of the house, disappearing down the foyer with the hostages.

Bolan ran to Shing, searching for a pulse on the carotid artery.

"Is he alive?" Crosswaithe asked. He was already on a cell phone, calling for medical help.

"Barely," the Executioner said, standing. "His pulse is almost gone. I don't think he'll make it to the hospital."

"I don't care about the weather!" Crosswaithe was saying over the phone. "This is an emergency!"

Bolan stared down at Shing, helpless to do anything but watch him die. One of the squad moved up to Shing and squatted before him, rolling the man onto his back.

"What are you doing?" the Executioner asked.

The aging bald man stared up at him. "Before I joined your army, Charlie," he said, "I was a doctor, a surgeon. I can help."

"Thanks. Use anybody and anything you'll need. There's a sturdy slate-top table in the kitchen if you need it."

The doctor nodded, bending back to his patient. Bolan hurried out the front of the house to join members of his squad. They watched the taillights of a black Mercedes disappear across the yard, the huge gate creaking open to allow passage.

Behind him the second floor and roof of the house were burning out of control. The remnants of the squad wearily trudged outside, toting computers and disks, anything that might contain damaging information.

Crosswaithe joined him in the yard, closing up the phone and putting it on his belt. "We've got medical and PD on the way," he said.

"Can you get us another chopper?" Bolan asked.

The man shook his head. "They're all grounded because of the wind," he replied, then pointed to the exiting vehicle. "Who the hell was that?"

"A dead man," Bolan said. "Let's get after him."

He walked across the yard to the Mercedes parking area, the inspector right with him. At least they'd all drive to hell in style. "Did you see which way he went out of the gate?"

Bolan opened the driver's door of one of the vehicles and climbed inside, Crosswaithe taking the passenger seat.

"It doesn't matter," Bolan replied. "I know where he's going."

"Where?"

"Home to roost on the seventy-fourth floor of the Bank of China."

ANGELA MAO SAT behind the wheel of the Mercedes, slowly taking the Eastern Corridor Highway as the man who called himself Werner sat on the passenger side, two children jammed between them. The other hostages were stuffed into the back seat atop one another.

"Do the speed limit, Angela," he purred, his arm resting on the seat backs so he could twist her hair in his long, delicate fingers. "Your friends can't help you now."

"Let the children go," she said, not for the first time. "You've got me, the other women . . ."

"You have to understand, dear, that I do not share the sentimental attachment that most people have for toddlers. All they are is extremely portable meat to me, meat that no one else will shoot. They are all that got me out of that house alive. So, can we go on to another topic? You're beginning to bore me."

She desperately watched the rearview mirror for any signs of the American, but realized that he wouldn't show himself even if he was near them.

"Where are we going?" she asked.

"Bank of China, where else?" Werner said. "I think this game's gotten too hot. I simply need to cash in my chips and move along. And I cash in my chips at the bank."

"What's going to happen to us?"

The man shrugged, his gun hand resting on his lap. "I don't know. Maybe the others will go back to where they came from. You, I think, will be quite a different story. Mr. Wang will want to keep you for a while before he kills you. He's really quite perverted for a good Party member. If you doubt me, just ask the ladies in the back seat."

Mao didn't need to ask. She'd seen them in the house, bruised and battered, their eyes hollow and lost, the kind of eyes she'd seen in survivors of great catastrophes. She'd already resigned herself to the fact that her life wouldn't end quickly or easily, but without Shing, she didn't want to go on anyway.

When Werner shot him, she'd felt her heart had been cut from her body. All that was left was the horror. No, death held no fear or surprises for Angela Mao. She had only one wish: that before she died, she'd have the chance to avenge Shing's death. Her one hope at attaining that goal lay strapped to her ankle with duct tape—Wang's gun.

She'd taped it there just before the battle, a last-ditch backup in case everything else went sour. She would have killed herself with it had they lost the battle. Now it could be her instrument of vengeance.

If she could just get to it.

And get a clear shot.

"THERE THEY ARE," Crosswaithe said, pointing two lanes over on the Eastern Corridor, "five cars lengths ahead."

"Got them," Bolan said, dropping back, not wanting to stir the pot. As long as Werner had the children, they were at a total impasse. He could do nothing but hope that Mao kept her head and didn't go crazy with thoughts of revenge.

"What now?" Crosswaithe asked.

"Wait it out," Bolan replied as the new day came up cold and windy all around them, the morning rush hour poised to begin. "Angela's good. She'll handle herself."

"Do you really believe that?" the inspector asked.

"I'm trying hard. Did we get a count on casualties?"

"Besides us, five of your squad were standing on their feet at the end of it," he replied sadly. "Damn, all this could have been avoided if the politicians hadn't gotten involved."

"You got enough information now to put a stop to it?"

"I hope so. With what we pulled out of the house before it burned, plus the report I'm going to write, we can probably shake the entire British government to its roots if we want to."

"I don't care about that," Bolan said. "All I want is for this to end and for one very brave woman to live to have her own children."

"They're exiting," Crosswaithe said. "Now we'll see."

MAO TOOK THE EXIT onto Gloucester Road, focusing her mind on her options, ignoring Werner as he slid closer, leaning over the seat to nibble on her ear.

"Maybe I won't give you to Wang," he whispered. He roughly turned her face to him. "What would you think about that?"

"You'd have to kill me first," she said through clenched teeth.

Werner laughed, his wire-rimmed glasses making his eyes look too large. He was like a big-eyed bug, alien and without feeling of any kind. "Done that before. Women are a lot more fun when they're alive. But I'll be perfectly frank with you. As tasty as you are, you're no match for the money and the new passport Wang is holding for me. No, you'll be his, and I'll be on a plane out of here. It's a bit cold in Buenos Aires this time of year, but Argentina is kind to people like me. I'll be a *porteno,* flirting in the open air cafés, long after you're dead and stinking."

"No, you won't," she said, making the turn from the early rush of Gloucester onto the relative quiet of Garden Road. "You've already doomed yourself by the choices you've made."

"Do tell?" he replied as she pulled up to the concourse of the Bank of China and cut the engine.

She turned and smiled at him. "You've made two bad mistakes. You've trusted Wang Wushen with your money, which makes you a fool, and you left Charlie alive, which makes you a dead fool. You'll never leave Hong Kong alive, crazy man. Argentina will have to survive without you."

He didn't smile this time, his face turning dark and ugly. He reached out and slapped her, snapping her head to the side, which made her laugh.

"Big man," she taunted, pushing it now, hoping to make him angrier than she was. "I'm glad you're giving me to Wang. That means I'll get to be there when you ask him for your money."

"Get out of the car!" he growled, his teeth bared like fangs.

"Idiot." She opened the car door and climbed out.

Keeping her head still, she let her eyes sweep the streets around her. She saw it, parked a block away, another black Mercedes. Charlie hadn't let her down.

It would have to happen quickly. She didn't want to be swallowed up by the bank building. Once she entered those doors, all was lost. It would have to happen on the stone pedestrian mall. She steeled herself. If the opportunity didn't present itself, she'd have to push it. There was no longer anger or fear in her. She'd do what had to be done to save the hostages and could mourn Shing later.

Werner climbed out the passenger side, not bothering to conceal the gun he carried. He was antsy now, in a hurry. He pulled the women and children out of the back seat by their chains, hurrying them onto the mall, walking quickly.

Now was the time, before he wrapped the chains around his arm again. He had one boy of about ten by the scruff of the neck, dragging him.

Abruptly Mao stopped walking, putting her arms out to stop the others . . . just for a second, just long enough to separate them physically from Werner.

The man reacted instantly, swinging around with the Glock. Mao let herself fall backward even as she heard the screech of tires in the distance.

A dozen steps separated them. Werner only controlled the boy now as his Glock tracked her to the pavement, his finger tightening on the trigger as he pulled the boy to him.

She reached to her leg, pointing it toward the man's barely exposed thigh and grabbing, going for the trigger right through her clothes.

BOLAN HAD BEEN watching intently from a block away, trying to put himself in Mao's brain, to think her thoughts. The moment she put her arms up to stop the progress of the hostages, he hit the gas, knowing she was making her move.

Two seconds later she was on the ground, a flash erupting from her blue-jeaned leg, the man crumpling back, blood squirting from his right thigh.

Pedal to the floor, Bolan hit the stone curb, bouncing over it as a wounded Werner aimed his weapon at Mao. Then he heard the car and whirled just as Bolan slid the Mercedes between Werner and the hostages and slammed on the brakes.

The man fired once, wild, then retreated toward the building, his free arm wrapped around the boy's neck, dragging him.

Bolan was out of the car, the man thirty feet distant now, closing on the building. Blood drenched the concourse, running in rivulets toward the street. Mao had to have hit something major.

Just as Werner reached the building, dragging his leg and the hostage with him, the boy grabbed his arm and bit into it hard. Werner screeched like an animal as the boy jerked away from him and ran.

Knowing futility when he saw it, Werner turned and hobbled through the bank's door.

Bolan rushed around the car to Mao. She lay on the ground, holding her leg. The flash from the gun had burned through her jeans, and her leg was charred and blistering, bleeding slightly. "Are you all—?"

"Shing," she said, grimacing in pain. "Is he...?"

"I don't know," the Executioner answered honestly. "He was alive the last time I saw him. How about you?"

"Never mind about me." She struggled to sit up with Crosswaithe's help, the man using his free hand to call the hospital on his cell phone. "Get that son of a bitch before he gets away!"

Bolan nodded and headed toward the door, Crosswaithe right with him.

The terrified boy who'd bitten Werner ran to the Executioner and threw his arms around his waist, unwilling to release his salvation.

It was at that moment a dozen security guards, guns drawn and pointed, charged through the bank's doors.

OSKAR WERNER LEANED against the elevator wall and tried to keep from crying with the pain as he removed his belt and cinched it around his right thigh to act as a tourniquet. The Chinese woman had to have hit an artery. He'd lost a lot of blood and knew it. His dreams of a quick and quiet exit were now shattered. He'd have to depend on Wang to protect him.

He was light-headed from the blood loss and briefly wondered if just a small dose from the extra endorphin syringe he carried in his pocket would give him the energy to go on. He couldn't quite think straight and was still making the decision when the elevator deposited him in the middle of the seventy-fourth-floor reception area. Bank officials and secretaries stopped in their tracks to stare at him.

He staggered out of the elevator, leaning against the wall for support as he drew the Glock from his blood-soaked waistband, the .45 he'd taken from the woman falling to the floor, his arm quivering as he held it out before him. "Just stay away from me," he rasped, and stumbled from desk to desk as he tried to reach Wang's secretary.

"Dr. Werner," she said as he fell heavily against the desktop, the right side of his body totally numb. Then she launched into a long speech in Chinese that he didn't understand, but she stood and opened the door to Wang's office for him. If there was ever a sanctuary for him in this world, that was it.

He made it to the doorway, his hands leaving a bloody smear on the frame, then stumbled inside to be greeted by Li and Pei Chai, who sat on the couch watching the closed-circuit television.

He nearly blacked out as he made it to the couch. He was getting very cold, and for the first time it struck him that the woman may have killed him. The realization snapped him out of his stupor.

He was half standing, half lying over the couch back. Pei was standing, a hand to his mouth, while the colonel sat casually, glancing at Werner over his shoulder.

"Wang," he said, his voice weak.

The colonel pointed to the television. On the screen Wang was watching his secretaries passing out reams of paper. The *hong* were in attendance, all anxiously poised with their pens to begin the laborious job of penning their signatures in a hundred places.

"Need help," he mumbled, fighting the cold, fighting to stay awake.

"Indeed," the colonel said, smiling.

"What happened?" Pei asked, leaning down to stare in his face.

"The American and the . . . Chinese bitch."

"Where?"

"Down . . . down . . . stairs."

"Oh, no," Pei groaned, straightening. "What's being done?"

"S-security," Werner said, true fear overtaking him. He reached out, snaking Pei's arm but unable to raise his head enough to stare at the man. "He-help me!"

Pei jerked Werner's hand from his sleeve and looked down at Li. "Do something," he said. "Do you have troops on forty?"

"*You* do something," Li said. "You set all of this up, so it's up to you to step in and take control. Go ahead."

The man was shaking badly. "Please, Colonel," he said. "I implore you."

"Why not just threaten me?" Li asked. "Maybe tell me what terrible thing you'll do to my brother. The only trouble is—" Li stood, nose to nose with Pei "—you'll have to dig up his grave first!"

Without a word Pei turned and strode from the room. Li watched him leave, then moved to stand before Werner, squatting to get into his line of vision. "How are you feeling?" he asked.

"Please," Werner said, his voice so weak it was almost a whisper. "Help me."

"I will be happy to be of assistance," Li said, cocking a large fist. Werner saw it coming. When it hit him on the jaw, he felt no pain, nor did he feel pain when he slid heavily to the floor, knocking over a wooden chair. The world folded in on Oskar Werner until there was nothing but darkness.

LI WAS STARING DOWN at the unconscious man when Wang entered the office from the connecting door to the conference room.

The man hurried over, startled upon seeing the unconscious Werner on his carpet.

"What happened?" Wang asked.

"I am not exactly sure," Li replied, returning to the couch to watch the signing ceremony. "If the doctor is to be believed, he was shot downstairs by either the American or Angela Mao."

"Downstairs?" Wang repeated, bending to the man. "Should we move him or something?"

"Only if you want to get blood on your nice silk suit."

"Good point," Wang said, straightening and looking at Li. "Will security be able to handle them?"

The colonel shrugged. "You tell me."

"Where's Pei?"

"Gone."

He watched Wang looking around the room, as if he could find a place to hide in the office. "Go into the reception area," he said, avoiding eye contact with Li. "Stop them if they come up here."

The colonel laughed. "So I should go die for you now?" he asked. "My inclination is certainly otherwise. In fact, if I didn't think there was something much nastier in store for you, I'd kill you myself."

"Don't be insubordinate," Wang said, reaching for the phone on his desk.

"I'm being honest. Honesty. Now, there's a topic you and I could discuss at length."

"I don't know what you're talking about," Wang said, punching numbers on the phone.

"Chao's not here," the colonel told him. "He's away on some secret mission you sent him on, something I wasn't told about."

"Ah." Wang slammed down the phone, then picked it up again to try another number.

"Looks like they're finishing up in the conference room," Li said, pointing at the television screen. "Do you not need to sign some papers yourself?"

Wang slammed down the phone again. "Security's not answering." He took a long breath, reaching some internal decision. "All right. What do you want? I'm getting set to become a very wealthy man. I can make you rich and still be rich myself. Put a number to it, Colonel. You've got me over a barrel."

"I don't know...what's a brother's life worth...a million pounds sterling, two million?"

"Dammit!" Wang yelled. "Would you make a deal with me?"

"I will make you a bargain," Li said, standing to face him. "You may choose. Either I kill you the way I did your bodyguard in Lhasa, making you look at the heart I've just plucked from your chest as you die, or you walk out of here, potentially dealing with the American."

Wang walked to the door that led to the reception area, the floor devoid of people now. They were alone. He shut the door and walked back across the room, staring once at Li before entering the conference room. "You'll not survive this," he said over his shoulder.

"I do not intend to," the colonel answered, but Wang had already closed the door and didn't hear his response.

Li returned to his seat in front of the television, watching as Wang laughed and joked with the somber *hong* as if nothing had happened, shaking hands and guaranteeing the quick return of their families.

The desk phone rang, and Li got up to answer it. It was one of the red ties calling in, and what he had to say poured some gladness into the colonel's empty heart.

"Would you say that again?" he asked, basking in the crystal-pure light of justice.

"Headquarters is gone, burned to the ground. Everyone in it is dead, all killed in a firefight."

"Thank you," Li said, hanging up.

He moved to look down at an unconscious Werner. The doctor had been at headquarters. What stories he must have to tell. Things were working out nicely. He moved to sit again, watching as Wang worked at signing a stack of papers before him, the man playing his hand all the way out. And somewhere in the building, the American stalked him.

Things were finally getting interesting.

BOLAN ASSUMED the classic shooter's position as the security force surrounded them. But Ian Crosswaithe had other ideas, putting a hand to the Executioner's arm.

"Put the gun down," he whispered. "This is my job. Let me try it."

The inspector strode forward, pulling out his ID and holding it up. "Who speaks English?" he asked loudly.

Several men took a step forward.

"Then listen up and tell your co-workers. My name is Chief Inspector Ian Crosswaithe, and I am in pursuit of a fugitive. Under the authority granted by Her Majesty's government, I am going to enter that building. Anyone who interferes will be subject to arrest and will face charges."

"We were told to stop you," a man said.

"By a wounded fugitive on the run," Crosswaithe replied. "The Hong Kong Police have no quarrel with any of you unless you break the law. Now you will step aside and allow us passage."

Still holding up his shield, he walked right into the midst of the security force, Bolan close behind as the line of defense broke, the men moving aside.

"Wait a minute," Bolan said, and turned back to the hostages as an ambulance appeared to help Mao.

He waved them forward. "Your husbands and fathers are in here," he called, and all of them hurried forward.

"What are you doing?" Crosswaithe asked as all of them moved into the bank.

"Reuniting families," he replied, striding to the elevator and pushing the Up arrow.

A car door opened, and all of them jammed in.

"But you don't know what we're facing up there."

"That's why you're getting off on seventy-three," Bolan said. He pushed the button, and the elevator started up.

The doors slid open to silence, and no one made a sound as Crosswaithe and the hostages moved out of the car.

Bolan held the door, pointing to a nearby desk. "Give me the extension number on that phone."

Crosswaithe walked to the desk. "Seven three six eight," he said, nodding. "Good luck."

"Come up when I call," Bolan told him, moving back into the elevator, the doors closing.

He took the ride to seventy-four with guns drawn and primed, but the doors slid open to the same silence that had greeted them on seventy-three.

A trail of bright red blood splashed the floor and the desk of Wang's secretary. The bank officer's door frame was smeared with it, as well.

Bolan moved quietly to the office door, his hand reaching for the knob, when he heard muffled voices in the adjoining conference room.

Straightening, he hurried over and put his ear to the door, listening as a man within was demanding that Wang produce his son immediately. The discussion sounded interesting, so Bolan walked in.

He looked around the table, knowing who they were without having met them. Wang stood, eyes wide, at the head of the table.

"We're conducting business here," he said.

Bolan ignored him, walking around the table, the .44 held loosely at his side in case Wang had replaced the .22. He stared at Wang. "How's the ear?"

"Gentlemen," Wang said, shakily, "Thank you for meeting with me this morning. Everything seems to be in order. I'll contact you in an hour about our...other business."

"Does 'other business' mean the kidnapped women and kids?" Bolan asked. The men at the table jumped, startled.

"What do you know of this?" one of them asked.

"Plenty. You gentlemen represent the *hong*. Several days ago Mr. Wang kidnapped your wives and children to force you into selling out your investors by turning control over everything financial to him."

"If you know so much," Wang said, "then you know the problems your interference could mean to these gentlemen."

"I have to hand it to you," the Executioner told Wang, "you keep right on hanging in there. But it's already been taken care of. We've rescued the children and burned down your fortress on the cape."

The men were all talking at once, but Wang shouted above them. "Prove it!" he yelled. "If you have saved these people, let me see them. Bring them in!"

"I'll be happy to." Bolan moved to a table containing a phone. He picked it up, punched in the extension number and turned to the *hong*. "You don't have to fear Mr. Wang anymore, gentlemen. His infrastructure is collapsing, and his portfolio has rolled over and died. Bankruptcy of the soul. Foreclosure on the body."

He heard Crosswaithe pick up the phone. "Yeah, Ian? Bring them up now. Their fathers are anxious to see them."

He hung up and shrugged at Wang. "Your stock options have all expired."

"You've really got our families?" one man asked, fear straining his face.

The Executioner nodded just as the elevator doors opened and the children ran out, charging into the conference room. Bolan walked slowly around the room to block the door to Wang's office.

There was half a minute of gleeful reunions, then the *hong* began to notice the condition of their families—the women bruised and battered, the children shell-shocked with fear—and knew immediately whom to blame.

They turned as a unit to face Wang as the man slid along the wall toward the door. "You see?" he said. "They've been returned unharmed."

One of the women spoke up. "That man raped and beat me," she said. "He made me do horrible things."

Wang turned toward the door, Bolan raising the .44, pointing it at the man's chest. "It's not going to be that easy," he whispered.

Londy Than strode up to Wang. "Someone take the children out of the room," he said, never taking his eyes from the man who'd had his wife murdered.

"Gentlemen," Wang pleaded, "we're all business-men here. I'm sure we can reach an accommodation."

"Yes," Than said. "We will accommodate. Take the children out."

"Ian," Bolan said, "go back to seventy-three with the children. I believe this room is outside of your jurisdiction."

"So it is," Crosswaithe replied. At the urging of their mothers, the children followed the inspector out of the room.

The *hong* and two battered wives moved slowly toward Wang, boxing him in.

"My friends," Wang said, "don't be hasty. Let's call off the deal. I'm sure if I talk to my government, they will be happy to—"

The crowd jumped on Wang, who screamed in pain and went down under the relentless attack.

He was picked up and thrown onto a conference table, face already bludgeoned, his clothes ripped to shreds, and they weren't through yet.

Just then the door behind Bolan flew open under a tremendous force, knocking the Executioner against the wall, then to the floor.

He shook his head to clear it, looking up to see a blood-soaked Oskar Werner growling in the doorway, an empty syringe still clutched in his right hand.

Werner jumped into the room, pouncing onto the Executioner as he tried to rise, bloody drool running from his sputtering lips, the man no longer human in any sense as he bent to try to rip Bolan's throat out with his teeth.

The soldier's gun hand was trapped between the two of them. His left hand clutched Werner's throat, holding back human jaws that were mankind's deadliest natural weapon, capable of exerting hundreds of pounds of ripping pressure.

As Wang screamed pitifully from the table, Bolan was locked in the struggle of his life, his arms quivering under the attack of drug-induced, superhuman energy.

Werner's face was an inch from his, bloody breath hot on his cheeks. As his arm gave way, Bolan knew he had only seconds left before his jugular was severed.

Straining on his right wrist, the Executioner tried to tilt the .44 caught between them just enough to catch Werner and not himself. As the man's teeth scored his neck, Bolan fired. He felt the flash burn on his stomach, but the doctor jerked only slightly as the Magnum shell tore into his belly.

But when he jerked, Bolan got the barrel right into his stomach and fired again. Werner rolled off him but sprang immediately to his feet to pounce, his stomach laid wide open, viscera bubbling out.

"You!" screamed a voice from the doorway. Bolan looked behind him from the floor to see Angela Mao, leg bandaged, staring down the barrel of her bloody .45. "You're mine!"

She fired, hitting the man in the neck, not stopping him. He bounded for her as she fired twice more, grabbing her in a bear hug, straining to rip into her throat.

Bolan jumped to his feet as the pair twirled in a *danse macabre* in the middle of the conference room.

Reaching them, he jammed the .44 into the base of Werner's skull and pulled the trigger, taking off the back of the man's head.

Werner released Mao, his body spasming, jerking wildly, what was left of his head lolling back and forth as the woman took a run at him, hitting him with a body block that staggered him toward the windows.

Werner hit the floor-to-ceiling glass hard, going through, plunging from cloud level to sea level without a stop in between.

Mao threw herself into Bolan's arms, crying from relief as the *hong* moved away from the table, revealing the battered body of Wang Wushen.

They all filed out of the room, Bolan closing the door.

They climbed into the elevator together, all of them knowing without saying that the incident would never be mentioned again. Order had been restored. That was enough.

Except for the nightmares all of them would have to live with for the rest of their lives.

They climbed off the elevator at seventy-three, and parents moved to their children, taking them gently in their arms to begin the long process of healing. What Wang had done so callously, so casually, would take many years to undo.

And the Executioner hoped that it wouldn't have to be done under Communist Chinese rule.

Crosswaithe was on the phone, talking animatedly, putting up a hand to hold them off while he spoke.

"What now?" Mao asked.

"We finish it," Bolan replied. "This won't be over until every red tie is dead."

"We lost most of the squad," she argued.

"Yeah," Bolan said, "we did. But it doesn't change what's happened. Blood in, blood out. It must be finished or it'll never go away."

"I understand."

Crosswaithe hung up the phone. "I just got off with the hospital. Thanks to expert help on the scene, Shing's going to be all right."

Mao fainted dead away.

CHAPTER EIGHTEEN

Bolan, Crosswaithe and Mao walked out of the Bank of China into a blinding rainstorm. The wind was up, too, gusts so strong they had to fight their way through.

The wind was in control, sending trash cans, papers and laundry, capriciously airborne, into the flooding streets and whipping the rain into stinging tentacles that slashed at their faces and hands.

"Does it get worse than this?" the big man asked.

"Worse?" Crosswaithe repeated. "It hasn't even gotten started yet."

"Great."

They made their way to the Mercedes Bolan had commandeered on the cape, climbing in soaking wet and closing the doors to a solid thunk that sealed them in. The Executioner turned on the engine to get the heater going.

"I want to see Shing," Mao said, her arms wrapped tightly around herself as she shivered in the cold.

"We can do that," Bolan replied, "but we can't stay. We need to rest up for tonight."

"Old chap," Crosswaithe said, "you don't really think that this will continue now, do you? What with

Wang dead and their headquarters destroyed, plus all the publicity, I—"

"This won't be over until all of them are dead," Bolan said calmly. "I understand that, and Colonel Li understands it."

"Are you saying that the colonel wants the rest of his troops killed?" Crosswaithe asked. "It makes no sense."

Bolan sat behind the wheel and watched the rain sheet down the windshield. "I understand Li," he said, "and the man understands me. This is a war of attrition, and it won't be over until one side has wiped out the other. Tonight on the government docks, we'll have our chance."

"Tonight?' Mao said. "In this weather?"

"Can't be helped," Bolan told her, then turned to look at Crosswaithe in the back seat. "It's time to use your volunteers. Can you still get them?"

The man nodded stoically. "With the information collected from the cape, I can even get official help. The *hong* kidnappings will sell the prime minister more than the plight of the dissidents. Money is involved, and when money is involved, there is no second place."

"Good," Bolan said. "I want you to clear the docks of workers and bystanders. I'll move my people into defensive positions this afternoon. When the red ties come tonight, you can move in with your men. We'll back you up."

"How many do you think are left?" Crosswaithe asked.

The Executioner shrugged. "Twenty-five...maybe thirty. We've thinned them out pretty well. Is it a go?"

The inspector stuck his hand over the seat. "You can depend on me," he replied as he and Bolan shook hands. "If you can give me a ride to the precinct house on Arsenal Street, I'll start the ball rolling."

"Good," Bolan said, putting the car in gear and pulling away from the stone wall. "Angela, I want you to talk to all of your people. I want you to give them a guarantee from me."

"What guarantee?"

"That this ends tonight. After tonight I'll guarantee them safe haven. No more running. No more hiding."

"How can you make that promise?" she asked.

"My secret," he said, turning north on Queensway toward the police station three blocks away.

"How will your government react to Wang's death and the end of his financial deal with the *hong?*" Crosswaithe asked.

"I'm not going to tell them about that," Bolan answered. "I'm going to let them stew for a while."

He made the turn onto Arsenal Street and pulled up in front of the station.

"Well, here we are," Crosswaithe said, opening his door and stepping into the driving deluge, a bundle of computer disks wrapped in plastic under his arm. He leaned back in. "I'll see you tonight on the docks."

"Right." The inspector shut the door and hurried across the street. The worst was over, and the mop-up was about to begin.

CROSSWAITHE RAN through the rain and into the Arsenal Street station. He was tired, worn-out, but had never felt better in his life. It had taken a crazy American to put him back in touch with himself and make him a good cop again by realizing why he'd become one to begin with. Over the years too much bureaucracy had worn him down. Not anymore. He was a new man, flush with satisfaction of doing the right thing no matter what the consequences.

He moved into the usual confusion of the Wan Chai headquarters, all of the cops turning to stare.

"Look, there's Ian!" one of them called, the others—Britons and Chinese alike—broke into a rousing cheer. His men rushed over to pat him on the back and congratulate him on his exploits.

And in that instant he knew that all of them had felt the weight of politics grinding them into the ground while horror was allowed to exist unchecked. All of them had felt as ineffectual as he, and all had been renewed by his dedication to doing the right thing.

He headed to the receiving desk and looked up at the smiling duty officer. "The chief in?" he asked.

The sergeant nodded, jerking a thumb toward the offices. "We're all behind you, Ian."

Crosswaithe winked at the man and moved down the hall toward the administrative offices, tapping on and then opening the door with the words Superintendent of Police stenciled in gold on the frosted glass.

A small man with half glasses resting on the end of his nose looked over the frames to raise his eyebrows at Crosswaithe. A stack of reports sat before him on his desk. The inspector didn't need to ask what they were.

"Ian," he said, "you've generated more paper-work in the last few days than the Hong Kong Police Force has seen in its entire history."

"Well," Crosswaithe said, dropping the package of floppies onto the desk, "here's some more. And you're going to want to see it before you bust me down to the vice squad."

Thirty minutes later Police Superintendent Elton Ward sat back and took off his glasses, tossing them on the desktop. "Ian, this is dynamite. When this is all over, you should get a major promotion."

"I'll make you a deal. I'll trade you the promotion for one favor."

"A favor? Name it."

"I have strong reason to believe that tonight, on the government docks, the remainder of the red-tie army will be attempting to finish off the dissidents."

"In this weather?"

"This is a fight to the death, sir. What does weather have to do with it?"

"I see. And you want department support in place?"

"Yes, sir. It's time we gave the Chinese the message that it isn't their island...not yet. And as long as it's a free land, we will fight to the death to keep it free. It's what we should have done to begin with."

Ward nodded. "I'm not as courageous as you, but I don't need to be. The evidence you've presented me indicates a clear and present danger to social stability in the territories, an organized assault on the economics of Great Britain itself and a world-sickening advance of hooliganism." The man stood, putting out his hand. Crosswaithe shook it. "No, Ian, it's not your lonely fight anymore. You've got your support."

"Good. Will you do me one more favor?"

"Of course."

He pointed to the disks. "Make several copies of these, hide them in different places and mail one set *directly* to the prime minister."

Ward smiled a fighter's smile. "You want the governor out of the action on this."

"I especially want Governor Purdy out of the action, sir. Much of the evidence I can present may implicate him in the crimes committed by the red ties."

"I'll take your word for that, Ian, and will proceed immediately to implement your wishes." The man put his arm around Crosswaithe's shoulders, drawing him closer and lowering his voice. "Don't worry, old man, I'll put copies in the diplomatic pouch *and* express mail. I'll do it myself. It will be out of here in thirty minutes."

"Thank you, sir."

The man shook it off, returning to sit at his desk. "Guess you've made me reconsider how I do my job, too. We're all just trying to do the right thing. Now go home and get some sleep. You look a wreck. Come back in later and take full authority in putting together your team."

Crosswaithe left the office, feeling the burden lifted from his shoulders as department policy took over.

Ward had done it, officially authorized him to treat the red ties as criminals. All the doors had finally opened.

With the weight of the problem gone, the tiredness and the soreness set in. He was too old for this.

He turned up his collar as he walked out the door and into the storm. It wasn't until he reached the parking lot that he remembered he'd left his car parked at the chopper pad on the harbor. He'd have to get a ride over there.

As he turned back to the building, a gray Rolls-Royce slid up beside him. It had solid rubber tires, steel-reinforced doors and hood and tinted bullet-proof glass on all the windows: the governor's car.

The back window slid down, Governor Purdy's smiling face poking through the space. "What luck," he said. "You're just the man I was looking for."

"Really?" Crosswaithe replied without inflection, the door opening.

"Were you leaving?" the governor asked.

Crosswaithe shrugged. "I was until I remembered my car was at the heliport."

"I'll give you a lift," the man said, sliding over. "Come on, then. The rain is getting in."

Crosswaithe climbed into the car, the back seat roomy and smelling of leather. They drove on immediately in the driving rain. A small bar occupied center floor, and the governor was drinking straight Scotch whisky.

"Like a drink, Inspector?" he asked.

"Sir, it's 9:00 a.m."

"Right," Purdy said. "Too early." He finished his drink and poured another, his hand shaking the whole time. He couldn't look Crosswaithe in the eye. "Guess I'm in sort of a pickle."

"Sir?"

"I've been seeing some horrible stories on the telly and—" he took another drink "—I realize that my, er, connection to this mess will make me look guilty of...you know."

"Complicity, sir?" Crosswaithe asked, waiting for the man to get on with the pitch. First would come gentle prodding, then an escalation to attempted bribery. If Purdy had dug his own grave, he was now in the process of throwing the dirt over himself.

The governor stared at him, a shaking glass held poised before his lips. "Certainly not complicity...no, no. Not at all. I was caught in the middle, Crosswaithe. You can understand that. On one hand was official policy from Downing Street, which was capitulation, and on the other hand was the possibility of getting along with the Chinese, perhaps making democratic changes through the friendship, eh?"

"Do you know that Wang Wushen is dead?" Crosswaithe asked.

"He can't be. I just spoke with him last—"

"Unless he can hold his breath for a really long time, sir, he's dead."

"This just gets worse and worse," the governor said, then set down his drink and turned to Crosswaithe, putting a hand on his arm. "I implore you. Everything is working itself out. Is there really any reason to include me in all this? Complicity, indeed. I didn't know what to do. I made a mistake. Can't we just let it go?"

Step one—the begging—was complete. "Sir," Crosswaithe said, "I must report everything that happened in regards to the red ties. You are a part of what happened. I can't forget that."

"Come on, old man," Purdy urged, tagging him on the shoulder. "How can this matter in the long run?" He leaned conspiratorially close, stage two under way. "You know, I have a lot of pull with the royal family... we go way back on Mum's side. For your part in all this, I'll bet I could swing a knighthood for you. With the knighthood, I'll bet I could acquire the property to go along with the name, and a reasonable government pension every month... say, five thousand pounds?"

"You should know better, Your Lordship, than to add bribery to your list of offenses," Crosswaithe said with satisfaction. "My testimony will be honest and untainted. It is for others to decide your fate, not me. Talk to them. I'm just a cop."

"Blast! I knew you'd say that. You working-class types are all the same."

"Sir?"

Purdy tapped the driver on the shoulder. "Pull over," he said, the Rolls sliding easily onto the curb near Exchange Square on Connaught, two blocks short of the helipad. Damn. Now he was going to get drenched. He should have let the man talk longer.

Purdy threw open his door. "Excuse me," he said, getting out of the limo as a man with a gun slid into his place.

"Hello. My name Chao."

The governor leaned back into the Rolls. "Nothing personal, old man," he said. "I just can't let a stupid policeman drag my family's name through the mud."

He slammed the door.

It was the last sound Crosswaithe would ever hear.

COLONEL LI STOOD in the overflowing lobby of Kai Tak Airport on the Kowloon side of the harbor. The terminal was jammed with frantic, angry passengers, tourists mostly, wanting to get out before the big typhoon hit.

But there was an inevitability at work here that Li found deliciously ironic. They were all trapped in Hong Kong, the whole blasted island chain, everyone having to stay to see out the finish of the human chess game they'd been playing for a week. The planes weren't flying; it was too late, the wind too high.

The gods of his ancestors were laughing right now with the depth of tragicomedy Li was involved with. For the Communists there were no gods and no irony. There was only confusion. And that confusion, he knew, would deliver Pei Chai into his hands if he simply waited long enough.

He wore his side arm, but no one confronted him about it. Not yet, anyway, though he had a feeling that the irony of the moment would dictate its dramatic impact.

What a fool he'd been. He somehow had thought that if he was a good and loyal soldier and a staunch Party member, life would run itself out like a swan floating on a lake. Whether he was fighting the Vietcong encroachment of southern China or protecting the long border with the hated Russians, he always did his job and loved his mother country. And it was all a lie.

He saw his quarry then.

Pei, looking harried, scrambled through the front doors with a small carryon, clutching a passport that was the same size and color as the ones the Japanese tourists carried. Not a retreat, then. An escape. Delicious.

He followed the man to the airline counters, the personnel there pointing up to the departure boards with the canceled notations. The man then moved off, looking, no doubt, for private transport that wasn't afraid to fly in a typhoon.

Staying ten feet behind Pei, Li thought about the charade of his own life. His father had died when he was ten and Yun was still in his mother's womb. He had died like a rabbit, fast and quiet, with a lot of unfinished business left behind. It had fallen to Li to become the man of the house and earn what it would take to support a woman and small baby.

Pei reached the private-transport counters, talking animatedly with people who simply shook their heads at him. He kept jamming his passport, then money, at them, the attendants shrugging at the notion there was enough money in the world to risk death for.

At the last counter Pei began to yell, slamming his hand on the counter and demanding service the way he would do in Party headquarters in Beijing. But this wasn't Beijing. It was a free country whose people answered only the calls of their own hearts and souls. No matter how much screaming Pei Chai did, he couldn't get what he wanted. More than delicious.

Li had joined the army at sixteen as a way to keep his family alive, and he had found a home. In the army there was no class system, no mandarins to take what they wanted and leave the scrapings. He'd been dedicated and worked hard, and the work had been appreciated. Meanwhile Yun had been growing up, his mother idolizing the boy as the embodiment of her dead husband. Through Li Soo's growing influence, Yun was able to go to university, later to teach at the university level. Education had been his downfall—so many different ideas to choose from. He'd been killed for choosing the wrong ideas.

Pei, dejected, moved away from the last counter, his last chance of escape, and was walking back toward the front doors. That wouldn't do.

Li hurried to intercept him, catching the man twenty feet from the anonymous freedom of the out-of-doors.

The man jumped, startled at seeing the colonel. "Li," he said, fighting to compose himself. "What are you doing here?"

"Everyone must be somewhere," Li replied, enjoying the interplay as the wheel of justice slowly turned. "Were you trying to leave?"

"I have to get back to the mainland."

Li pointed to Pei's hand. "With a Japanese passport?"

"Oh, this?" he replied, sticking the passport into the carryon. "It's nothing."

"This isn't about money, is it?" Li asked.

"M-money? I don't understand."

"All this," Li said. "The kidnappings, the assassinations. Was this just some way for you and the late Mr. Wang to make money?"

"You don't know what you're talking about," Pei said. "But listen, it's fortuitous that we ran into each other. I've just gotten word from Beijing that we are to dismantle the operation in the face of such bad publicity and go home immediately. With Wang dead, we can blame our failure on him and probably come out of this all right."

"And then you'll free my brother, right?"

Pei smiled, patting Li familiarly on the shoulder. "I believe he's suffered enough, don't you? It's time to forget the past and move forward. Perhaps I can even get them to renew your commission as a general."

"I called the prison. I know what you did."

Pei started backing up immediately, his eyes wandering to the doors just ten feet from him, freedom so close. Li stayed with him, matching his steps, always just a reach away.

"I remember you wheezing as you climbed the stairs at Lhasa," Li said. "You're out of shape, sir. It's a discipline you should have cultivated. You cannot get past me."

And indeed, with every step Pei took, he was moving farther from the doors, not closer. Giving that up as an option, he simply walked faster into the interior of the airport, a closed environment.

"Why are you doing this to me?" he asked over his shoulder. "You should thank me that you got to at least stay in the army. My bosses wanted to decommission you completely."

"Thank you," Li replied, stalking, moving closer. "And you should thank me. I'm getting ready to end your years of dishonor."

"What do you mean?"

"I'm going to kill you."

They were moving down a long hallway now, people lethargically leaning against the walls or sleeping on the airport chairs. They were moving through the Cathay Pacific terminal. The baggage-check area was nearly vacant with one lone security guard watching the metal detector and conveyor belt.

Li smiled. Pei was already winded, his breath coming in quick, short spurts.

"You can't kill me in here," he said, laughing without humor. "The place is full of armed security." He moved through the metal detector clutching his bag, the guard taking note.

"You've created the atmosphere," Li stated, moving through the detector, his gun setting off an alarm. He took one look at the security guard, who averted his eyes, ignoring the two men. "You've sent us through this city like dark angels, killing everyone we see. You wanted Hong Kong to fear us. Well, they do, and no one is going to help you now.''

''I've got money in the bag,'' Pei said. ''Not much, but—''

''I'll burn it over your grave,'' Li replied, moving forward as Pei struggled to draw breath. The bag fell from his hands, Li kicking it aside as he increased his pace.

''Help!'' Pei cried. ''Somebody help me! Murder!''

His screamed message had just the opposite of its desired effect. People moved away, leaving the two men alone in a cocoon of hate and fear.

They had reached the boarding concourse, where grounded planes filled the window spaces on both sides of them. Pei was looking around frantically for help that wasn't going to come.

Li watched his eyes as he would an animal's, waiting for the second the man would panic and bolt.

He did.

Stairs led downward from the boarding concourse and onto the tarmac. Pei charged headlong down the stairs, gasping for breath, Li jogging, keeping up easily.

His quarry hit the downstairs push bar, running into the rain, slipping to fall in a puddle as Li came out the door, unsnapping his holster and drawing his Ruger. A huge 747 sat just beside them, its wings stretching wide to catch the rain. A fuel truck sat beside the aircraft.

"You used me in the worst way," Li said, priming the weapon, "a most inhuman way."

"It was Wang," Pei cried. "He talked me into it." The man rose, gasping, his suit dripping mud and gravel.

"You just told me that's what we could say to save ourselves," Li replied, shaking his head. "It's over, Pei."

"I appeal to you as a man of honor," Pei begged, getting down on his knees in the mud. "Please don't kill me."

"I have no honor. I have been your lackey for years, doing your killing for you while you laughed behind my back. I will deal with my own dishonor later. I will deal with yours now."

Pei's eyes gave him away as he jumped up, trying to run again.

Li fired a round into the back of the man's left knee. Pei crumpled in anguish to the ground, rolling in the mud, crying like a baby.

The colonel moved to stand above him as Pei tried scrambling once again, putting a bullet into his other knee. The man collapsed then, lying on his back, arms outstretched, tears flooding from his eyes.

Li holstered his weapon and walked to the fuel truck. The terminal windows were crowded with faces pressed to the glass. "You've taken my humanity and my brother's life," he said, unhooking the nozzled hose from the tanker and returning to stand over the man.

"P-please," Pei moaned, blood flowing from his shattered knees.

Li bent to him, patting down his pockets, looking for the matches anyone who was close to Wang had to carry to light his cigarettes. He found a box, still dry, in Pei's vest pocket. He stood.

"You brought the horrors of war to this island for no other reason that to profit financially from people's misery. No more."

Li opened the nozzle on the gas line. Clear, pungent jet fuel splashed all over Pei, who screamed when he felt the fuel hit him.

"Be a man," Li said, releasing the nozzle and replacing it on the truck. "Face up to the consequences of your own actions. Make peace with your ancestors."

He carefully lit a match, protecting it with his hand from the pounding rain. Pei screamed hysterically.

"What? No last words? So be it, then."

He tossed the match and backed away, Pei's body exploding in bright white fire, the man's arms flailing wildly as he screamed out the agony of his retribution. Li watched without feeling as the screaming gave way, the man's body a charred twig, arms still frozen in the air, caught in the death posture.

Li looked at the remnants, feeling cold. Pei had indeed taken his humanity from him; life and death were all the same to him now. But he could still salvage his honor with the help of the American.

Drenched, he walked slowly back into the airport, back along its crowded hallways, the people, the real, living people backing away from the specter of death as it walked among them.

He had only one more deed to accomplish before this night and his appointment with destiny, one more loose end to tie up before his spirit could be free to embrace the void.

CHAPTER NINETEEN

Bolan put down the receiver of the hospital telephone and turned to Mao and a bedridden Shing. "Ian's missing."

"Missing?" Mao said.

He nodded. "We dropped him off at the Arsenal Street station this morning. He walked back out of the place an hour later and hasn't been seen since." Bolan looked at his watch. It was already after four. They needed to be in motion. "His car's still parked at the helipad."

Mao was involved with Shing, staring into his eyes, smoothing the hair out of his face. "He'll turn up," she said.

"I can't depend on that." Bolan picked up the phone again, using the government code to call Brognola's home.

Shing lay semiconscious on the bed. He was swathed in bandages from chest to chin, his breathing aided by oxygen fed through a tube into his nose. He was pale but had stabilized, and looking much better than he had when they'd seen him that morning.

The line was ringing on Brognola's end. Bolan let it ring, knowing that the big Fed would never allow himself to be totally out of contact.

A sleepy voice answered several rings later. "This better be good," he said, trying to sound intimidating through a yawn.

"It's me, Hal."

"Striker," Brognola said, instantly alert. "What's up?"

"I want you to get the U.S. consul to Hong Kong on the horn right now."

"What do you need?"

"I had a deal with a Hong Kong cop with some pull, a man named Crosswaithe, who was putting together some police help for us down here. Now Crosswaithe's missing, probably dead. I want the U.S. consul to get over to the station and put the pressure on them to honor our deal."

"It sounds like you've got a war going down there."

"Yeah. Will it help if I tell you all of this will be over in four hours?"

"Over?"

"One way or the other. We need those cops."

"I have Consul General Merchant's cell number," he said. "I'll get it taken care of."

"A lot of people are depending on you," Bolan said.

"I understand."

"Thanks, Hal."

"Thank me next time you see me," Brognola said gruffly, then hung up.

Bolan returned the phone to the cradle and put a hand on Mao's shoulder. "It's time to go."

She stared at him in irritation but stood anyway, leaning down and giving Shing a tender kiss on the mouth.

"What's eating you?" he asked as she straightened and walked out of the room with him, both of them carrying heavy hooded overcoats.

"You want to know what's eating me?" she asked, taking him by the arm and dragging him to the seventh-floor window. The rain was pounding from the sky at nearly a forty-five-degree angle, the wind bending the trees surrounding the hospital nearly to the ground. It was a steady wind now, gusting between forty and seventy miles per hour. The streets were deserted.

"That is what's eating me, Charlie. No one is going to come out and meet you on the docks tonight. There's going to be no fight. By tonight there may not be any docks!"

"He'll be there," Bolan said, leading her back to the elevator and punching the button. "Colonel Li isn't bringing his troops to the pier to fight. He's bringing them there to die."

The doors slid open, and several people got out before they climbed in and took the ride down. "I don't understand."

"Wang has been using him," Bolan explained as the elevator reached ground level with a slight shudder. "He's had enough time to check on his brother's death by now and knows the truth."

The doors slid open, and they exited, hurrying to the glass front doors that had chairs propped in front of them to keep them from blowing open.

"He's an honorable man caught in a dishonorable situation," he said, pushing into the slashing rain and wind, grabbing Mao as a stiff gust threatened to blow her away. He shouted into the wind. "He wants to die a warrior's death. But before he does, he wants to right all the wrongs that he's perpetrated."

They reached the Mercedes, climbing in, both of them soaked to the skin, their hair plastered to their heads.

He started the car and threw it into reverse, hitting the gas. "He knows he's walking into a trap," he said, skidding backward in the rain, dropping into gear and driving slowly off, water halfway up the hubcaps.

"Why in the storm?" she asked, pushing her hair back.

"No innocent bystanders," he said. "Just us and them. This has to be finished. The red ties have forfeited all rights as human beings and have to be destroyed."

Mao didn't say anything, and he turned to look quickly at her before returning his gaze to the road. "Only people who want to come will come. I'll force no one."

"Then nobody will come, Charlie," she said sadly.

"Then *I'll* face them," he said. "We've got to finish what we started."

She leaned over and kissed him on the cheek. "Then there will be *two* of us facing them."

"Good girl," he said, patting her on the leg. "See? We've already doubled the size of our force."

She leaned to her window, using a scarf to wipe at the fogging glass to try to clear it. "Let me ask you a question. Why didn't you tell your friend about Wang Wushen or D'Aguilar Cape?"

"I would have just had to explain more things than I wanted to explain. He'll find out when he goes to work in the morning," Bolan said. "And by then all this will be nothing but a memory."

"I hope it's us who gets to have the memory," Mao added hopefully.

"I DO NOT CARE what the governor told you," Li said through the two-inch opening on his driver's-side window. The gate guard was leaning down to it, holding a slicker over his head to protect him from the rain. "You are to open this gate immediately. We have an appointment."

"The best I can do, Colonel," the British soldier said, "is to call up to the house and double-check my orders."

"Do it, then," Li said, rolling down his window all the way as the man walked into the small gate house and picked up the phone.

The colonel raised his Ruger and shot the man in the head from four feet away, all sound swallowed immediately in the wind as the man slumped over his control panel. Li climbed out into the rain, reconnoitering, then going into the gate house.

Li pulled the corpse from the panel to drop it on the floor, then pushed the gate control. The reinforced ornamental ironworks creaked slowly open.

He got back into the car and drove slowly onto the lavish estate nestled high on the mountain. The paved road leading to the house was winding and tree lined, the trees whipping back and forth in the gale-force winds. The grounds encompassed many acres, with the house situated at a high point well back on the lot. It was pseudo-Victorian, three stories, painted white. Huge. He wondered who would live in it after 1997.

Li pulled up in front of the house, the lone car sitting in an immense circular driveway. The building itself almost looked deserted, its windows boarded against a wind that was far stronger up here than it was below.

Gusting with increasing force, the winds nearly took his legs out from under him as he climbed from the car. He had to use the handrail up the stairs to keep his feet until he got onto the porch, then bend at a severe angle to get to the door.

It was locked.

He began banging and kicking at it until a man pulled it open. It was Stewart Miles, Purdy's personal secretary. They'd met before. He stood with a loosened tie and a large glass of Scotch whisky in his hand.

"Bloody hell," he said. "What do *you* want?"

"I must see the governor," Li answered, shoving his way into the foyer. "Where is he? I have something I must give to him."

Hearing a voice, Li moved toward a large study on the left of the massive entry hall, Miles moving deftly to block his entry. "Colonel Li."

"General," Li replied.

"*General* Li . . . yes. Well, there're some things you need to understand," Miles said, putting his arm around Li, attempting to lead him away from the study door.

"Is he alone?"

"He's speaking at the moment to the prime minister of Great Britain," Miles said, lowering his voice. "Things have come unraveled around here with this business with the *hong* and the death of Mr. Wang. I'm telling you, he's back there fighting for his political life."

"I see," Li said, and headed toward the doorway again, Miles blocking him again as he quietly unsnapped his holster.

"What you don't see, er, General, is that the cooperation that may or may not have existed between your people and the governor is over if it ever existed in the first place, which I don't think it did."

"I have something to give the governor," Li repeated, and tried for the third time to enter the study unmolested.

"What do you have to give him?"

"You do not want what I have to give him."

"Give me a hint."

"Yes," Li agreed, bringing the Ruger out of the holster to slam against Miles's temple, just above his left ear.

Miles stood staring at Li for several seconds, his eyes blinking furiously, before crumpling, dead or unconscious, to the carpet.

Li entered the study and saw a large room with high-backed leather armchairs and a fireplace. A wet bar occupied the far wall, another door beside it. Light and the governor's voice spilled from the door.

He walked quickly to the door and peeked around the frame, staring at Purdy's back as he sat hunched over a desk, talking in quick bursts over a telephone.

"But, sir...I believe we can control the publicity on this. No, no...I understand. I was only expediting your own instructions, sir. No, I'm sorry sir, I didn't mean... It's just that everything's so confusing down here it might be possible..." He stuck a finger in his ear and talked louder. "I said, it might be possible to avoid any problems at all if the complexities can't be pinned down. No...of course I didn't. I'm just saying that it could all blow away with the typhoon. Those kind of things—"

"The prime minister," Li said. Purdy jumped, startled. "You certainly have important friends."

The man, shocked, put his hand over the receiver. "What the devil are you doing here?" he asked. Then he shouted, "Stewart!" but got no response.

"I want to speak to the prime minister," Li said, walking up to the desk and holding out his hand.

"Wait in the other room. Make yourself a drink. I'm in the middle of a very important conversation. Stewart!"

"I don't want a drink," Li said, pointing the gun at Purdy, "and Mr. Miles cannot hear you."

He stuck his palm out again, and Purdy handed him the phone.

"Hello, Mr. Prime Minister?" Li said, keeping his gun and his eyes trained on his prey.

"Who is this?" came the distant, staticky response. "Put Purdy on the line!"

"My name is Colonel Li Soo. I am the commanding officer of the regiment you know as the red ties."

"Go on," the voice said, subdued.

"I just want you to know that Governor Purdy is a dishonor to his family name and his government," Li said as Purdy gasped. "While working for you, he was also on the payroll of Wang Wushen, director of the Bank of China. I saw cash money, pounds, change hands between the two men on more than one occasion."

Purdy tried to rise, but Li shoved him back with the gun barrel.

"In return for what?" the prime minister asked.

"Administrative favoritism...such as protecting the red ties from police interference as the lists of dead grew larger."

"He took money?" the prime minister asked loudly.

"Blood money. He is a traitor to your people, sir."

He raised the gun until it was touching Purdy's forehead and pulled the trigger to a loud pop. "There," he said over the phone. "I've just saved you the trouble of executing this scoundrel. Goodbye, Prime Minister. Perhaps we'll meet on another plane."

With that he hung up, then leaned forward to Purdy's pale white tie. He used it to wipe the blood from his face.

BOLAN INCHED the Mercedes along Pier Road, the harbor access, though where the road ended and the harbor began was impossible to tell right now.

Pier Road was under a foot of rushing water as the sea rose with the typhoon, waves cresting, breaking against the warehouses that once sat a hundred feet from the shore.

The car's engine fought the water that threatened to drown it. If the sea level rose another few inches, the vehicle would be useless.

Mao sat beside him, the back seat occupied by Bui Tin, Chan Kun and the doctor who had saved Shing's life. Bolan had used the phone tree to contact everyone and had told them when and where the firefight would take place, giving them the option of meeting him there or not. So far, he'd seen no other cars.

"This is nuts, Charlie," Mao said, staring at the wrath of heaven. Visibility was nearly nonexistent, the winds gusting over a hundred miles per hour. The angry sea slammed against the line of docks that slid by on their right, sending spray fifty feet into the air. "They're going to find us washed up on the beach in Vietnam."

She pointed. "Government docks."

The Executioner took his foot off the gas, the car gliding slowly, engine coughing.

The pier was huge, seventy feet wide, nearly a football field long. It was fronted by a ten-foot chain-link fence that was closed and locked, the royal seal emblazoned on the gates.

"Let's get in there," Bolan said, popping the trunk, then climbing out and grabbing the bolt cutters. The water was rushing almost to his knees, the wind stronger than he'd felt in his lifetime. It was awesome, the power of nature in all its furious glory.

Heavy chain fixed with a lock held the gates closed. He took the bolt cutters and chopped off the lock, jerking the chains out to disappear in the water at his feet.

Bolan swung open the gates, feeling a part of nature's power. He wasn't one to believe in joss, but he found it possible to believe that the typhoon might have come to this land not to tear down but to reorder. The typhoon was there for him and for Colonel Li. Despite the weather, he knew that they would meet one last time. Here. Tonight.

He climbed back into the car and drove through the gates, engine sputtering the entire time. But the dock rose from the shoreline, angling upward, the Mercedes climbing from the water and onto dry land.

The setting was eerie. The deserted dock sported two large cranes for cargo retrieval, the hundred-foot crane arms wiggling like rubber in the driving winds as the spray drove furiously up the sides of the dock, grasping for them with palsied white claws. Both sides of the dock were filled with boats—harbor patrol and fireboats—everything grounded with the weather. He wondered what the boat people in Aberdeen were doing to survive on the other side of the island.

Driving into the center of the dock, he turned the car around and stopped, staring back down the pier. He looked at his watch—6:30 p.m. The sky was dark gray already, the gray edging to black.

"We don't have a whole lot of time at this point," Bolan said, half turning to face his companions. "Let me tell you what I've got in mind."

"Where are our friends?" Bui asked from the back seat.

"And the cops?" Mao added.

"There are five of us," the Executioner told her. "That's all I can guarantee you."

"But what can five do," the doctor asked, "against so many?"

"I'm not sure how many men they've got left," Bolan told him. "We've killed a lot. Colonels are regimental commanders, so that limits the size somewhat. What we've seen in our previous firefights have been against units, two, maybe three at a time, a good colonel never committing any more than a fourth of his regiment. I'll bet you that Colonel Li has no more than twenty-five or thirty men left at his command."

Mao nodded. "No more than thirty, huh? Six apiece. Fine."

"I will kill them all," Chan Kun said. He was clutching Shing's Remington, a woman's leather purse, stuffed full with 12-gauge shells, slung over a shoulder. His face was set in harsh lines.

"My brother was a good man. He was just...
weak," Chan said. "They made him do what he did,
and now I will use their bodies to restore my family's
honorable name."

Bolan reached over the seat and took the man's
arm. "I appreciate the sentiment, Kun," he said, "but
don't fire your weapon in anger. Suck it down into a
cold rage, then choose your targets carefully."

"I will," the man said, looking at him, and Bolan
was looking into the face of a man pushed to the edge.

"Look," Mao said, pointing down the pier.

Two sets of headlights drifted through the impene-
trable rain, turning to move through the gates and up
the pier, large, dark hulks looming behind the headlights.

"What is it?" Dr. Chin asked.

"Trucks of some kind," Bolan replied. "Come on.
We're target practice here."

They scrambled out of the vehicle and into the
winds, the trucks rumbling loudly down the dock toward them. They stopped thirty feet away, Bolan
peering over the fender of the Mercedes to look.
Dump trucks.

The tarps covering the back of the trucks were
thrown aside, and Mao's people jumped up, cheering, waving their weapons in the air.

"Charlie!" she said. "They did come! We got a
chance now."

"Yeah. We've got a chance."

Bolan walked up to the trucks, pounding on the
solid steel construction of the gondolas. The perfect

blind. The drivers rolled down their windows to listen.

"I want ten volunteers from each truck to work with me," he called. "Everybody else stays with the trucks. We're going to put one at each end of the pier to set up a cross fire."

"We heard the news, Charlie," one of the drivers called. "The governor of Hong Kong has been killed by someone wearing a Chinese colonel's uniform. Someone with that description also burned a man to death at the airport earlier today."

It was Li Soo tying up all the loose ends. Come hell or high water, the phrase went. Well, they had hell *and* high water. Despite them, Li would be on the pier this night, and he would get his wish by dying there. The question was, how many people would go with him?

"The weather!" Bolan called up to the driver. "Anything new on the weather?"

"Yes," the man called back. "It's going to get worse!"

CHAPTER TWENTY

Colonel Li sat across the desk from the Geomancer, the small man in the white robes hunched over the trigram dial, trying to read it in the candlelight that shone steady in the cold room. The electricity to the city was gone, the buildings dark, forlorn hulks out his fortieth-floor window. A *pat kwa,* the octagonal deflector of evil, sat beside the candle, reflecting its light in all directions.

"This is quite remarkable," the man said, turning the dial to the right, aligning the natural elements and the animal symbols, the needle moving around the eight trigrams representing the *c'hi* of existence. "Water is ever present in your life. Were you born in the year of the goat?"

"I was. Yes."

The Geomancer shook his head. "You forced me here to perform the seeing, but you should have done this a long time ago. The life force is long disturbed."

"You will make it right," Li said, the rain banging against the windows, the building swaying physically. Except for him and his men, the Bank of China building was deserted.

The man crackled, showing broken teeth, and sat back. "It is your joss that has brought the calamity of the typhoon upon us, and you want me to set it right. Do you know what name the English have given to the typhoon?''

The colonel shook his head.

"Lisa," the Geomancer said. "They call it, Li...sa."

Li stared at the tabletop. He was the last of his line, so tied to Party and family duties he had never married. His seed, his immortality, would die with him tonight. A fitting punishment for his stupidity.

"I must set this right," he told the Geomancer. "I must act tonight."

The man looked down, turning the wheel. He smiled. "Yang you have been...male...active. But your solutions lie in passivity...in your yin. Let's work together to find a positive prediction, shall we?"

CHAO LISTENED at Li's door as he talked to the Geomancer, but their voices were low and the rain loud, blotting out their words. He turned back to the wide-open room filled with desks, where the remainder of their regiment talked in small groups or played cards.

There were twenty-seven of them left. The colonel had lost nearly eighty percent of their force, and yet he still wanted to go out in the middle of a typhoon and try to take the remainder of the dissidents. It seemed pointless.

With Wang dead, they had no leadership to turn to for answers. They were directionless. He didn't know much, but he knew that somebody had to be in charge, and Li Soo seemed somehow inadequate to do the job.

He moved back to the group of men, all dressed in long black leather coats over their suits, their weapons bristling from coat pockets, holsters and waistbands.

"Something's not right," he said. "Why does Li consult with the Geomancer?"

Corporal Jiange-li looked up dully from a Chinese-language newspaper. "He just wants to do a seeing," the man replied with a shrug, "to ensure good luck."

"We've never done the ceremony before going into battle before."

"I suppose this is different," Jiange-li returned. "Why is this so important?"

Chao leaned down, motioning the men in closer. "We're supposed to go to the government docks," he said. "In this weather. At dark they are all supposed to be leaving from there. Who would take a boat in a typhoon? And what better place for a trap to be set than on a pier?"

"Perhaps that is what the colonel is trying to do... set a trap," someone called, the men laughing until Chao glared them to silence.

"It doesn't feel right," Chao said emphatically, moving to the desk he had commandeered for himself just outside Li's door. Without hesitation he opened the bottom drawer and removed a box, setting it on the desktop.

He opened the box and removed a syringe, holding it up. "A present from the late Dr. Werner," he said, then stared them all down. "I was authorized by Mr. Wang to take command of this regiment if I thought it was necessary. If I do that, you will all be under my command. I want each of you to approach me and take a syringe. Put it in your pocket. That's an order!''

They lined up then, reluctantly, all of them knowing the effects of Dr. Werner's drugs. ''Hurry,'' Chao whispered harshly. ''Trust me. This may save your life.''

He passed the drug around, the men restless now. They were thinking about it. Chao had just put the box back in the drawer when Li walked out of the office with the Geomancer.

''It's time,'' he said, then looked at the priest. ''The basement will be a safe haven for you until the storm breaks.''

''It will break soon,'' the man replied softly, and left the office.

''We go to the government docks,'' Li told his men, ''to remove the rest of the names from our list.''

''A question, Colonel,'' Chao said. ''No ships can sail from any docks while the storm persists. The traitors won't be there.''

''We don't have the luxury of making that assumption, Major,'' Li replied, staring at the man. ''We must assume they will be there or risk losing them. If they don't show up, they don't show up. But if they do show, we finish them tonight and go home tomorrow. Those are the orders I received just today.''

Chao wasn't nearly convinced. But he had his own little *pat kwa* now residing in each soldier's pocket, a little insurance against the cold, unfeeling world.

MACK BOLAN STOOD on the dock with his arm around Angela Mao, holding on to her in the heavy wind that threatened to blow her away.

He stood, surveying his defenses. A bullhorn, taken from a harbor-patrol boat, dangled in his free hand. He brought it to his lips and spoke into the howling wind.

"All right!" he called, his voice staticky, its volume dying in the winds. "Assume your ready positions!"

At his command the people in the dump trucks, one on each end of the pier, ducked into their gondolas, pulling the tarps over themselves. The remaining twenty-five members of the team ducked beneath gunwales and wheelhouses of the surrounding boats they occupied.

"Mr. Bui!" Bolan called. "I can still see you. Down more... there, that's it."

He and Mao turned a full circle, checking. The pier looked like a pier, nothing more, except for the Mercedes still parked in its center.

"Do you want me to hide the car?" she asked.

"No, it's part of the bait."

"Part of the bait? What's the rest?"

"Me," he said, bringing the bullhorn to his mouth again. "Listen up, people. The wind is high enough that it's going to affect your ability to shoot straight. Try for close shots. Aim into crowds."

"Uh-oh." Mao tugged on his sleeve.

He turned to see her pointing farther down Pier Street. Through the ever-descending darkness and curtain of rain, he could see tiny pinpoints of light slowly moving closer to their position. Headlights.

"Friend or foe?" she wondered aloud.

"We'd better consider them enemies," he replied, walking her toward the fireboat she'd picked as her cover.

He spoke into the bullhorn. "This is it! Everybody hold your positions. Don't fire until all of them are on the pier. If we handle this right, it won't take long."

He moved her onto the bow, Mao turning to stare into the darkness. "We're going to just shoot those men down, aren't we?"

"It's them or us, Angela," he said. "They'd do it to you and your friends."

"It makes us act like them," she said.

"It's what keeps free people free. Take your position."

"That's where you come in, isn't it? Dirty work."

"I do what has to be done," he replied.

"When this finishes, my life goes on. Yours stays the same."

"Let's talk philosophy some other time, okay?" he said, watching the headlights drawing closer.

He handed her the bullhorn and walked back down the pier, the water creeping higher up the dock. The waves were washing over it now, the patrol boats almost even with the top of the pier.

He shucked the heavy coat, cumbersome for fighting, and dropped it to the ground to wash away on the next swell. A light jacket covered his harness.

He reached the rear dump truck, parked among other construction vehicles off to the side, and tapped on the driver's door. The driver popped up from his place on the floor of the vehicle and rolled down the window.

"Don't forget your part," he said.

"Box them in."

"But not until they've moved past the Mercedes on the pier, okay?" The big man turned and looked, the Mercedes barely visible in the darkness. But he'd fix that.

"Got it, Charlie," the man replied, rolling up his window and disappearing again.

Bolan made the curve down at the end of the pier and found himself in water nearly up to his waist. The cars were less than a block away—Mercedes. He'd been hoping for, but not expecting, the police. They could have used the help.

The cars were inching forward, barely moving in the rushing water. Bolan slipped into the space between two warehouses and waited until they got closer, unholstering the Beretta and priming it, waiting for the right second.

He wouldn't be able to see anyone in the car, would be lucky to find the windshield. He simply intended to unload the clip in that general direction and see what happened.

He peered around the building. The lead car was ten feet away. The Executioner took a long breath and sloshed out of hiding, aiming the Beretta at the car's windshield.

"DOWN!" CHAO YELLED as he and Li spotted the American at the same time.

The colonel had already been in motion before the gun's continuous blasting took out the windshield and the two men in the front seat.

He crouched low, reaching up to open the back door as Chao tried to fold his huge frame onto the floorboards.

The door opened to a rush of water, Li almost swimming out as the firing stopped. He stood. The American had turned and was wading back into the darkness, moving toward an open gate.

All the cars stopped and Li's men moved into the water, several of them firing futilely into the night, their target already a specter in the driving rain.

"Formation!" the colonel called into the teeth of the wind. "I will have a formation!"

The men, wading with their guns held above their heads, tried to form up at the open gateway.

"Why are we marching in?" Chao yelled at him, getting within an inch of his face. "Let's scout it, check for traps, divide into squads."

"These are soldiers, Major," Li stated. "In this, our last action together, we will behave as soldiers. Now kindly silence yourself." He turned to his men. "Column forward!"

He turned to Chao. "Walk with me, Major. We'll lead the column."

"What are you doing?" Chao asked, joining Li at the head of the ranks, the men slogging forward.

Li drank in the typhoon, his typhoon, and felt the grandeur of heaven and earth coming together to enact justice. "I am leading my regiment, Major. Just as I have all my life."

The ground sloped upward, taking them out of the water and onto the government dock.

"One of our cars," Chao said as they approached a black Mercedes, "set out for us like cheese for a rat."

Li, ignoring the man, had turned and was walking backward, facing his column. "Keep the formation tight, men," he ordered. "March at attention."

Even in the rain, they still looked proper, military. He had trained them well for a task unworthy of a unit so sharply honed. They weren't good men, but had been dependable, loyal soldiers. For both their good and their bad points, they now had to die. His life force had to be restored, his honor reaffirmed. He was doing the work of destiny.

They passed the car, marching down the center of the wide, unlit pier, marching to nowhere.

"Where's the American?" Chao asked.

"Hiding. We'll flush him out."

The colonel looked around. They were standing close to a mechanized metal platform containing two tall cranes. Government boats banged against the dock all around, large swells spilling onto the deck, threatening to bring the boats with them. He smiled at the dump truck parked near the end of the dock, remembering he'd seen one parked near the dock's entry with other heavy machinery. The American was doing well.

The next step would be to close up the box by bringing up the other dump truck.

"Colonel," Chao said, pointing back down the dock.

Li turned to see a dump truck backing up the pier to stop beside the Mercedes, effectively cutting off any escape. The trap had been sprung.

"I suggest," Li said loudly, "that we make peace with ourselves and call on our ancestors—"

"It's a trap!" Chao yelled, pointing to the dump truck as he reached into his pocket to jerk out his syringe, holding it high in the air.

"Take your dose!" he called. "Take it now."

Li looked on in horror as Chao plunged the needle into his arm right through the sleeve of his coat, the others frantically trying to do the same.

"No!" he roared. "I order you not to take that drug! Put it down! Follow orders!"

Chao looked at him, his eyes edging darker, a line of drool already hanging from a corner of his mouth. "You brought us here to die," he growled.

"You should welcome death," Li said, pointing his Ruger at Chao's chest. "I do."

At that moment the area exploded into dazzling light from above, capturing them like rabbits in headlights.

The end had begun.

BOLAN POWERED UP the master board on the cranes and hit the loading lights that ran off the machine's batteries. The red ties fell into his spotlight, their initial vision chilling his blood as he saw them injecting themselves with what could only have been Dr. Werner's drug.

From his vantage point fifteen feet above them in the tiny control room, he ripped the .44 from his harness and fired into the middle of the pack, trying to see the effects of the wind.

He hit a man, not the one he was aiming at, in the shin, driving him to the deck as Angela Mao stood up in the wheelhouse of her pumper boat and fired her .45 into the crowd.

Where were the others? This was the time. Didn't they know—

"Fire!" Mao's voice yelled through the bullhorn. "Kill the red ties!"

They jumped up then, from the wildly swaying ships and from the dump trucks, firing into the circle of men caught in their beams, two going down, a third.

The pier itself was no longer visible, the red ties appearing to be standing atop open seas as Bolan gauged the windage and fired again, taking out the man he'd been aiming at.

But the man didn't go down. The bullet tore through his chest to no apparent effect.

CHAO DIVED at Li Soo, the colonel firing several shots into the man to no reaction except anger. As the harbor swept up to their legs, they went down, splashing, Li losing his wind as his subordinate landed on top of him. He gagged as Chao pushed his head beneath the swirling waters, only instinct keeping him from trying to struggle for breath right through the liquid as his mind popped with bright white fireworks.

Li slapped at his sides, his right hand finding the gun under the water even as his consciousness faded. Trying to hold on to the light, he wrestled the gun up between them, jerking the trigger to a muffled pop.

The weight fell off his chest, Li fairly bursting out of the water, pulling in air in a long, sucking wheeze.

Chao lay partly across his legs, shaking his head while emitting a continuous low, wolflike growl. His eyes turned to Li even as the men of the regiment bellowed in pain and animal passion, bullets pinging all around them.

Li's shot had hit Chao on the left cheek at point-blank range, burning that side of his face, taking out cheek, teeth and tongue, then blowing out the back of his neck just beside the spinal column. But he still had strength enough to attack.

The colonel pulled the trigger again, but the gun was still jammed with the last shell. He rolled, then got to his feet in time to get hit by Chao's bulk, which drove him backward to slam into the hull of a harbor-patrol boat that had floated, still moored, onto the dock.

Fire seared Li's leg as a shot from the civilians hit him just below the knee. He crumpled, dazed, to the pier, water up to his chest, a ribbon of red winding through it.

Chao kicked out, and Li took the blow to the side of the head, his brain exploding white light. He idly realized his head was in the water and struggled back to consciousness in time to see Chao pounce again.

BOLAN JERKED the controls, bending the left crane into the wind, fighting it as the battle raged below. Half the red ties were down, floating like pond scum on the harbor, but the others were climbing onto the boats, howling into the wind as the sea rose, lifting the boats, which threatened to slip their moorings.

The crane won its battle with the wind, jerking down heavily to bash the center of the submerged dock. Bolan quickly levered the lateral control, swinging the arm to the sides. It caught two red ties, decapitating one man and breaking the other in two.

The Executioner swung back the other way, snapping the legs off one man as he tried to scramble onto a boat. Then he saw Li Soo, pinned beneath the towering bulk of one of his own men. The crazed soldier was tearing at him with his fingernails, trying to rip him apart.

Chao half rose on his haunches, ready to plunge into Li's throat, when the crane hit him, catching him full on the upper torso, his arms wrapping around the crane's skeletal framework as it swung away on an upward arc.

Bolan looked down, a battered and dying Li struggling to his feet, waist deep in water. He looked up at Bolan and somehow came to attention. Arm shaking, he raised a stiff hand to salute the Executioner. Bolan snapped off a quick return salute as the colonel was hit by several more bullets and went down, disappearing immediately beneath the waves.

The crane arm was creaking badly as it listed in the raging winds, Chao still attached to it, his legs furiously kicking empty air as he hung on.

Bolan tried to raise it to no avail, the metal screaming loudly, then bending slowly, like a wilting flower, from the base. Its tip bent back to the water, the big Chinese dropping onto one of the fireboats, getting hung up.

The red tie scurried across the top deck just as Bolan saw Mao firing from the wheelhouse at two more men who were hanging onto the rails, trying to board. She didn't even see the big Chinese.

The Executioner moved through the control room's entry, ignoring the steps down, walking onto the surrounding scaffolding that held the crane, the winds threatening to take him away.

He climbed onto the bare steel arm and made his way across its length, straight at first, then sloping downward. The rain slashed at his face like razor blades, blinding him, as the wind snatched at his hands, trying to throw him from his delicate perch.

Muscles straining to hold on, he inched forward, sensing rather than seeing the downward slope.

A patrol boat rammed into the crane arm, hitting hard, shaking, nearly vibrating Bolan from where he clung. When he felt rushing water close to him, he squinted into the rain, trying to protect his eyes with an upraised hand.

He was staring at the third deck of the fireboat, the ship itself gouged by the arm on the upper gunwale, held fast there.

Scrambling down the framework, he climbed on deck beside the seawater pumper, just in time to hear Mao screaming from below. He hurried to the ladder down, the .44 out and ready in his hand.

He jumped to the deck and charged down the gangway to the wheelhouse, the boat foundering as it took on water because it was hooked into the crane armature, unable to roll with the sea. The wheelhouse door crashed beneath the force of his shoulder and fell into the room. The big Chinese had Mao in a bear hug, her legs and arms flailing as his teeth sought to tear into her exposed neck.

Bolan leaped to his feet in the enclosed space, Chao slashing out at him, knocking him hard against the wall, then to the ground, the .44 skittering away.

The red tie dropped Mao and turned to his attacker, the entire side of his face shot away. He sprang on the Executioner, pinning him, as the woman tried to struggle back to her feet.

"Run!" Bolan rasped. Mao instead threw herself on Chao's back, bringing her nails around to claw his eyes.

With an animal roar the man jerked back, grabbing at his eyes, Mao kicking him in the face as Bolan shoved the man off and grabbed her hand.

"Come on!"

They ran out of the wheelhouse, another crazed red tie moving quickly down the gangway toward them. The Beretta cleared leather just as the man reached them. Bolan fired three times point-blank into the man's forehead, the third shot lifting off the top of his head and driving him over the gunwale and into the swirling waters.

"Charlie!" she screamed.

Bolan turned back to see the big Chinese, blood running from his eyes, lumbering out of the wheelhouse.

The Executioner raised the Beretta and pulled the trigger to a click.

"Go...go!" he yelled, dropping the clip from the Beretta as Chao charged him.

"Up or down?" she yelled, holding on to the rail in the buffeting winds, the boat now listing badly to the port side.

"Up!" he shouted, noticing two more red ties on the deck just below.

Chao hit him hard, grabbing his wrist and squeezing until his hand went numb and the gun dropped. He punched the man's jaw and broke away from him again, following Mao up to the pumper deck.

She was arching her back painfully as she held on to the gunwale. He ran to her. "Where's your gun?"

"I blacked out when he squeezed me," she said, grimacing with the pain. "It got lost."

"We've got to get back to the wheelhouse," Bolan told her just as Chao topped the stairs and growled at them, his gaze rowing back and forth, taking in the situation.

He charged them, Bolan diving away from him as Mao slid along the rail, the huge man lunging for her.

Bolan ran to the side pumper and fired up the controls. He swung the water cannon toward the huge man and hit the hand controls.

A pressurized jet of water slammed into the man, driving him to his knees as Mao hobbled away from him.

The Executioner eased up on the stream long enough for the man to climb back to his feet. "Come and get it," Bolan gritted through clenched teeth.

Chao charged, Bolan opening the pumper wide when the man was a foot away, knocking him backward, the spray dead center on his chest.

He backpedaled all the way across the deck under the relentless push of the hose, finally slamming into the crane arm with a loud thud, impaled on the arm in a rush of guts and blood.

The movement rocked the boat off the crane to float away, leaving the huge man behind, two feet of steel sticking through his belly, his arms and legs trying to run as he stared down stupidly at his new appendage.

"There's more on board," Bolan said. "We've got to get back to the wheelhouse and our weapons."

"I'm glad you said 'we,'" she responded, grabbing hold of his arm, walking gingerly.

They moved toward the stairs, the fireboat twisting in a circle as it got caught in the current. Just before they reached the stairs, another red tie crested the top, red drool spilling from his lips, his dark eyes stark and inhuman.

Bolan kicked out furiously, smashing the man full in the face, cracking his jaw, unhinging it. The man didn't seem to notice.

They were in the midst of an insane flotilla, twenty patrol and fireboats out of control, drawn like flotsam in the angry current as the rain continued to beat down, stinging, turning their faces red with welts.

Bolan and Mao retreated to the water cannon as a patrol boat bumped into them, knocking everyone to the battered deck. The pilot deck of the patrol boat was jammed with red ties and civilians locked in a life-and-death struggle. An old man, gun empty, was bashing the head of a red tie who was attempting to tear out the throat of a fifteen-year-old girl. The Executioner got to his feet and manned the cannon again.

He swung the barrel to the other boat, banging the fire control to a loud, hissing spray that bridged the gap between the boats, hitting the red tie square on the head. The force of the blast turned him around, the old man swinging the M-16 at his eyes, blood spurting.

"Charlie!" Mao screamed.

The Executioner swung the barrel back to his own deck as the flotilla cleared the docks and floated into the downtown streets, the buildings rising tall and dark, like stone trees, out of the boiling water.

The red tie on their deck was coming at them, working at keeping his balance on the tilting deck. Another enemy was just clearing the stairs.

The cannon hissed when the red tie was three feet away, catching his right shoulder and spinning him like a top across the deck to tumble over the gunwale and into the churning water.

The other red tie was on top of them, but Bolan swung the cannon just in time to angle up and hit him point-blank in the face. The Chinese's head snapped back, breaking the neck.

"The guns!" Bolan yelled, swinging the cannon to starboard. The patrol boat carrying Chan Kun floated by, the old man calmly sticking the Remington under the chin of a red tie and pulling the trigger, taking the man's face off as the Executioner sprayed low on an enemy approaching the old man from behind.

Mao fought the wind to the stairs, hanging on to the rail as she moved down a level.

The red tie on Chan's boat hit the deck when the water leveled him. The old man turned and calmly pumped the shotgun, aiming it at the top of the downed man's head. He pulled the trigger, splattering brains all over the deck, then turned and flashed the thumb's-up sign to Bolan. He'd cleared his boat and moved off, looking for someone to help.

Mao returned to the deck, her own .45 stuffed in her belt, her coat long discarded. Bolan's guns were in her left hand, her right locked in a death grip on the handrail as the boat scraped the second-story facade of the new, huge Hong Kong Convention Center.

Bolan made his way to Mao's side and grabbed her, taking her back to the relative security of the water-cannon turret and the round steel wall that surrounded it.

The end of the building screeched closer, Bolan pulling Mao back to the turret, reloading and holstering his weapons as a boatload of red ties behind them hit the building on the forward hull. The patrol boat smashed against the wall, jerking hard, throwing the remaining red ties off the top deck and into the dark water.

They cleared the convention center, the boat immediately twisting hard to starboard, the current sweeping them toward the mammoth glass front of the Harbour View Hotel.

"Get down!" he yelled, both of them ducking into the turret and trying to get beneath the machinery of the cannon. Like the dragons on their way to bathe in the harbor, the fireboat would pass through the glass. Unlike the dragons, however, the boat wouldn't pass through unnoticed.

They hit it aft, massive sheets of glass exploding on contact, showering on them.

They were struck but unscathed, and they both jumped up to find themselves just below the mezzanine level of the hotel, startled staff and guests, wrapped in blankets, surrounding them. Mao waved gamely at them, then turned to the Executioner.

"Can we throw a rope?"

He shook his head and pointed fore. They had twisted back on contact with the mezzanine and were heading out the other side of the building.

"Here we go again!" Mao yelled, and they dived under the cannon, reliving the explosive glass to worse results, both of them sustaining cuts to their arms as they covered their heads. Out in the open they would have been sliced to pieces.

The current carried them onto Fleming, plunging into the heart of Wan Chai, where huge shopping malls rose like rectangular boulders on the wide street. Light standards poked out of the water, several of the boats now solidly moored to them from lines thrown by survivors. Bolan smiled at their resourcefulness.

"The wind's dying, Charlie!" Mao called. "I can stand in it!"

She was right. And the rain was lightening, too. He moved fore and stared into the dark city. They were angling across the wide street, heading for the intersection with Gloucester, the main thoroughfare through Wan Chai.

The rain was a sprinkle now, the moon lighting the night. The bulk of other ships were visible all around him.

They reached Gloucester, the stone forest thick here, buildings sprouting everywhere. All at once light spilled onto the tableau. Portable stadium lights set on the tops of buildings flared in the darkness as rappeling lines were shot from hundreds of windows to fall across the bows of the wayward ships.

"Come on!" Bolan yelled, charging across the now-steady pumper deck and down to the main deck in time to grab hold of a line that arched across the bow.

Mao grabbed the line with him, holding it as Bolan furiously tied it to the pumper housing, the line going taut quickly as they swept onward.

It jerked hard, knocking them to the deck, the ship creaking but holding fast.

On their feet in a flash, Bolan and Mao worked in unspoken cooperation as they pulled the line, laboriously hauling themselves back against the current, the Executioner looping the rope around a firehose spool and locking it to hold.

All around them, dozens of uniformed cops sprang from the tops of buildings on ropes, automatic weapons at their sides.

They landed on the decks of ships, firefights flaring up all around Bolan on patrol boats as the Royal Hong Kong Police Force finished the mop-up.

Straining, Bolan and Mao pulled themselves to a three-story electronic store, uniformed men reaching out of the second-story windows to help them.

They climbed, soaked and shivering, into a dark room full of audio equipment. The electricity came on as the police led them through the building, beeps and whistles going off as systems came up.

The water levels dropped quickly, and all of the remaining dissidents gathered in the center of Gloucester Road, now littered with harbor trash and boats.

There might have been fifty of them left. The numbers weren't that important. Even one left alive would tell the Red Chinese they couldn't have everything they wanted. That would be enough. For now.

They were all exhausted, gathering, embracing, speaking softly. This was no joyous occasion; they'd all lost too much. But it was positive, and that was also better than the alternative.

A diplomatic limousine with American flags on the fenders pulled up to the group, followed by two flatbed trucks. The back doors opened, and two men stepped out. One was dressed in a silk suit, the other in wool. Bolan figured one to be the American consul, the other probably the chief of police.

The Executioner moved out of the crowd to face the man in the silk suit.

"You Belasko?" the man asked.

"Sure."

The man stuck out his hand and smiled. "My name's Charles Merchant, American consul general. This is Chief Ward of the Hong Kong Police."

Bolan shook both men's hands.

"I must apologize for our late arrival," the chief said. "Our cars couldn't make it through the water. We did what we could."

"Which was plenty," Bolan replied. "Thanks. Anything on Ian?"

Ward looked at the ground. "We found him about a block from here just before the storm." He looked up at the Executioner. "He'd been shot nine times in the head at point-blank range."

Bolan nodded, turning to Merchant. "I assume you're here to complete America's end of the bargain."

"Indeed I am," the man said. "The whole world is cheering this on. But, ah, I was told you had something for me."

"I've already taken care of it."

"But, I was told—"

"Look, you can debrief me tomorrow, okay? It's been a long day."

"For sure. What the hell. Let's load them up."

"Now, you're talking." Bolan turned to the people he'd come to respect as much as any he'd met. "I have a deal to offer you."

They all gathered quickly, but there was no hope in their eyes, only curiosity.

"The United States government has come up with a solution to your dilemma. If you choose, you may go with Mr. Merchant, the American consul, to his consulate. That is American soil and protected from intrusion. There you will stay and be taken care of while you go through a crash course on U.S. citizenship, the President himself shortening the required residency time to the length of your lessons. Once you've become American citizens, you will be flown, first-class, to Los Angeles, where a government representative will make sure you have housing and jobs. You will be entering the United States as full-fledged American citizens, not Chinese criminals."

There was no need to take a vote. The cheering spoke for itself.

"Then climb on the trucks, people!" he called. "The sooner you get on American soil, the sooner you're safe."

They moved, laughing, for the trucks, U.S. Marines helping them aboard as Angela Mao moved up to take Bolan's arm.

"Consul General," Bolan said, "I'd like you to meet a very special lady, Angela Mao."

"I'm so sorry about your father," Merchant said, shaking her hand.

"What's your name?" she asked, tilting her head.

"Merchant," he said. "Charles Merchant."

"Charles!" she said loudly.

He smiled, holding up his hands. "No formality, please. We're all going to be spending a lot of time together the next year or so. Call me Charlie."

Mao turned to the crowd. "His name's Charlie!" she called.

"Hi, Charlie!" all of them said.

Mao took Bolan by the arm and led him away from the trucks. "This was all your doing, wasn't it?" she said, pointing over her shoulder at Merchant.

"What does it matter?" he returned. "What's important is that I told you the United States government wouldn't let you down, and it hasn't. Enjoy your good fortune."

"I'll never see you again, will I?"

"Your life has somewhere else to go," he said. "Mine is here." He pointed to the death and destruction all around him. "Get Shing healthy. Have lots of kids and grow old together."

"I will," she promised.

"I know," he replied. "I hope you'll like America." They hugged then.

She broke the embrace. "You will live through my children and their children, for I will tell them stories they won't believe." She touched his lips. "Goodbye, crazy man."

She turned then strode up to Merchant, locking her arm in his. "So, Charlie," she said, winking at Bolan, "when can we get our injured transferred from the hospitals and into the consulate?"

"Injured?" he said. "I don't know what—"

"And you're going to have to have a fully staffed medical center on the grounds."

"But I—"

She turned him back toward his limousine, dragging him. "Let me outline to you how our living conditions should be," she said, all but shoving him into the limo and closing the door.

Bolan watched as the rest of them climbed aboard the trucks, Bui and Chan Kun helping each other to a new life. Even through the pain of loss, new relationships were being born. The circle of life closing back in upon itself.

People were taking to the streets now, rebuilding their lives with resignation and good humor, Bolan losing himself in blessed anonymity.

As he walked, he thought about General Li and how he'd died, concluding that whenever the time came for him to cash it in, he'd want to go out just the same way as Li. The warrior's death. Somehow he found that thought comforting.

With terror at home and a nuclear nightmare, Stony Man is the President's last hope

STONY MAN™ 24
BIRD OF PREY

At Stony Man Farm in Virginia, world trouble spots are monitored around the clock. And when watch-and-wait tactics aren't enough, the elite field teams go behind the lines—and beyond the law.

Available in September at your favorite retail outlet.

Take
4 explosive books
plus a
mystery bonus
FREE

Mail to: Gold Eagle Reader Service
3010 Walden Ave.
P.O. Box 1394
Buffalo, NY 14240-1394

YEAH! Rush me 4 FREE Gold Eagle novels and my FREE mystery gift.
Then send me 4 brand-new novels every other month as they come off
the presses. Bill me at the low price of just $15.80* for each shipment—
a saving of 15% off the cover prices for all four books! There is NO extra
charge for postage and handling! There is no minimum number of books I
must buy. I can always cancel at any time simply by returning a shipment
at your cost or by returning any shipping statement marked "cancel." Even
if I never buy another book from Gold Eagle, the 4 free books and surprise
gift are mine to keep forever.

164 BPM A3U3

Name	(PLEASE PRINT)
Address	Apt. No.
City State	Zip

Signature (if under 18, parent or guardian must sign)

* Terms and prices subject to change without notice. Sales tax applicable in
NY. This offer is limited to one order per household and not valid to
present subscribers. Offer not available in Canada.

AC-96